MARKED BY MAGIC

A NEW ADULT FANTASY NOVEL

JASMINE WALT

DYNAMO PRESS

Cover illustration by Judah Dobin

Cover typography by Rebecca Frank

Edited by Mary Burnett

Electronic edition, 2016. If you want to be notified when Jasmine's next novel is released and get access to exclusive contests, giveaways, and freebies, sign up for her mailing list here. Your email address will never be shared and you can unsubscribe at any time.

1

At first, I didn't understand what woke me. I was so exhausted from the long trip across the country that as soon as my head hit the pillow, I was asleep like the dead. But as I was tugged back to consciousness, the thick, pungent smell of smoke overwhelmed my nose, and the crackle of flame disturbed the late-night silence. Realizing the danger, I bolted upright in bed, my throat already half-closed, my heart beating twice its normal rate. The smoke was so thick I couldn't breathe, and I fell back against the mattress as a coughing fit erupted from my chest.

Breathing shallowly through my mouth, I blinked against the stinging smoke and scrabbled for my discarded T-shirt so I could shield myself from the haze permeating the room. It was growing thicker by the second, and if I didn't want to suffocate, I needed to get a move on.

With the T-shirt pressed to my face, I slid, belly down, off the bed and onto the floor. Three inches of relatively smoke-free air allowed me to breathe more freely, and I crawled over to the door, trying to get a feel for my situation. I pressed my hand to the thin, painted wood, gritting my teeth against the heat that scalded my palm. The smoke billowing from beneath the door triggered another coughing fit even with my impromptu mask, and I retreated hastily, considering my options.

I had two choices to escape death. I could open my bedroom window and jump down the fire escape, or I could try braving the fire raging beyond my bedroom door.

Crawling to the window, I hauled myself up so I could peer over the ledge. Unfortunately, the thickening haze made it difficult to see outside even with my shifter vision, and a cloud had drifted over the moon, blocking out my main source of light. Even so, a tingle skipped down my spine, causing the hair on the back of my neck to rise. There was somebody out there, watching, waiting for me to escape by using the path of least resistance. If I climbed out this window, I'd likely run straight into an ambush.

Then again, it was entirely likely that if I braved the fire and made it out into the hall, there would be an assassin from the Resistance waiting for me out there too. If I took my chances with the fire escape, at least I wouldn't have to endure third-degree burns.

But then, I remembered I wasn't the only one at risk here. My neighbors were in danger too – it was only a matter of time before the fire spread to the other apartments. There was a newlywed couple next door to my place, who had a six-month-old child. I needed to help them get out. After all, it was my fault they were in danger in the first place. Unless the fire inside my apartment was ignited by some kind of freak accident.

Then again, the Resistance had left a note on my apartment door only hours ago, telling me in not so many words that they were going to kill me. A freak accident would be a hell of a coincidence under these circumstances.

Mind made up, I pulled on some clothing, grabbed my weapons, and yanked open the door. The overheated metal doorknob blistered my hands, but I ignored the pain. Instead, I surveyed the damage through stinging eyes. My entire kitchen was in flames, and the fire had blazed a path over to my living room furniture. Smoke was escaping through the window above my kitchen sink, which someone had broken. Flames blocked my path to the door, rising high enough that, considering my low ceiling, I wouldn't be able to jump over them without setting my pants on fire.

Oh well. There was a first time for everything.

I took a deep breath, which was a mistake, and immediately doubled over as I coughed up the scalding black cloud that entered my lungs. Dammit. Angry now, I swiped at my watering eyes and straightened as best I could.

Stop wasting time! People might be dying.

I braced myself, then dashed for the exit, taking a flying leap over the growing pillar of flame. As expected, the fire lashed out at my legs, traveling up my ankles to wrap around my calves. I clenched my teeth on the scream that threatened to tear from my throat, angling my body feet first as I crashed through the doorway. As soon as I landed, I dropped into a roll, moving back and forth until the flames devouring my legs were extinguished.

Wincing, I climbed to my feet, then cloaked myself in the illusion of an old woman. My legs burned like...well, fire, as I ran down the hall and began pounding on doors, shouting in a quavering, but shrill, old-lady voice that everybody needed to evacuate the building. Alarmed voices began to fill the air, but people weren't moving fast enough for my purposes, so I yanked open the newlyweds' door, breaking their flimsy lock in the process. Smoke filled their apartment, and I covered my mouth as I ran to the bedroom in the back. The fire was going to eat through the wall and spread to them in no time.

"Get out!" I threw open their bedroom door, and the couple shot straight up in bed, eyes wide with shock. The baby in the crib instantly started crying, and I raised my voice so they would hear me over her wails. "The building is on *fire*. Grab your kid and get out!"

The couple stared at the haze of smoke creeping into the room, and the man nodded. "Get the baby, Dalina," he ordered, hastily rising from the bed. "Let's go."

I dashed from the room, then went to herd other people from their beds. Thankfully, several of them were already moving toward the fire escape at the end of the hall, which was what I wanted. Not just to save them, but because I needed to get myself lost in the crowd of residents fleeing the building. If I came out first, even in my old-woman guise, the Resistance was more likely to be suspicious and guess it was me. Once enough people started swarming for the exit, I dashed down the stairs to the second floor, then repeated the process, banging on doors and shouting at people to evacuate.

By the time I got to the first floor, I was staggering, my legs burning like mad from the pain. They were probably only second-degree burns, which meant they hurt like hell because they hadn't killed my nerve endings. Even though they were healing thanks to my shifter heritage, it was going to take some time. Luckily, the people here were already roused and heading for the exit, having heard the commotion from the upper floors.

"There now." A man hooked an arm around my shoulder, supporting me. I glanced up, startled, and found myself staring into the face of a thirtyish human with spectacles on warm brown eyes. "An old lady like you shouldn't be the one trying to evacuate everybody. You look like you're in pain. Let's get you out of here before you get hurt any worse."

"T-thank you, young man," I quavered, leaning against him. I allowed him to gently lead me outside. This was perfect. Nobody was going to suspect me now, not as an injured old woman being practically carried out by a helpful human. We followed the crowd out into the lobby and through the front doors.

I stiffened at the sight of two men in khaki uniforms standing outside. Swords drawn, armbands gleaming bloody red beneath the moonlight, there was no mistaking them. They were Resistance soldiers, operating in public view right here in Solantha. Things were worse than I had imagined.

"It's okay," the human murmured, squeezing my shoulder a little. "We're going to be fine."

We passed through the front doors, right beneath the watchful gaze of the two soldiers. Gawkers and survivors lined the sidewalk, a growing crowd, and I twisted around to face the soldiers, deciding to use the situation to my advantage.

"You *stupid* boys," I shrieked, shaking my small fist at them. "How dare you set fire to this building, instead of fighting the mages like real men? Do you have any idea how many innocent people you endangered tonight?"

"Shut your mouth, old woman," the taller soldier growled, his eyes flashing in the moonlight. The sword in his hand twitched, and my human escort began dragging me away in earnest.

"You almost killed a baby," I yelled as he hauled me away, and the crowd began to murmur in agreement. Those murmurs soon turned into angry shouts, and I smiled inwardly as I disappeared into what was rapidly becoming a seething mob. Not that I was into mobs, but I wanted the population to understand just how corrupt and ruthless the Resistance had become. The less people trusted them, the harder it would be for them to take over the Federation.

"Nice play," the human murmured in my ear as he pulled me to the back of the crowd. "But I would have appreciated it more if you'd waited until we were clear of their swords before you started insulting the soldiers."

I turned to face my 'rescuer', a warning bell going off in my head. "I don't know what you're talking about." I sniffed. "Those young men needed a talking to, and that's what I delivered!"

"I'm Forin Olmos from apartment 309," he murmured. "The one directly across from yours. I saw you come out and transform, and I followed you down here to see what you were up to."

"Fuck," I muttered, dropping the old-lady voice. I leveled a glare at him. "I'm not going to have to knock you out, am I?"

Forin snorted. "I'm on your side. I don't support the Resistance, who thinks nothing of killing the rest of us to get at you, and has just attempted to burn down my apartment. Besides, I don't agree with how you've been treated. You're a hero, Sunaya Baine, and you need to be free so you can keep doing your thing." He released me, and I gaped at him in astonishment. Nobody had ever said that to me before. "Now go."

Nodding, I turned away, then fled into the night.

2

S ince running through town in the guise of an old woman would draw suspicion, I ducked into the first dark alley and allowed my disguise to drop for a moment. Leaning my back against the wall, I slid to the ground behind the safety of a dumpster, then pulled up my pant legs to check the damage on my legs. The sensation of the leather scraping against my shins was painful, but not as much as it should have been. Patches of skin had been burned away, leaving the areas raw and bloody, but they were already scabbing over.

I debated whether to use my magic to heal the wounds the rest of the way, or if I should allow shifter nature to take its course. I would be able to move faster without the pain, but since I didn't know the proper Loranian words or the techniques involved to invoke a proper healing spell, it would drain more energy out of me than was wise. I had no idea what else I would encounter tonight, and I was already using enough magic on my illusions as it was.

The clouds above me parted, allowing the nearly full moon to shine down, and a wave of energy swept through me, reminding me I didn't need to draw on my own magic for this. I could shift to heal my wounds. But I had to be careful.

Retreating to the back of the alley, I checked to make sure there was no one nearby, then shifted into my panther form. White light engulfed my body as the change took place, and I gritted my teeth against the pain as the transformation sealed my wounds shut. But when the light finally faded, I felt a million times better, my burns completely healed.

I gave myself ten minutes to rest, senses alert for any kind of danger. But nobody was looking for me here, and at this time of night, most people were in their beds. I caught a few whispers, the sound of feet clopping against pavement, but no one came in this direction. Relatively assured of my safety, I shifted back into human form, then cloaked myself in the illusion of a pimply teenage boy and headed out again.

Part of me wished I could stay in beast form as I made my way to the Palace. But the Resistance would be on the lookout for a black panther, and though I would blend in with the darkness well enough, traveling as a shifter still wasn't the wisest move.

Yeah, and neither was staying in your apartment after receiving a death threat.

I scowled. Yeah, so maybe I should have headed for Solantha Palace right away, where I would have been safe. But I'd been away for so long. After the arduous adventure of the last few weeks, traveling across the country to rescue the Chief Mage, dealing with political assassination attempts, and other bullshit, I'd just wanted the solace of my apartment. Besides, I wasn't about to let the Resistance think I was scared of them by running straight for the Palace with my tail tucked between my legs at the first sign of trouble. I wasn't scared of them, and I wasn't going to let them intimidate me.

But I *was* scared for my friends, and for the people around me, and I couldn't let the Resistance hurt them again because of my pride. Even though the last thing I wanted to do was take up residence in the Palace again, I would do it if it meant saving lives.

As I walked toward the Mages Quarter, whose towers I could see jutting into the moonlit sky even from this distance, my eyes wandered, taking in the city. Sadness filled me at the cracked windows and boarded-up storefronts, at the trash littering the streets, at the threats and curses sprayed onto formerly pristine walls and shutters. This wasn't the Solantha I knew, the clean, bustling city that oozed with character. This was a city under attack, besieged by terror and fear. People were scared to walk the streets at night, and even during the day they averted their eyes and stayed as far away from passersby as possible. It was a little terrifying to see just how far downward Solantha had slid in the time I'd been gone.

Heading toward Solantha Palace, I caught flashes of light in the distance, and my sensitive ears picked up distant explosions, screams, and battle cries. The commotion was coming from the direction of Shiftertown, where the Resistance had established their base, mainly in a couple of abandoned factory buildings close to the Rowanville border. Many shifters had fled the city when the Mages Guild had gone on a rampage, arresting anyone they suspected of having ties with the Resistance. Those who remained had sided with the Resistance out of defiance. I had heard the residents were even letting the Resistance use the vacated homes in their sector of the town, and that shifter children as young as six or seven were proudly displaying the red armbands signifying their support.

My thoughts turned to Boon Lakin, the tough-as-nails Shiftertown Inspector who had become a friend to me. Would the Resistance have been able to take Shiftertown as easily if he, or my aunt Mafiela, the Baine Clan Chieftain, had not been swept up in the arrests? The clan chieftains were divided on the issue, but Mafiela had always been very much anti-Resistance. In the past, I'd always scorned her for it, but that was before I realized the truth about the borderline terrorist organization. Her son, my cousin Rylan, was a prominent member of the Resistance, and my aunt had written him off as soon as she'd learned he'd joined.

You'd think I would welcome my aunt's misfortune, considering she'd thrown me out of my home and clan at the age of twelve, and done her best to make my life difficult. But it still seemed unfair for the Mages Guild to imprison her without cause. As for Lakin, he was just doing his job. The Tiger Clan chieftain had shared their fate, as well as a number of other shifters who hadn't escaped town, falsely confident that their innocence would protect them from the mages' wrath.

Iannis had ordered the wrongfully imprisoned to be set free, but that had been less than twenty-four hours ago, and it would take time to process their release. Many of them were probably still languishing in their cold, dark cells on Prison Isle. I shivered at the thought – it was a place you did not wish on anyone but your worst enemy.

A wave of magic rippled through me as I crossed the invisible line separating Rowanville from the Mages Quarter, and I realized wards must had been activated around the perimeter. That explained why these elegant apartments and town homes, with their magically enhanced trees and shrubbery, remained untouched. Old resentment burned inside me at the fact that, while the rest of the city was burning, the mage families slumbered in safety in luxurious homes behind their magically reinforced doors. They weren't subject to pain and terror like the rest of us.

That's not really fair, I told myself. If shifters and humans had the ability to ward ourselves from Resistance soldiers, we damn well would have done the same thing. All the mages did, or so I guessed, was put up a boundary that stopped any non-mage from coming through. The same thing would hardly work for the rest of the city, which was mostly comprised of non-mages. But still, I wished there was some kind of magical protection we could give everyone else, to keep them safe from the Resistance.

The neighborhood around me changed again, apartments and townhouses giving way to elegant homes and mansions butting up against the coastline, vying for the coveted view of Solantha Bay. Solantha Palace rose above them all, a sprawling white stone edifice with red tile capping the roofs and turrets. Casement windows sparkled in the moonlight, and rune carvings shimmered on the edges of various ledges. To my surprise, there were no guards stationed outside. As I passed through another set of wards and walked up the garden path to the entrance, I could see none guarding the front door either. Strange. I'd never seen the Palace without guards before.

I took the wide staircase two at a time, wanting to get inside as quickly as possible. The massive double doors were closed tight against the evening, and with no one around to help me, I was forced to pull one open myself. An impossible feat for a normal human, but my shifter muscles managed. Closing the door behind me, I leaned against it to catch my breath, allowing my illusion to drop with a sigh of relief.

The reception area was deserted as well, but at around four in the morning, that was hardly a surprise. Still, with the city under attack, I'd have expected guards to be around. The complete lack of people made me uneasy, which was saying something since I really didn't like Privacy Guard employees. They tended to slice first and ask questions later. A few of them had ganged up on me the first night I'd stayed at the Palace, and they'd nearly succeeded in killing me. Strength in numbers and all that.

Shrugging my unease off, I continued past the reception area, heading toward the south wing where the Mages Guild was located. The reception area for the Guild was empty as well, but I found a note pinned to a corkboard just inside the hall that led toward the Guild offices. It announced that by order of Chief Mage Iannis ar'Sannin, all routine apprentice activities were suspended until further notice, and that everyone available needed to report to the Guild Director for special assignments.

Well, well, well. Guess every cloud really did have a silver lining. Not that I was especially looking forward to taking orders from Lalia Chen, the Director of the Mages Guild, and in fact, I was going to go out of my way to make sure those orders came from Iannis instead. But my old apprentice duties had been boring as fuck, and I was glad to be rid of the grueling paper-pushing and mind-numbing grunt work, at least for a while.

Since nobody was around to report to at this hour, and it was too early to get anything done by myself, I made my way down to the kitchens to grab some food. The scent of freshly baked bread teased my nostrils even before I hit the stairwell, and my stomach growled in earnest. Food would give me an energy boost, something I really needed since my sleep was cut short.

"Good morning," I sang as I sailed into the kitchens. The kitchen staff didn't like me, mostly because I inhaled so much food every time I came in, so I tried to combat their dark looks and sour mood with extra cheeriness. "You got anything for breakfast?"

"Miss Baine!" I nearly toppled over in shock as the head chef bustled toward me. She was beaming, and the effect made her look like a sweet, middle-aged lady instead of the lemon-sucking matron I knew her to be. "I can see you're famished. Why don't you have a seat, and I'll get you something?"

"Uh... sure." My tone was cautious, and I wondered what kind of alternate reality I'd walked into. I allowed the chef to steer me over to the small wooden table in the corner where I usually ate my meals to avoid the other mages who congregated in the upstairs dining hall for mealtimes.

"Let me get you a glass of orange juice. I'll be right back."

I stared after her round figure as she hurried away, watching as she barked an order to one of her juniors. Oranges were plucked from a basket, sliced open, then pressed with a citrus juicer into a tall glass that the head chef herself carried back to my table.

"We'll have your food out soon," she promised.

"Wait." I grabbed her wrist as she was turning away and glowered at her. Maybe not the most appropriate response, but I was severely sleep deprived. "Why are you being so nice to me, Mrs. Tandry?"

A guilty look flashed in her pale blue eyes, and her round cheeks reddened a little. "I'm sorry we misjudged you when you first joined the household," she said, lowering her voice a little. "After the way you rushed out so fearlessly to save Lord Iannis when he went missing, and all the work you've done to help keep the city safe, it's obvious you're a true friend of the Palace, and Solantha. Thank you for everything you've done."

I caught the glimmer of tears in her eyes as she hurried away, and was surprised to find a lump swelling in my own throat. An odd feeling welled in my chest, one I couldn't quite describe, and it was threatening to bring tears to my own eyes. Strange that, after mostly holding it together in the face of all kinds of bullshit these past few weeks, this simple act of acceptance from a human woman was enough to make me cry.

You're just tired, I told myself, shaking my head a little. *Tired, and on the verge of heat.* I grabbed the glass of orange juice and downed it in one go. The sugar hit my system fast, giving me a tiny burst of energy, and my engines revved, ready for more.

By the time the food came – a mountain of scrambled eggs,

fried sausage and potatoes, and toast slathered with butter – I was ravenous. Only the fact that I didn't want to damage my new friendship with Mrs. Tandry stopped me from throwing myself on it like a starving animal. But I made damn good use of my fork and knife, shoveling as much food into my belly as possible. And when my plate was empty, I asked for seconds.

By the time I was finished with my third helping, I felt much better. Satisfied, I leaned the back of my chair against the wall and considered a nap. It would be another couple of hours before anybody worth speaking to arrived at their offices, so I might as well catch up on sleep.

Before I could get up, the sound of footsteps in the stairwell caught my attention. A moment later, a grey-robed apprentice with carrot-red hair staggered in, soot smeared across his freckled nose and exhaustion rimming his blue eyes.

"Coffee," he gasped. "I need coffee. Please, Mrs. Tandry," he begged.

"Coming right up," the head chef said, not even bothering to turn around. "Go ahead and have a seat."

I canted my head. I was never down here at the same time as any of the mages, so I'd never seen the head chef interact with them. It was interesting that the head chef treated him as if he were one of the Palace staff, instead of a mage. Yes, he was an apprentice, but he was still a mage, and she was a human.

Then again, she did control the food around here. So maybe that afforded her more status.

The apprentice staggered into the chair opposite me, and I wrinkled my nose as I caught a whiff of singed hair. "You catch fire or something?" I asked.

"Something," he agreed, dragging a hand through his hair. If he was trying to fix it, he failed – the action only caused it to stick out in all directions. "A group of Resistance members attempted to steal several ships from the harbor tonight, and the fight got pretty ugly. When they realized they weren't going to be able to get away with it, they set fire to them instead."

"What kind of ships?" I asked curiously. "Passenger ships?"

"No, cargo. They were mostly loaded up, set to leave tomorrow morning for Garai."

"Huh." I pursed my lips as I thought about that. If the Resistance was stealing cargo ships, it was likely one of the ways they were getting their supplies. Maybe they weren't as well funded as I'd thought. "It sounds like the battle going on in Shiftertown might be a diversion."

"No, it was the Mages Guild's idea to attack there, to try to hit the Resistance during the evening when the humans among them are more vulnerable. The Resistance might have decided to time the theft to divide our forces, though. They were prepared for our attack, which likely means they still have spies in the Palace."

"I see." I didn't like the idea of the Mages Guild mounting an attack against Shiftertown, where I'd grown up, but since the Resistance had taken root there, it wasn't as if they had a choice. "I'm guessing our new 'special assignments' have to do with defending the city and attacking the Resistance?"

The apprentice nodded. "Lord Iannis himself is organizing the defense. He was out there with us tonight, along with that savage wolf of his, and a group of other mages too." A frown creased his brow. "We should have taken them easily tonight, but the blasted humans have managed to get their hands on real firepower."

"Guns?" My eyes widened at that. Guns were banned in the Northia Federation, and the penalty for possessing firearms of any kind was death. The Federation had a department specifically dedicated to the prevention of illegal firearms smuggling, as did the local Mages Guilds. Not even the enforcers, or any of the privately owned security companies such as Privacy Guard, were allowed to own guns. And there had been none at the Resistance Camp we'd infiltrated, at least that I'd seen.

"This is very bad news," I murmured, dragging a hand through my hair. "If the Resistance has guns now, they've got a foreign contact somewhere that's helping them." Foreign affairs weren't really my thing, but even I knew there were a few countries in the Far East where you could get anything for the right price, no matter how illegal, while their authorities looked the other way. The firearms were likely coming in by way of the docks, which would explain why the camp I'd run across didn't have any yet; they were in a landlocked state. "You guys need to start monitoring the docks more closely."

The apprentice glared at me. "This is the first time we've seen guns of any kind being used in an attack by the Resistance. I'm sure Lord Iannis will be urging the Department of Firearms Control to get to the bottom of this."

He better be doing more than urging, I thought, but I kept that to myself.

Closing my eyes, I focused in on the *serapha* charm that rested against my chest, carefully tucked away beneath my clothing. The tiny stone grew warm as I activated its magic, and a tug on my chest confirmed the apprentice's story. It was pulling me in the general direction of Shiftertown, which meant Iannis was there right now. Part of me was annoyed he'd gone without me, but I understood that Iannis wouldn't want to put me in a position where I might have to fight my friends and relatives.

Finished in the kitchen, I headed down to the East Wing to grab a shower, and then a change of clothes from my old bedroom. The huge corner room still looked exactly the way it had when I'd left it – decorated in pale greens and earthy browns, a huge four-poster bed draped in green silk dominating the far side and a sitting area with a fireplace directly in front of me. Three rectangular windows framed with gossamer curtains provided a gorgeous view of Solantha Bay, and through them, I could see just a hint of dawn beginning to creep over the horizon.

Glossy wooden floorboards creaked beneath my weight as I crossed the room and entered the walk-in closet. It was mostly bare, since I'd cleared this place out after I'd gotten my own place, but, luckily, I'd left a few items of clothing here in case I needed to change after my magic lessons – a deep red button-up shirt, black leather pants, underwear, and a pair of sturdy boots. Sighing, I dropped my towel and changed into the clothes. My mood sank as I realized that aside from the dirty clothing I'd stripped off, my weapons, and my harness with its many pouches, these were the last items I owned. Everything else would have been destroyed in the fire by now.

Tears pricked at the corners of my eyes. I wasn't all that attached to physical possessions, and certainly hadn't owned that many of them, but still. I felt like the Resistance was determined to take everything from me. They'd already taken Noria Melcott, my best friend Annia's sister and a lovable genius scamp I'd grown quite fond of. They'd tried to kill Iannis, forcing me to fight tooth and nail to rescue him. And now, they were trying to take my life, too.

Suddenly exhausted, I left my boots on the floor and crawled into bed. This defeatist attitude wasn't going to get me anywhere. A couple of hours of sleep would get me in the right frame of mind, then I was going to regroup and plan a counterattack of my own. No one took what was mine and got away with it. No one.

Four hours later, I awoke to the sight of daylight streaming through my gossamer curtains. Groaning, I shielded my eyes against sunlight that was far too cheery considering the circumstances, and rolled out of bed. Coming to stand in front of the mirror, I realized my hair was an insult to rat's nests, and my skin was still pale with fatigue.

I could sleep for a week, I thought, scrubbing my face with my hands. I slapped some color into my cheeks, then wet my hair before pulling the brush through my damp mane, taming the unruly locks as quickly as possible. I needed to get down to the Mages Guild and find out what my 'special assignment' was supposed to be.

The brisk walk from the East Wing to the Guild reception helped wake me a little more, and by the time I got there, I realized the four hours of sleep had done me more good than I initially thought.

"Good morning, Miss Baine." Dira, the receptionist who often acted as an aide to Iannis, greeted me. She didn't smile, but her voice was pleasant. "I'm glad to see you've returned safe and sound."

"Thank you." I inclined my head, resigning myself to the fact that I was just going to have to get used to the fact that people were starting to be nice to me. First, the man who'd helped me escape the apartment building, then the head chef, and now the receptionist. Who was next? Canter, the grumpy old mage who manned the front desk at the Palace entrance?

Ha. Yeah, right. I didn't think anything would break through that old man's derision.

"Do you know where I might find the Chief Mage?" I asked Dira.

"He's in conference right now, with Director Chen and Captain Galling."

By Magorah. Doesn't he ever sleep? "What about?"

"I'm not privy to those details," she said firmly. I knew that was a lie, but I also knew I had a better chance of getting Iannis to dance naked across the Firegate Bridge than I did of getting her to tell me what she knew. "I would suggest you ask him yourself, when he's done."

"All right then. Thanks for being so helpful." Careful to keep the sarcasm out of my voice, I sauntered to the hall on my left, the one that led toward the Guild offices.

"Miss Baine, you can't just barge in!" Papers shuffled and a chair scraped back against the marble tile as Dira hurried to her feet.

I shot her a withering look over my shoulder. "Don't be silly. I'm just going to wait in Director Chen's office. After all, I still need to receive my 'special assignment', don't I?"

The receptionist gave me an aggravated look, but she didn't say anything more, and I moved on. I was dead certain that entering Director Chen's office without her knowledge or permission would displease the Garaian-born mage, but considering that the Guild owed me big time for bringing Iannis back, she was hardly in a position to object too strongly.

The door to her office was locked, so I ducked into another one, then returned with a paperclip. It was easy enough to jimmy it open, and since she hadn't thought to activate her wards, I slipped inside easily. Casting a dirty look at the incredibly uncomfortable visitor's chairs I'd already been acquainted with, I crossed directly over to the wall on the opposite side, sat on the floor, and pressed my ear to the silk wallpaper.

I hadn't actually come to Director Chen's office because I wanted to report to her for an assignment. The conference room Iannis was using was directly on the other side of her wall, and I wanted to listen in on the conversation.

"Captain Galling, please put your understandable resentment aside in the interest of the greater good," Iannis was saying. "I am willing to consider suitable amends for the Council's mistake of imprisoning you. In their panic at my disappearance, they did not know whom to trust, but such an error will never happen again. You have my word."

"And mine," Director Chen added in a tight voice.

"Hmm." Galling appeared to be wavering.

Iannis persevered. "By refusing to do anything, you're aiding and abetting terrorists. Can you square that with your conscience, to know you're effectively aiding the wrong side?"

Captain Galling barked a laugh. "That's easy for you to say, that I'm on the wrong side. You weren't here when the Mages Guild was sweeping through the streets and snapping up anyone who was even remotely defined as a suspect. They took some of my best enforcers too, and they'll be just as angry."

"I apologize for that," Iannis said. Anger simmered beneath the sincerity in his voice, and I nodded, satisfied. He hadn't let the matter go yet, which meant that those who were still unjustly imprisoned would be freed soon, if they hadn't been already. "But the first priority at this moment is to re-establish order and safety for all citizens in Solantha. That becomes nearly impossible if the Captain of the Enforcers Guild won't lift a finger to help me drive the Resistance from our borders."

"Even if I wanted to help you," Captain Galling growled, "I can't. Most of the enforcers hate the mages even more now, and they want nothing to do with this war." Exhaustion entered his deep voice. "Besides, the apothecaries have been shut down, and I have no access to the medicine that my wife so desperately needs. I'm not interested in resuming my office while she is suffering."

"What if I could cure your wife?" Iannis asked softly. "Would you be more inclined to help us then?"

There was a long pause. "You can do that?" Captain Galling asked, and there was no mistaking the surprise in his voice. "Don't you think I have already tried everything? I was told repeatedly that such an advanced liver disease was beyond the skill of magic healers."

"As it happens, I'm one of the most talented healers in the country," Iannis admitted without a hint of hubris. To him, he was simply stating a fact, not bragging. "There are very few maladies I can't heal, but because I am unable to heal everyone, I do not advertise that fact."

"Well, it would have been nice if you'd offered before now," Captain Galling grumbled. "My wife has been suffering for years."

"I did not know," Iannis said. "But I am more than happy to help her now."

There was another long pause. At last, Captain Galling grunted. "Very well. I'll help you. I don't like the way the Resistance is dealing with things anyway. So much unnecessary chaos and destruction does not bode well for us, and if they should actually seize power..." He trailed off. "I'll help you," he said again, more firmly.

"Excellent."

I listened as they hashed out the details further. Captain Galling grudgingly agreed to haul the enforcers back in line, getting them to police the looting and withdraw their support from the Resistance. In exchange, Iannis promised to release a public apology for all the wrongful arrests, and to double the bounties for looters, rapists, murderers, and other miscreants while the crisis lasted.

"I believe we're done here for now," Iannis said at last, followed by the sounds of chairs scraping back from tables. "Make the arrangements to have your wife transported to the Palace without delay. Director Chen, please find two mages to go with her as an escort. I would hate for something to happen to Mrs. Galling along the way."

"Yes, sir," Director Chen acknowledged.

The door opened, and I hastily deposited myself into one of Director Chen's visitors' chairs, wincing as the carved dragons dug into my back. I didn't want her to know I had been eavesdropping, even though I doubted I'd heard anything all that confidential aside from the bit about Galling's wife. And even if I had, Director Chen knew she could trust me. Or so I hoped.

A few minutes later, the door to Director Chen's office opened, and the woman herself walked in. Her waterfall of fine, dark hair was pulled up into a high bun secured with ivory chopsticks, and the robe she wore today was emerald-green silk, with tiny, golden petals scattered across the fabric.

Her almond-shaped eyes widened as she caught sight of me. "Miss Baine. Who let you into my office?"

"I let myself in," I said casually, looping my left leg over the chair's arm as I twisted to face her. It creaked under the unorthodox distribution of my weight, and predictably, Director Chen's eyes flashed, though her impassive expression did not otherwise change, and I bit back a tight smile. If she was going to force me to sit in such a shitty chair, then I was going to abuse the hell out of it.

"I believe that when a door is locked, it's a signal that the occupant does not wish for others to 'let themselves in'," she said stiffly, gliding around the cherry-wood desk to sit in her own high-backed and much more comfortable leather chair.

I shrugged. "The sign in the hall said to report to you for special assignment, so here I am. Give me an assignment."

Director Chen took a deep breath and squared her shoulders. "Simple enough. Your assignment is to stay out of the way."

I straightened in my chair. "Excuse me?" I couldn't be hearing that right. "You want me to sit back and do *nothing*?"

"I didn't say that," Director Chen said tersely. "You are free to join the enforcers in their efforts to restore order in the city, or help any of the secretaries, since we are badly understaffed. But I need you to stay away from Lord Iannis."

I nearly toppled out of my chair at that. "Why?" I spluttered. "Have you forgotten that I am his apprentice? He's supposed to give me direction! I almost lost him, Director Chen, and *I'm* the one who found him. Until my magical training is complete, I'm not leaving his side."

Director Chen sighed. "I am grateful you recovered Lord Iannis safely, and I'll even apologize for not taking you along on the rescue mission, as you had requested. But I am now thinking of Lord Iannis's best interests, as you should be too. Rumors are spreading throughout the city that the two of you are lovers, and they will only be exacerbated the more often you two are seen together in public."

"T-that's ridiculous," I sputtered, heat rising to my cheeks. "We're not lovers." *Kisses don't count,* I reminded myself firmly. Sure, they'd been some of the hottest, most erotic kisses I'd ever experienced, but they were still kisses. No actual lovemaking had ensued. *Yet.*

"I believe you," Director Chen assured me. "The Chief Mage would never forget himself to the point of engaging in carnal relations with an apprentice. But Lord Iannis is reasserting his control over the state of Canalo, and such scandalous allegations are most unhelpful at this critical juncture." She plucked a copy of the Herald off her desk, flipped it open to the social section, and passed it to me. "Take this article, for example."

I took the paper from her and quickly scanned the piece. It detailed how the Chief Mage had taken his 'feline mistress' to the Convention and shocked the other delegates by dancing with her in public view. There was even a photograph of the two of us waltzing, and I blinked, hardly recognizing myself in the resplendent ball gown I was wearing. We made an incredibly handsome couple, I admitted to myself, and the way our bodies were pulled so close together, nearly touching, certainly suggested 'carnal relations' as Chen had put it.

Too bad appearances could be so deceiving.

"Other papers across the country are displaying similar stories," Chen said, drawing my attention back to her. Her lips were pressed into a thin, disapproving line as she stared down at the image, and anger flared in my chest. I was tempted to tell her just how wrong she was about Iannis and me, but what was the point? He still hadn't made a decision whether we should become lovers and the last thing I needed was to go around telling people we had a relationship, only to later find out that he'd rejected me. The humiliation would be devastating.

"There is great public interest in Lord Iannis right now," Chen went on, "so upholding his reputation is more important than ever. Taking on a hybrid apprentice has already raised too many eyebrows as it is. Lord Iannis needs unified support from the Canalo mages. If they believe this is anything more than malicious gossip, it could ruin any chances of advancing his political career, or making more eligible connections."

"I see," I said slowly. "So you're saying if I wasn't a hybrid, that if I were a full mage like yourself, this wouldn't be a problem?"

Director Chen nodded. "Affairs between master and apprentice are frowned upon under any circumstances, but it is the fact you're a hybrid that pushes the issue over the edge. I'm sure you understand."

"I do," I said, and this time, I couldn't quite keep the anger from entering my voice. I got the subtext loud and clear – Chen was saying Iannis needed a respectable career mage by his side, someone like *her*. "But you know what?" I added, leaning forward a little to pin her with a stare that told her I knew what she was up to. "I think the Chief Mage is old enough to decide what he wants and needs."

Chen's eyes widened with pity and astonishment, and she let out a half-laugh. "You foolish child. How could you imagine that Lord Iannis would ever 'need' a hybrid like you? You may be growing into your powers, Miss Baine, but you are little more than a charity case in the Chief Mage's eyes."

I opened my mouth to retort, but my heated words died on my lips as I caught Iannis's scent. Footsteps sounded in the hall, followed by a knock on the door.

"Come in," I called, mostly to annoy Director Chen. She shot me a venomous glare, but quickly masked her expression as the door swung open and the Chief Mage stepped inside.

"I didn't realize this was your office, Miss Baine," Iannis said mildly. His expression was unreadable, as usual, but the briefest hint of amusement in his iridescent violet eyes made me grin.

"It's not," Director Chen said, drawing Iannis's gaze away from me. Her dark eyes brightened, almost imperceptibly, and I clenched my jaw. I'd suspected she had feelings for him, and I was seeing them now, loud and clear. She wanted Iannis for herself.

And why shouldn't she? a voice whispered in my head. *She's much better suited as a politician's consort than you'll ever be. If that weren't the truth, Iannis would have claimed you already.*

"Is there something you need from me?" Director Chen asked him.

"Actually, I came in here looking for Miss Baine," Iannis said. "I have a few matters I need to discuss with her."

"I was just about to assign her something –" Chen began.

"That can wait until later. Unless whatever task you were planning to assign is of paramount importance?" Iannis arched a brow.

"No, it's not." Director Chen's voice was smooth as a glassy lake as she inclined her head in deference. But the smile in her voice was gone. "Of course you are free to take her, Lord Iannis. I can always speak with Miss Baine later."

"Excellent. Come along," he said to me, then turned and strode out the office.

I hurried after him, pausing only to shoot a smug grin over my shoulder at Director Chen. I should probably have been worried at the fact that she was glaring daggers at me, but at the moment, I didn't care. I would be damned if I was going to let her tight, uppity ass come between Iannis and me. If Iannis wanted to keep me at arm's length, that was *his* decision, not hers.

I stepped into Iannis's office across the hall and shut the door behind me. His Guild office was much larger than the study he kept in the West Wing – the study was smaller, more personal, with only his workspace and shelves of books. This office was clearly meant for receiving guests, with a large picture window overlooking the gardens behind a magnificent desk, a sitting area in front of a fireplace, and even a small bar. Gold and blue was the décor here, of course – those were the state colors, after all. I wondered how many diplomats and Chief Mages had sat on the couches or in the visitor's chairs, sipping tea or drinking cognac as they discussed matters of state with Iannis.

"So," I began, but before I could ask what Iannis wanted to discuss, he pushed me up against the wall and crushed his lips against mine. My mouth opened in shock, and he took advantage, nipping my bottom lip as his tongue stroked mine, filling me with his dark, exotic flavor. The kiss was somehow gentle despite his aggressive body language, savoring rather than trying to devour. Warmth ignited low in my belly, then spread through me like wildfire, and I dug my fingers into his broad shoulders, clinging to him as my body begged for more. I was perilously close to heat, and I knew if Iannis decided to take things further, I would be powerless to stop him despite the ultimatum I'd given him back in Dara. The one where I'd said I wasn't going to sleep with him until he made a decision as to whether or not he wanted to be with me.

Eventually, Iannis broke the kiss, but his hands remained firmly curled around my waist. His violet eyes seared me as they searched my face, and more warmth flooded me as I realized that beneath the burning desire was relief.

"When I returned to the Palace and discovered you were sleeping in your room instead of your apartment, I asked an aide to do a little investigating," Iannis said. "They only told me the news a few minutes ago. Are you all right?" he asked, stroking my cheek. "Did those bastards hurt you in any way?"

Oh, I could just melt. The way he was looking at me, as if he could not bear the thought of losing me, made me want to just sink into his embrace and never let go. But I couldn't let that happen, not until he told me, with real words, how he actually felt. Besides, we had more important things to worry about.

"I'm fine," I told him, pressing the heels of my hands into his shoulders – a subtle sign that I wanted space. He moved slightly, but not enough to cool the inferno he'd sparked. "The Resistance set fire to my apartment to draw me out so they could kill me. But I got everyone out of the building and made sure to stick close to the crowd so they couldn't get a clear shot at me. I was disguised as an old woman, and with so many witnesses, they didn't want to risk killing bystanders, when they couldn't tell if they had the right target."

"Smart," Iannis said. "But they never should have come so close. And even if you have nine lives, Sunaya, they must be nearly used up by now. I'm assuming you'll abandon this foolish idea about living outside the Palace now? You'll be much safer here."

"Only until the crisis is over," I said coolly, folding my arms across my chest. I wasn't about to let Iannis think I was moving back in permanently. If he decided he didn't want me as a lover, that we were only going to be master and apprentice, then I most definitely wasn't willing to live in the same building as him.

Iannis's eyes darkened. "You're being ridiculous," he insisted. "Life would be easier for both of us if you lived here. We could –"

"If you start telling me that we could get more master-apprentice stuff done if I lived in the Palace, I'll punch you straight in the nose," I warned. Shock flared in his eyes, and I used the opening to plow forward. "You know damn well you've only got so much time in the day, especially now that you're out fighting the Resistance. How am I supposed to move on if I'm constantly living in your shadow? Hearing your voice? Inhaling your scent? And watching you and Director Chen make eyes at each other when she seduces you?"

He blinked. "*What?* That's not –"

The intercom speaker on Iannis's desk crackled to life. "Sir, the Minister is on the phone for you. He says it's urgent."

"Very well. Put him through." Iannis sighed, then moved away, giving me much-needed breathing room. "We're not finished with this conversation," he warned before picking up the ringing phone.

"No," I said softly as I slipped out the door. "I imagine we're not."

My feet took me from the Guild offices to the library on the lower floor of the West Wing. I'd been here before, seeking out Fenris so he could help me with the bank investigation I was conducting only three weeks ago. An investigation that had eventually led to the discovery of a group of kidnapped shifters who were forced into illegal fighting matches. Perhaps I'd find Fenris in the library again – he was generally a calming influence, and great for bouncing ideas off when I had a puzzle to solve. I had hardly seen him since Iannis and I returned from Dara, and truth be told, I missed him.

Unfortunately, the library was completely deserted, aside from a grey-haired librarian who sat quietly behind her desk, a fragile old tome open as she hand-penned notes from it. I glanced around the huge room that could have easily fit the entire Shifter Courier building inside it, scanning rows of bookshelves so tall they nearly touched the soaring ceiling, and wondered if there was anything in here that might be of interest to me.

You could always research the Tua.

Huh. That was an interesting idea. Not exactly relevant to the current catastrophe, but interesting. I'd recently discovered that Iannis was part Tua, and had extra abilities this heritage afforded him. I wondered if researching the mystical, long-lived race of his grandmother might give me better insight into Iannis himself.

Probably not. But what else do you have to do? It's not as if Director Chen is going to assign you anything useful.

"Excuse me, Miss Baine," the librarian said in a firm but friendly voice. "Is there anything I can help you with?"

"Oh!" I turned around to look at her, a little flustered that she knew me. The nameplate on her desk told me her name was Janta Urama, and that she was the head librarian of the Palace. A prestigious position... was she sitting at the reception desk because her staff was off fighting the Resistance? Her middle-aged appearance was unusual for mages, who could assume youthful beauty whenever they pleased, but perhaps she cared more about research and learning than her looks. "Umm..." I scrambled to come up with something, because Iannis had told me of his Tua heritage in confidence, and I did not want to accidentally reveal that to her. "The Chief Mage sent me here. He wanted me to research *gulayas*, as part of my apprentice training."

"*Gulayas*?" The woman's steel grey eyebrows rose in surprise. "That is advanced magic indeed for an apprentice in her first year of training."

I forced myself not to fidget underneath her searching gaze. Before Argon Chartis, the renegade mage who'd signed up with the Resistance, had used a *gulaya* to escape Iannis's wrath, I'd never even heard of them. It figured that they'd be an obscure subject. "Yeah, well, we came across one during the recent rescue mission, and I wanted to know more about them. So he said I should look here."

"Ah, I see." The librarian's face cleared, and she stood up. "We have an excellent encyclopedia of magical items that should have the information you need. Come, right this way."

She led me over to a low shelf that was fitted directly into the wall beneath one of the windows. The shelf was filled with a series of white, leather-bound books with the titles stamped on the spines in gold – twenty-six volumes total, one for each letter in the alphabet. Carefully, she selected the 'G' volume, then placed it on a bookstand on top of the shelf and opened it to a specific page.

I sighed as I scanned the small print. I knew it was the right entry because at the top of the page was a stylized drawing of a *gulaya* that looked very similar to the star-shaped object Chartis had used to vanish before our eyes. But the text was written in Loranian, the difficult language of magic I was still trying to master.

"It's all right," Janta said, noting my dismay. "I'll help you."

Slowly and patiently, she helped me translate the text. I was able to read every fourth word or so, and between the two of us, I worked out what the encyclopedia said. Some of it I already knew from Iannis – *gulayas* were anchored to the location where they had first been activated, and the wearer could use them to teleport back to that location so long as the *gulaya* was charged. They would activate on command, or in some cases automatically if the wearer were in deadly peril. The encyclopedia cited a mage who had been carried back to the nursery at the age of seven by a *gulaya*, when a grizzly bear was about to bite her head off. However, several centuries ago, *gulayas* had gone out of fashion because charging them required a two-day ritual after each use, and a single mistake in the execution of said ritual meant you had to redo the whole damned thing. Even worse, the ritual involved a rare plant called grusia that only grew in a mountainous area located between Sandia and Garai, and its sale and export were illegal in most countries.

"Why is it illegal?" I asked Janta.

"Because grusia is more commonly used in death spells," Janta explained. "Mostly by witches, of course, as they tend to rely on plants for their magic more than we mages do. The Federation banned the plant nearly three hundred years ago, when the Minister at that time was assassinated through a death spell that involved grusia."

"Makes sense." I shuddered a little. "I didn't know death spells were a thing." I mean, maybe in the back of my mind I knew it was possible, but I'd never really thought about it.

Janta smiled a little. "I'm afraid you'll find out that all sorts of things are possible with magic, both good and bad." She turned away, gesturing for me to follow her. "Come. We have several old *gulayas* in the library's artifacts collection that I can show you."

She led me to a back room lined with shelves filled with containers of varying shapes and sizes. They were all carefully labeled, but when I tried to read some of them, I found, to my frustration, that the labels were written in Loranian. Dammit. I really was going to have to master the language sooner rather than later.

Humming a cheerful tune under her breath, Janta scanned the shelves until she found a long, rectangular metal box. As she touched it, runes flared to life, glowing bright blue and red. I squinted against the glare, my eyes having adjusted to the dim interior of the library, while Janta murmured a few Words. There was a loud click, and the runes faded as the container unlocked.

"Here we go," Janta said, carrying the box to a table in the center of the room. She opened it and pulled out a smaller box from within labeled "*Gulayas*". Inside were seven of the silver, star-shaped charms, most of them as big as my palm, but some of them smaller.

"Oh, this is *terrible*," Janta cried as I laid the last one on the table. She was scanning a long piece of paper. "One of the *gulayas* is missing!"

"Somehow, that doesn't surprise me," I murmured, picking up each piece in turn and examining it. They smelled like magic, but very faintly, as if only traces remained. But one of them, a small one that was little larger than a gold coin, smelled more strongly than the rest. Was there a chance that it might still be charged? How long did it take for a *gulaya's* charge to wear off naturally?

"What do you mean, you are not surprised?" the librarian asked, suspicion clouding her voice. "Nobody is supposed to have access without one of my staff."

"As I mentioned earlier, I encountered one of these on my rescue mission," I told her. "Argon Chartis used it to escape when we found out he was allied with the Resistance, and it's entirely possible he stole it from this very library when he was still Director at the Mages Guild." I held up the small gulaya. "I need to take this one to Lord Iannis. It might be able to help us with something we're looking into."

"Yes, of course." The librarian had her hand pressed to her cheek, still shocked. "You'll need to sign the check-out log."

I did as she asked, then pocketed the borrowed *gulaya* and strode out of the library. I had no intention of giving the *gulaya* to Iannis – I was keeping it for myself, at least for a little bit. With the bright red target the Resistance had painted on my back, any ace in my sleeve was welcome. I just hoped that the *gulaya*, if it was in fact still active, would not whisk me all the way to Garai or some other place overseas where I did not know the language. But then again, any place was probably safer than where I was now.

5

I hurried back to the Mages Guild, intent on cornering Iannis and getting him to give me a useful assignment. But just as I was passing through the reception area, Dira, the front desk receptionist, called my name.

"Miss Baine, there's a message for you. From an Enforcer Annia Melcott."

I paused, then veered toward the desk. If Annia was calling me here, it had to be important. The last time I'd seen her, she'd been in a fog of grief over Noria's decision to join the Resistance, bitter and utterly defeated. I hoped she wasn't about to do something rash. "What's the message?"

Dira frowned, reading the message she'd scrawled down when she received the note. "She asked if you could please meet her at your mutual friend's house. And that it was urgent."

"Thanks." I nodded, then hurried down the hall, heading for the finance office. As I half-expected, most of the finance department's desks were empty, and the few people who were busy at their desks were mages, with the exception of one elderly human accountant. I couldn't help the small sigh that escaped me. Was *everyone* deserting us?

Noria did.

Pushing that thought out of my head, I veered left, toward the Finance Secretary's office, and knocked on the door.

"Who is it?"

"Sunaya Baine."

There was a pause. "Come in," he said eventually.

I pushed open the door, then closed it behind me. Cirin Garidano, Solantha's Secretary of Finance, was more striking and fashionable than the other mages of his stature. Like Iannis, he tended to dress in robes that flattered his broad shoulders and tall frame, and he wore his black hair long, far past his shoulders. Dark, piercing blue eyes were narrowed in concentration as he tapped out a report on his typewriter with long fingers that flew across the keys. I felt my approaching heat more strongly at the sight of a handsome male, but firmly pushed the sensation away.

"Isn't typing reports something you delegate to a lackey?" I asked, leaning my hip against the door.

He glanced up at me, a faintly annoyed expression on his face. "In case you haven't noticed, Miss Baine, we are in short supply of lackeys at the moment. Did you come in here to criticize my office?"

"No," I admitted, shoving my hands into my pockets. "I came here because I need to borrow a car."

His dark eyebrows winged up. "And what makes you think I'm in a position to help you? The Mages Guild doesn't use cars."

I rolled my eyes. "Give me a break. I spend enough time around this joint that I can afford to do a little snooping." My ability to wear illusions was a big help in sneaking into restricted areas, too. "You've got a garage full of them." I smirked a little at the surprise in Cirin's eyes. "Guess you mages aren't so averse to technology after all, are you?"

"*We* mages, Miss Baine, and not as much as we used to be,"

he admitted in a cool voice. "After all, we use telephones, type-writers, and dirigibles, don't we?"

"And apparently vehicles."

"They are for emergency use only," Cirin warned. "After realizing how much of an advantage technology has given humans, Lord Iannis has authorized, and even encouraged, the use of technology in the Guild, though not everyone is in favor of such innovation. Vehicles aren't the only things he's collected... but we've yet to publicly use them."

I rolled my eyes. "Oh, come on. It'll be okay. I know how to drive. It's not like you guys painted the Mages Guild emblems on your vehicles, have you?"

When Cirin didn't respond, I groaned. "Seriously?"

"They wouldn't be official vehicles if we didn't," Cirin pointed out. "We had it done recently."

That explained why I didn't remember seeing it. "Fine. Then give me a can of paint so I can cover it up. Just let me borrow a vehicle. I can't go running around on foot with the Resistance out to kill me."

Cirin sighed. "I can't give you a car," he told me. "But there is another kind of vehicle I can give you."

I perked up. "Oh?"

"THIS IS BULLSHIT," I grumbled to myself as I pedaled up one of the many very long, very *steep* hills that Solantha was known for. I was halfway to the Port now, pushing the bicycle the Finance Secretary had bestowed upon me as fast as I could. But even though I had extra-strong muscles as a shifter, they weren't used to bike riding, and certainly not over long distances with steep hills. A dull ache was starting up in my quads, and it was only going to get worse from here.

At least you're getting a workout.

I snorted. Yeah, like I really needed one. By Magorah, but I missed my steambike. I wished like hell I'd been able to recover it from Turain, but Danrian's cronies had probably sold it off to a chop shop weeks ago. I was never going to see my baby again.

You could probably convince Iannis to replace it for you, a little voice murmured in my head. I clenched my jaw at that idea. I was too proud to ask for that kind of gift from Iannis. I was already living in his Palace and eating his food, wasn't I? I wasn't going to ask him for money I hadn't earned on top of it.

No, when this was over and I could start earning money as an enforcer again, I'd buy myself another bike. For now, I had to deal with this hand-me-down. It was one of the bikes the guards used to circle the perimeter during their rounds, and since the guards were conspicuously absent, there was an abundance of bicycles available.

Eventually, I made it to the Port, and I cruised down the boulevard, studying the row of large, stone boathouses that marked the entrance to each pier. The smell of burnt wood still lingered in the air, and I could see wreckage floating in the water – leftovers from the attempted ship robbery the apprentice had mentioned last night.

I finally came to Witches End, and I skidded to a stop as I noticed the entrance to the pier had been barricaded, and was guarded by two stout shopkeepers bearing cudgels. Cautiously, I got off my bike and approached them.

"Hey," I said, adopting the voice of the acne-covered teenage boy I was pretending to be. "What's going on?"

The shopkeepers closed ranks, glowering down at me. "This area is off-limits to all humans and shifters," the one on the left growled in a thick Pernian accent that was much deeper than Comenius's. I recognized him as Caradin, a magical bladesmith who'd set up shop at the Port about a year ago. I'd been eyeing his wares for a while now, but hadn't managed to scrape up the coin to buy any as yet. The man next to him was his son. I'd bet those cudgels they wielded were capable of more than breaking bones and causing concussions.

"Look," I said, lifting my hand. Fire crackled in my palm, and the two jumped, startled. "I'm not a human. Comenius is a friend of mine, and he called me over here. Can you just let me in to see him? I promise I'm not here to cause trouble."

"How do we know you're not using a charm to produce that flame?" Caradin demanded.

I rolled my eyes and lifted my arms overhead. "Search me then, if you're so suspicious."

"She's not, Da." The son's eyes glowed an eerie blue as he stared at me, and I had a feeling he was searching me. "She is wearing charms, and an illusion of sorts, but both fire and illusion are being produced by her."

"*She?*" Caradin demanded, and I tensed. I wasn't prepared to drop my illusion, not in broad daylight.

"Da, just let it go," the man hissed.

They shared a long look, then Caradin sighed. "Very well. You may pass." He moved his big bulk out of the path. "But if you try to blow up any shops, I'll have your head." He lifted his cudgel, and I gaped as it morphed into a short sword right before my eyes.

"Damn," I muttered as I turned away. *I've gotta get me one of those.*

I walked my bike up the pier, noticing that all the shops were boarded up now. This was likely in response to the skirmish that went down by the Port last night. I couldn't blame the shop owners for being cautious – I would have done the same – but it still made me sad to see the usually thriving shops battened down. It felt like they were huddling close together, bracing for a storm.

A storm that was already in full swing.

Com's place was boarded up as well, so I trotted up the side staircase and knocked on the entrance to his apartment. Since he was the only close mutual friend Annia and I had, I figured she had to be here.

The door opened, revealing Comenius. His ash-blond hair was messy, and there were bags under his eyes, as though he'd risen from a sleepless night and hadn't bothered to brush his hair.

"It's me," I said, using my normal voice, though I didn't drop my teenage-boy disguise.

"Come in, come in," he said hurriedly, waving me inside. He shut the door behind me and double-locked it. I stared at the two strangers sitting on his couch. One was a tall, lean man in his thirties wearing dark sunglasses and a leather jacket, and the other a petite blonde dressed head to toe in denim.

And they both smelled strongly of magic.

"It's us, Naya." Annia's voice came out of the blonde, and I started. "Annia and Elnos."

"Elnos?" I swung my gaze back to her companion and goggled. The man I stared at looked nothing like the fresh-faced, gangly young mage who was Noria's boyfriend. "Why the hell are you two disguised like this? What's going on?"

"The two of them have decided to infiltrate the Resistance," Comenius said from behind me. I turned to see him standing near the small, round dining table, arms crossed and an uncharacteristic glower on his handsome features. "Something I am in complete disagreement with, by the way."

Sighing, I turned back to face Annia. She might have been wearing a different guise, but the steely look of determination in her eyes was all her. "I'd ask why you're doing this, but I already know. You two are going to try and get Noria back, aren't you?"

"Yes," Elnos answered, his voice hard. "By force, if necessary. She has gotten in way over her head."

"We're going to try to persuade her first, though," Annia added.

I snorted. "Do you really think persuasion is going to work at this stage of the game?"

Annia opened her mouth, but Elnos beat her too it. "No," he said glumly. "She won't listen to reason at this point, and we don't have time to convince her. We need to get her out before the Resistance is defeated, and she is killed."

"You seem pretty convinced of that," I commented. Not that I disagreed, but I was interested in hearing his reasoning.

Elnos nodded, his expression grave. "Modern humans and shifters have no idea what cornered mages are truly capable of. The mage community has not been forced to use the full extent of its powers since the Conflict, and neither human nor shifter memory is that long. The Resistance and their supporters think that between their superior firepower, greater numbers and the handful of magic users they've recruited to their side, they have what it takes to successfully overthrow the Federation government. However, offensive and defensive magic is still very much a part of every apprentice's curriculum. We have lethal spells that can wipe out entire armies if they're not set up to properly defend. These spells are currently forbidden, but if the Resistance continues their provocations, that is going to change."

I paled at that. "So you're saying that, if it came down to it, the Federation could just send a group of mages to wherever Noria's at and wipe out her entire camp?"

Elnos nodded. "Easily. The Federation has refrained from such action because they did not consider the Resistance a large enough threat, and also because they know the kind of public-relations nightmare indiscriminate mass killings would cause. But they will only exercise restraint for so long. This is why I've always pleaded for peaceful and voluntary reform. I kept hoping that if I had enough time, I could convince Noria to change her outlook." He sighed, his stern expression crumpling with sadness. "But I failed, and now I must get her back before it is too late."

I nodded slowly, impressed with Elnos's maturity, then went over and laid a comforting hand on his shoulder. "All right. What can I do to help you guys?"

"I need some assistance with our disguises," Elnos admitted, a little sheepishly. He gestured to Annia, who pushed her sleeve back to reveal a bracelet with a single charm hanging from it. "I created a charm for Annia's disguise, in case we get separated. While I believe the look itself is solid, I haven't quite gotten the hang of masking her scent, since my own nose is not sensitive. There will be shifters at the camps, and since she has already infiltrated a Resistance camp with you and Fenris, there is always the chance someone might recognize her scent. Not to mention that we need to disguise the scent of my magic, or the Resistance will know for sure that we're not two rebel humans running off from our homes to join the fight."

"Yeah, you'll definitely want to mask that." Sitting down on the couch between them, I guided Elnos through the necessary steps required to change their scents. It was interesting, that I was teaching a full-blooded mage how to direct his magic in a specific way, when I'd only just learned this trick myself a few months ago. Iannis had mentioned that my sensitivity to scents must be why I had such an aptitude for disguising them – it was a talent that usually took a long time to master. I wondered what other types of magic my shifter heritage might give me an advantage in, but I filed that question away for later.

"Okay, you two should be good now."

"Thanks." Sighing, Annia leaned her head back against the

couch, then eyed me. "You know, it's a little weird to hear your voice coming out of a teenage boy's mouth."

"Oh. Right." I dropped the illusion. Almost as soon as I did, I felt a surge of warmth, followed by a soreness in my breasts and a tingling ache in my lower belly.

"Naya? Is something wrong?"

I pressed a hand to my belly. "My symptoms. They disappeared for a while." At Comenius's blank look, I explained, "I'm about to go into heat, and for the past couple of days, I've been experiencing the onset. But when I put on the teenage-boy disguise, the symptoms reduced so drastically I barely noticed them."

"Fascinating," Elnos said. He tilted his head, regarding me like I was one of the machines in his shop. "I wonder if it's because you are more in tune with your mage half than your shifter half when using magic? Or if your use of a male illusion is tricking your female body to some degree?"

"All plausible explanations," Comenius agreed. He had a strange look on his face as he stared at me. "Do you think you're going to be okay this next week? Dealing with this insurrection as well as your...heat?"

His face flushed, and I grinned a little, understanding. I'd gone to Comenius twice in the past when my heat had become too unbearable to ignore, and even though we'd no longer been in a relationship at that time, he'd been more than happy to oblige. But now he had Elania and that was no longer possible, so he was concerned about what I might do without a ready outlet.

"Don't worry about it, Com," I told him. "I'll figure out a solution, even if it means I have to walk around like a teenage boy for the next week."

"Why are you disguised as a teenage boy, anyway?" Annia asked. "Are you also on a reconnaissance mission?"

"I wish." I sighed, thinking back to Chen's directive – that she wanted me to stay out of the way and not do anything. "Honestly, I'm just trying not to die." I stood up and began to pace as I told them about the warning message the Resistance had left on my door yesterday, and the fire I'd narrowly escaped in the early hours of the morning.

"*Heiliger Strohsack*, Naya!" Comenius exclaimed. "You waited to tell us about this until now? You could have been killed!" He wrapped me in a tight hug.

"I know, but I wasn't." I hugged him back, briefly resting my cheek on his chest as I inhaled his woodsy, herbal scent. The ache in my lower body flared up in proximity to a male, and I hastily extricated myself from his grip. Logic and heat didn't really go together, so it was better if I didn't touch Comenius, or any other male I wasn't planning on taking to bed.

"Anyway, I've got to stay in disguise when I go out in public, which sucks. But at least it helps with the heat, so that's something."

"You could always jump the Chief Mage," Annia said, waggling her eyebrows. "I'm sure he'd understand your...situation. He'd probably even be happy to help." She grinned.

"*Annia*," Comenius scolded.

"I'm afraid he's a little busy," I said, not sure whether I should laugh or cringe. "Don't worry, guys. Seriously. I'll figure it out."

"I might be able to help." Elania's musical voice drifted from the stairwell, and I turned as I heard her footsteps creaking on the wooden steps. She sashayed in a few moments later, and I was surprised to see her in a black top and pants rather than the tight, low-cut dresses she preferred. Over her clothing, she wore a stained apron, and the smudges of dirt on her usually perfect face and the duster in her hand told me she'd been cleaning downstairs.

"Help with what?" I asked as she glided over to Comenius. "The heat?"

"Yes." She planted a kiss on Comenius's cheek, then turned to face me. "My mother used to make an anti-aphrodisiac that was quite effective. Her customers were usually tired women who wanted to stave off their randy husbands. They would mix a few drops in their man's beer when he came home from work, and unless said man had an extraordinarily powerful libido, he was content to leave her alone for the evening."

"Huh." I'd never even considered such a scenario between married couples, but I could understand an overtired housewife wanting to go to bed early every so often without spreading her legs. "Well, if you've got some, I'll try it out."

"It'll only take a few moments to make," Elania promised. "Let me just get washed up."

She disappeared into Comenius's bedroom, then returned a little bit later with the dirt removed from her face, wearing a long, high-waisted black dress with no sleeves. She tied a glittering purple apron over her dress as she went into the kitchen, then bustled around, chopping up herbs and boiling water.

Resigned to the wait, I sat down in the wicker armchair next to the sofa and turned back to Elnos and Annia. "So are you two already packed, then? Do you need help with any other preparations?"

"No, we're good," Annia said softly. There was a faraway look in her eyes as she stared at the opposite wall. "I'm not sure how long we're going to be gone for, Naya. It could be a week, or it could be months. Part of me feels I'm being selfish by doing this, that I should be staying here to help defend the city and fight off the Resistance."

"It's okay." I reached over and squeezed her hand. "You've done a lot already, between helping me with the Shifter Royale case and rescuing the Chief Mage. And depriving the Resistance of Noria's talents has got to be worthwhile in itself. No one would dream of faulting you for wanting to go after your sister." I turned my head to glare at Comenius. "Right?"

He sighed, looking away. "I suppose not," he admitted. "And perhaps while you're there, you may learn something useful that will help the Federation in their fight against the Resistance."

"We are planning on gathering as much intel as possible," Elnos acknowledged. "Comenius has agreed to receive my transmissions by ether pigeon and deliver any urgent information to the Mages Guild."

I arched a brow. "Ether pigeon?"

He nodded, then held out his hand and spoke a few Words. Magic swirled above his palm before taking the shape of a ghostly, glowing blue pigeon. "Mages used to send these to carry messages between war camps, during the Conflict. They're used much less often since the advent of telegrams, but the spell is far from obsolete."

"That's fascinating." I crouched down to get a better look at the pigeon. It turned its head to look at me in that strange, stilted way birds have about them, and I could swear I saw it ruffle its feathers. But when I reached out to touch it, my finger simply passed through it, though a magical tingle skipped up my nerves. "So how does it work? And can it travel very long distances?"

"Not more than a few hundred miles, unfortunately," Elnos admitted. "And imbuing it with the message you want to transmit is a tricky business. You certainly can't send more than a few sentences. Thankfully, from what we've been able to determine, Noria is still in Canalo for now, so we should be able to use these."

"But won't somebody notice a glowing blue pigeon flying through the air?" I asked. "If someone catches you at the camp, you'll be outed for sure."

Elnos shook his head. "When the pigeons are launched into the air, they turn into a blue mist that blends in with the atmosphere, and they don't regain their shape again until they arrive at their destination. Once they deliver their message, the spell is finished, and the pigeon will disappear. I'll have to be careful I'm not seen when I send messages, and I won't be able to receive them, but otherwise, this should work."

"Well, it's very brave of you to be willing to do that, and I hope you're extra careful," I told him. Should I warn him not to underestimate the Resistance? But no, Annia already knew how dangerous they could be. Between an experienced, wily enforcer and a resourceful mage, surely they would be all right. Besides, someone needed to go knock some sense into Noria, and I couldn't go. Annia was the best person for the job, and who was I to stop her from going after her little sister?

"Here you are." Elania brought me a steaming mug of faintly purple liquid. It tasted like lavender, mint, and something so bitter that I nearly gagged at the first sip. "Drink up." She winked at me.

I downed the entire thing in one go, then sat back in my chair and waited.

"Well?" Elania arched an eyebrow. "Anything?"

I smiled apologetically. "It's helped a little," I said, and that was true. The ache had eased off slightly, and I didn't feel quite so hot. "But not that much. I'm afraid my shifter metabolism is working against me in this case."

Elania pouted. "Well, that's unfortunate. I'll see if I can work on an alternate version that can stand up to your stronger system. It should be ready the next time you come by."

I shook my head, standing. "I appreciate the offer, but that won't be necessary. I don't think I'll be coming by again until the danger has passed and I can be sure the Resistance no longer has me marked for death."

"But Sunaya," Comenius protested.

"No." I turned to face him. "I can't risk putting you and Elania in danger by association. The Resistance has already proven on more than one occasion that they're not overly concerned with killing bystanders, and I'm pretty sure they consider anyone who aids me to be their enemy as well. They won't hesitate to harm any one of you to get to me."

Comenius sighed, raking a hand through his ash-blond hair. "I can't argue with that," he said ruefully. "But promise you'll keep up your teenage-boy disguise when you're out and about."

"Yeah," Annia agreed. "Nobody would dream of mistaking that disguise for the great and powerful Sunaya Baine. You looked even nerdier than Elnos."

"Hey!" Elnos complained, and we all laughed, the tension broken.

"I think 'infamous' might be a better adjective than 'great and powerful'," I told her, coming over for a hug. "But I'll keep it in mind. Good luck on your trip, both of you. And if you need anything from me at all, let me know."

I gave everybody goodbye hugs, promising I would see them again once this was all over. Elania pressed a flask of the anti-aphrodisiac into my hand, and I tucked it into one of my pouches before donning my teenage-boy disguise and heading out.

Director Chen had said I was free to join the enforcers if I wanted to make myself useful. So that was exactly what I was going to do.

6

I kept the teenage-boy disguise long enough to make it past the two shopkeepers who guarded the entrance to Witches End, then ducked into the first available alley and changed my illusion to that of Riley Tansom, an enforcer who had retired earlier this year. I hoped that the real Riley hadn't decided to get back into action, because he'd been well known enough that people would definitely notice if two of us showed up at the Enforcer's Guild. But since he was getting old and wanted to be with his family, he probably would have gotten them out of the city at the first sign of disaster rather than stay and fight.

I got back onto the bicycle, then headed down to the Enforcer's Guild in Rowanville. Thankfully, the trip was mostly downhill this time, and the legs pumping the pedals were still my own even if they looked like Tansom's. Before too long, the tall, dingy grey building that represented Solantha's law enforcement system came into view, an ugly but necessary eyesore that stood at the edge of Rowanville, and the center of the city. It was rectangular, four stories high, and there were cracks and miniature craters blown out of the stone exterior that hadn't been there before. All the windows had been boarded up except for one at the very top.

Taking a deep breath, I secured my bike. As I did so, Captain Galling pulled into the lot, parking his steel-blue steamcar in his reserved spot right in front of the entrance. He looked freshly showered and clothed as he stepped out of his car, a large, imposing man with close-cropped grey hair. To my surprise and gratification, he was wearing mercenary leathers. He must have gone home to shower and change, then transport his wife to the Palace. It was a smart move for him to dress in leathers rather than the suits he usually wore – it would show the rest of the enforcers that he was prepared to join them in securing the city and standing against the Resistance, rather than hiding behind his desk as he'd become accustomed to doing in recent times.

Eager to see what he was planning, I hurried in behind him. The two enforcers guarding the door let me in without complaint, their nods of acknowledgement much better than the reception I would have gotten if I'd arrived here as myself. Yeah, so the Palace staff was being nicer to me, but I doubted the enforcers were prepared to welcome me back with open arms, especially since many of them hated the mages right now. It didn't matter that I'd worked at the Enforcers Guild for years – right now, most of them only saw me as the hated Chief Mage's apprentice.

Captain Galling called for a general meeting in the main hall on the first floor, and I filed in there along with the rest of the enforcers. The few who saw me clapped me on the back and asked me about my wife and grandkids, questions I tried to answer as evasively as I could, as I didn't know Tansom that well.

"What the hell are you even thinking, Tansom, coming back out of retirement at a time like this?" Taren Widler, a Main Crew Enforcer who I usually found obnoxious, asked with a grin. "In case you haven't noticed, most of us have already hightailed it out of here, and the rest of us are just biding our time for when the Resistance finally takes this place over."

"I have noticed," I said casually, my eyes sweeping over the crowd that had gathered in the hall. Only about a third of the Enforcers Guild was present, most of them humans, and none of the very few mage enforcers had remained. "But it's hard to get accurate data about what's really going on in this town, what with the papers being slanted this way and that, and nobody wanting to poke their head out of doors to have a conversation. So I thought I'd come here and see what I can find out. Looks like I've got good timing, too," I added as Captain Galling stepped up to the small podium at the front of the room.

"All right, boys and girls," he addressed us once the room had gone quiet. "I know there's been some disagreement about what to do in the face of this catastrophe, but it's time for us to pull together and do our job. The Enforcers Guild was originally founded to serve the people of Solantha, and the whole state of Canalo. Regardless of whether or not we think the Mages or the Resistance are in the right, the people still need our protection, and our help."

"What about us?" a female enforcer close to the front shouted. "Don't we deserve protection and help too? Or is the Mages Guild going to continue to arrest us and treat us like criminals? Let them fight their own battles. I've had enough!"

Several enforcers began to shout their agreements with her stance, and soon, the entire hall was in an uproar. Anger filled me at some of the more inflammatory statements, and I wished I could march back to the Palace and shove my boot up the asses of the idiotic Council members who had caused all this bitterness to begin with. Hopefully, Captain Galling could sway the crowd, because if not, we were in big trouble.

"See?" Widler muttered into my ear, pitching his voice so he could be heard despite the shouting. "It's crazy town over here. You should go home."

"*Enough!*" Captain Galling boomed, silencing the crowd again. "I understand your grievances, perhaps better than anyone else in the city. In case you've forgotten, I, too, was arrested, and in fact was only released this morning. The rest of the enforcers who were wrongfully imprisoned, and the citizens as well, are going to be released sometime today. I've spoken to the Chief Mage, and we've come to an agreement."

"Is that why you're so willing to forgive them?" someone sneered. "A pouch of gold is enough to make up for all the bull-shit they've pulled?"

"It isn't," Captain Galling said, his voice hard as his gaze snapped to the enforcer who'd spoken. I smirked a little as the man in question hunched his shoulders beneath Captain Galling's intense stare. "But this isn't about me, you, or any one of us individually. This is about making sure the people in this city stay safe, regardless of the outcome of this civil war. The Mages Guild has agreed to issue a public apology for the wrongful arrests, and now that the Chief Mage is back, things will be under control on their side once more. They've also agreed to double the bounty for any criminals we apprehend during this emergency – *actual* criminals," he added with a scowl. "I don't want to see you guys hauling in citizens unnecessarily, or for inflated or imagined infractions. We don't have the time or the resources to deal with that kind of bullshit, and besides, we're no better than the Mages Guild if we start pulling that kind of shit."

There were a few cheers at the mention of the increased bounties, and the tension in the room began to ease off. Only a handful of the enforcers, mostly shifters, called Captain Galling a sell-out and stormed out of the hall, refusing to co-operate with the mage regime regardless of financial incentives. But once they were gone, the others seemed to relax. More questions were shouted, and details were hashed out between Captain Galling and the crew foremen. Eventually, an agreement was reached that the enforcers would concentrate on policing the streets, discouraging looting and other criminal activity. It was also agreed that in the event of an attack, the enforcers would be responsible for ensuring civilian safety, though they were not required to engage in any battles themselves. The paperwork for claiming the increased bounties would be simplified, so as to waste no time with red tape.

One of the shifters making his way out of the hall bumped into my shoulder. He was about to move off, but he froze, nose twitching, then swung his yellow wolf eyes in my direction.

"Oi," he protested. "Who are you? You don't smell like Tansom."

I stiffened as suspicious gazes swung in my direction, cursing inwardly. I'd tried to get Tansom's scent right, but evidently, I hadn't quite succeeded.

"Well?" the wolf shifter demanded, crossing his arms. "Show yourself!"

Reluctantly, I dropped my disguise. Gasps echoed through the crowd, followed by exclamations of surprise and anger. The words 'bitch,' 'whore,' and 'traitor' echoed through the halls, and I fisted my hands at my sides, claws digging into my palms as I fought to remain calm.

"Nice to see you guys too," I sneered. "You're welcome for bringing the Chief Mage back in one piece, and for rescuing all the shifters who were being kidnapped and enslaved by the Resistance."

Quite a few of them – the shifter who'd called me out included – shifted uncomfortably and averted their eyes.

"We shouldn't be so harsh to judge her," one of them murmured.

"She *has* done good work lately," another one said.

"*Very* good work," Captain Galling confirmed in a louder voice, and I flashed him a look of gratitude and relief across the room.

"Who gives a fuck?" Widler shouted, and it was then I noticed that he'd backed away, a look of disgust on his face. "She still works for the mages, doesn't she? I bet they sent her in here as a spy, to make sure we're good little peons and to report any of us if we don't do what we're told!"

There was a roar of agreement at that, and the crowd surged forward, murderous looks on their faces. The captain shouted at them to stop, but nobody listened.

I held up my hands, and the crowd halted as blue flame sprang to my fingertips. "Hang on, guys," I said, holding them at bay with my magical fire. "I'm not here as a spy, dammit! I came here to help. My main objective is to find the Benefactor, the person who is financing the Resistance, and I have a lot of good information that could help you guys out."

The crowd seemed to hesitate for a moment, but then somebody spoke up. "Aren't you on the Resistance kill list? They're going to think we're helping you if we let you back in here, and then what? I've got my family to think of!"

More voices chimed in with agreement, and the crowd surged forward again, heedless of my magic as they cursed and yelled that they didn't need the help of a filthy traitor like me. As one, they pushed me out of the main hall and slammed the doors shut on me as I landed on my ass in the entrance hall.

I stared up at the scarred, closed doors, hands braced on the equally scarred linoleum tile. I'd worked so hard to get into the Enforcers Guild. I'd wanted to be one of them since I was sixteen, had dreamed of fighting against injustice and making the city a better place. And now, they were throwing me out, calling me a traitor and telling me that my help wasn't good enough for them.

Stop moping, Sunaya. There isn't time.

I sighed. There never seemed to be time for wallowing in self-pity, was there? These days there were always lives at stake, and a big, bad guy that needed to be stopped. I wished that my enemy, for once, actually had a face. I hadn't known Yantz was the guy behind the silver murders until the very end, and the same went for Danrian and the Shifter Royale. But even they were just puppets, their strings yanked behind the scenes by a greater force – the Benefactor. And we still seemed to be no closer to finding out who the hell he was.

I got to my feet, checked to make sure my weapons and harness were still in place, then left the building. As I passed through the entrance, I caught the scents of the male enforcers who were still guarding the entrance, and stiffened as my body throbbed in response. If even these guys looked good, I was in a bad way.

Fuck. I'd been thrown so off balance by my ejection from the Guild that I'd forgotten to put my illusion back on again. The two guards started at the sight of me, and I took off running. I wasn't sure if I was running because I needed to get out of sight before someone from the Resistance took a shot at me, because I didn't want to humiliate myself in front of those guys by letting my hormones get the better of me, or because I couldn't stand to be near a group of people who, despite everything I'd done, still thought I was scum.

All I knew was that I needed a fucking break.

7

I found a quiet place to change back into my teenage-boy disguise, but even that didn't seem to help with the heat much. I was on edge, hungry, aching, my fangs and claws elongating beneath my illusion despite my efforts to stay in human form. I needed to take the edge off. I needed release.

I needed Iannis.

Leaning my head against the alley wall, I laughed softly to myself. Iannis? Even if he weren't too busy fighting and governing to see to my needs, I couldn't let him if he wasn't prepared to commit. If I did, then he was no better than the string of other guys I'd used in the past when the need had taken me. Was this what I'd been reduced to? Skulking in alleys and pining for a guy I couldn't have?

Angry now, I straightened up. I was better than this. Maybe I was in hiding, but I was still Sunaya Baine, and I'd never had a problem getting a guy into my bed when I needed one. If Iannis couldn't help me, I'd find someone else who could. Even just once a day would be enough to take the edge off so I could focus and get some real work done.

It's for the greater good, a voice whispered in my head, and I nearly laughed out loud. How absurd, the idea of having sex 'for the greater good'. But there was no denying that something needed to be done, and it needed to be done with someone else. Masturbation didn't work – it was that living, human connection that the heat sought, and the heat responded to. After all, self-pleasure didn't result in procreation, now did it?

I hopped on my bike and headed to The Cat's Meow, a diner run by the Tiger Clan. After parking my ride in the back alley, I changed my illusion to that of the blonde tiger shifter female I'd used the last time I came here. But instead of a sweater and jeans, I put on a skin-tight leather corset beneath a black blazer, leather pants, and boots. No, it wasn't the kind of attire one usually wore to a diner, but I wanted to make my intentions clear to the males inside.

It was mid-afternoon, so I didn't expect the place to be packed, but it was still a lot emptier than it should have been. Over two thirds of the tables and booths were empty. But as soon as I stepped in, every single male's gaze swung my way. Yellow, orange, and blue shifter eyes glowed with hunger as their nostrils flared, catching the scent of my heat. Other eyes, female ones, flared with jealousy, and several females bared their fangs in my direction as I walked past, swinging my hips a little as I headed for the bar in the back. The mated males all hastily averted their eyes as I sauntered past, but several gazes remained glued on my back. The single male seated at the bar, a hand-some tiger shifter with orange eyes and shaggy dark hair that I remembered meeting here the last time, licked his lips, showing a hint of fang as he looked me up and down.

"Hey," he greeted me as I sat down on the barstool next to him, his deep voice rougher than I remembered. He leaned in, nostrils flaring as he inhaled my scent. It would be nearly irre-sistible to him. "Visiting from Parabas again?"

I pretended to look sheepish at the reproach in his eyes – I'd lied to him the last time about where I was from, and had given him a false phone number to call. Because I'd used my magic to disguise my scent, he hadn't been able to tell, a fact that no doubt confused him.

"Sorry about that, but I was involved with someone else at the time." I didn't even really have to lie about that – I *was* involved with someone else. Just not the level of involvement that I wanted it to be. "I'm alone now, though," I added with a feline smile. "You could buy me a drink if you like."

"How do I know that's actually true?" he asked, arching a brow as he picked up his glass of *teca* – one of the few substances that could intoxicate a shifter, and that would kill a human if served to them. "You seem to be extraordinarily good at lying."

I shrugged a little. "You don't." Pretending to ignore him, I turned away and ordered five cheeseburgers and a boatload of fries from the man behind the counter. I was famished from the constant use of illusion magic, and besides, I had no intention of working for tiger-boy's affections. There was plenty of interest around here – in fact, two other males were approaching the bar already. One of them tried to sit down next to me, but tiger-boy bared his teeth and let out a ferocious snarl, and the other male backed off. I pretended not to notice, but inwardly, I sighed in relief. If the other male had been more dominant, a fight would have broken out, and I had come here for sex, not bloodshed.

"So, is this your spot?" I asked as the first two burgers arrived.

"Huh?" he asked as I bit into the food.

"Mmm," I moaned, closing my eyes as I savored the juicy burger. The reaction was genuine, but I played it up a little for him. And then I made him wait until I'd finished the burger.

"That barstool you're sitting in." I pointed a greasy finger at it. "You were sitting in the same one the last time I was here. Does it have your name on it or something?"

He grinned. "If you can actually remember which stool I was sitting in, then I must have made a big impression."

"You're cute," I said with a shrug as I picked up burger number two.

"The stool doesn't have my name on it, but it's a little more comfortable than the others, so I always use it." He smiled a little. "My father owns this diner, so I'm in here a lot."

I nearly choked on my burger at that. *So much for picking a random guy,* I scolded myself. If he were telling the truth – and my nose told me he was – then he would be well known in the community.

Suddenly, I had a flash of an earlier memory, from six years ago. It was one of the times I'd been in here with Roanas, and a gangly teen with shaggy brown hair had been serving us. He was probably no more than nineteen at the time, his face still thin, his shoulders too wide for his still-growing body, but there was no mistaking him. He'd always been our server, and he had been one of the few shifters to go out of his way to make me feel welcome.

"You're Nimos Barakan?" I asked, putting my burger down.

His eyes widened in surprise. "You know my name?"

I swallowed hard. "Yeah, I do." No longer hungry, I slapped some coin on the counter, then slid off the barstool. "I've gotta go."

"Just one second," Nimos growled, grabbing me by the upper arm. "You've already walked out on me once. I'll be damned if I let you do it again."

"You're making a scene," I hissed, mostly because of the pain. His claws were digging into my flesh, something I couldn't fault him for – I'd exposed him to my heat and brought out his territorial instincts. "Let me go. You don't even know my name."

"No, but you know mine." His eyes bored into mine. "I want to know why."

I sighed a little, then forced myself into a submissive pose – shoulders relaxed, eyes downcast. "Fine. But can we go somewhere else? Please?"

"Sure," he said easily, sounding satisfied. He thought he'd won. "Let's head to the back."

The entire room watched us as I followed him down a hall and up a staircase that led to a hall lined with three doorways. Upper-floor apartments, I guessed. My breath quickened as I tried to resist the heat – my body knew I was being led in the direction of sex, and it was clouding my judgment, making me forget the reason I'd decided to leave the diner.

Nimos opened the second door, and I followed him into a small apartment with dark, masculine furnishings. Nothing expensive, but well built. His scent was everywhere in this place, and it only made the ache between my legs worse.

He shut the door behind me, chest heaving, eyes glowing, and I braced myself to fend him off. But instead of pouncing on me, he leaned back against the door and crossed his arms.

"So. How do you know me, and what are you really doing in my family's diner?"

I had to applaud him for remembering the important questions in the face of raging hormones. If he, a full-blooded shifter, could do it, then so could I.

"Because I used to come here with my foster father every Sunday," I said quietly allowing my illusion to fade.

Nimos went slack-jawed, his eyes widening as he took in the real me. "Su...Sunaya Baine?"

"Yep." I mirrored his pose, crossing my arms against my chest to fend off the scathing insults and criticism I knew were coming.

"By Magorah, you really did make it back!" The next thing I

knew, he'd swept me up into a big hug. I squeaked as he lifted me off the ground, more because he was crushing my ribs with his powerful arms than because I was surprised. "I wanted to thank you for what you did, but you'd left before I had the chance to contact you."

"Thank me?" I pushed against his shoulders so that I could look at his face, bewildered now. "Thank me for what?"

"For rescuing all those shifters." He set me down, but his hands remained on my hips. "My cousin's son Sapian was among them."

"Oh." There had been so many victims of the Shifter Royale that I couldn't remember them all, but I vaguely recalled there had been at least two tiger shifters in that dark basement. "Well, you're welcome. I was just doing my job."

He shook his head, "You did a hell of a lot more for the shifter community that day than the Enforcers Guild has done in the last century," he insisted. Tilting his head, he sniffed, and the hunger in his gaze deepened. "You're in heat. Let me help you." He brushed his lips against mine. "That's what you came here for, isn't it?"

I clenched my jaw against a whimper of need, resisting the urge to lean into him. "It was a mistake," I said hoarsely.

"Why, because you thought I would reject you?" His lips moved to my jawline, trailing fire across my too-sensitive skin. "I won't deny that a lot of the shifters here dislike you, Sunaya, but there are others who are grateful for what you've done. Most have fled Solantha or are still imprisoned, but they exist. And I'm one of them. Let me help you."

Oh, how I wanted him to. His words were exactly what I needed to hear, his touch a balm on my overheated skin. It would be so easy to give in.

But I would never forgive myself.

"No," I growled. Placing my palms against his chest, I shoved

him, hard. He stumbled back, hitting the door, shock stamped across his handsome face. "I can't, Nimos. I...there's someone else."

His expression darkened. "I thought you said there wasn't."

I smiled sadly at him. "I lied. And the way my life is going right now, I'm just going to keep lying to you. Stay away from me, Nimos. You're better off without me."

Whirling away from him, I grabbed the latch of the back window and tore it open. And before he could say anything more, I was gone.

———

8

Three hours later, I reached the top of Hawk Hill, breathing hard as I pushed the bike up the path that wound up the hill on the other side of Solantha Bay. My legs burned and my lungs ached, but I was grateful – the long ride and the exercise had taken my mind off the heat, which was a good thing because my teenage-boy illusion still wasn't doing much to help.

I threw my bike down on the grass, then pulled out the flask Elania had given me and drank the last mouthful of bitter anti-aphrodisiac. Taking deep breaths of the fresh, lightly salted air, I gazed out at the bay, my eyes traveling over the magnificent Firegate Bridge, and the city beyond. The sun was kissing the horizon now, setting the bridge aflame and giving credence to its namesake. Just a few weeks ago, the Resistance had tried to destroy said bridge, affixing a bomb beneath it near one of the main supports. I'd managed to help evacuate the citizens and defuse the bomb, and for my trouble had been sent a warning from the Resistance via my own cousin, Rylan, to stay out of their affairs if I knew what was good for me.

Apparently, I didn't know what was good for me, because

now I had a kill target on my back. And looking back on how things went down, I still wouldn't have changed a thing.

From this distance, the city still looked much the same. I couldn't see the broken windows, the trash in the streets, or some of the smaller structures that had burned down. The taller, more visible buildings stood strong, just like the bridge. But how long would that last? How long, before the Benefactor got his way and took over the city, or the mages reached their breaking point and annihilated everyone who stood in their way? Either outcome meant the destruction of the city I loved, and I couldn't let it get to that point. Iannis's self-control was ironclad, and I trusted that he wouldn't let things get to that point either. But he wasn't infallible, and the council had already proven they were willing to go behind his back.

Another pulsing ache rippled through my body, and I gritted my teeth as I turned away from the view. Much as I loved it, I hadn't come up here to gaze down at the city. I'd come here to seek solace. Guidance. From a non-corporeal presence I still wasn't entirely certain existed.

Mages, shifters, and humans all technically worshipped the same god, though we all had different names and interpretations of Him. The mages called Him the Creator, but rather than praying to him directly, they often sought guidance from the spirit of the very first mage, Resinah. As I understood it, she was something like the Creator's mouthpiece. I wasn't totally certain I believed she was real, but I had imagined her voice once or twice, so I couldn't discount the possibility. And something had drawn me here to Hawk Hill, to her, so what was the harm in trying to seek guidance?

I am *real,* a voice whispered, and the air shimmered in front of me, indicating the location of the hidden temple I'd only visited once before. *Come inside and see.*

I spoke the Word Iannis had taught me, and the shimmering

increased, like intense heat waves rising from the grass. Even though I was prepared for it this time, it was still shocking to watch Resinah's temple suddenly appear out of nowhere. The domed building soared above me, the strange blue stone it was made of tinted purple by the sunset. The sunset also made the round, stained glass windows look like rippling fire, and I stared for a moment, my heat forgotten as I was transfixed by the beauty of this place.

Come inside, the voice whispered.

I stepped forward instantly, almost as though the movement was not of my own volition. My feet took me through the arch-shaped doorway, and like before, the heavy, carved door silently swung open to admit me. The fading sunlight streaming through the stained glass windows and the skylight set into the top of the domed ceiling illuminated the space, drawing the eye to the enormous white statue that stood in the center of the temple. Resinah towered there, at least thirty feet tall, her form carved of pure white marble. Long hair flowed over slim, but proud, shoulders, and her long robes hinted at a willowy figure as she cradled a book with one arm while she stretched out the other, palm up. A blue-white flame blazed above her palm, and I wondered just how that flame was maintained. Was it a spell that had to constantly be recharged? Or was the flame from Resinah herself?

You ask many questions, child. But few of them are the right ones.

I scowled. "Great," I muttered. "So now you're going to criticize me, too?"

A gentle breeze brushed my cheek. *Do not sound so petulant. You have many allies. You encountered some of them over the last few days.*

That was true. But it was hard to take comfort in that right this second.

"Are you usually so chatty with everyone who comes into

your temple?" I asked, genuinely curious.

There was a pause. Had I shocked Resinah with my cheeky question? Maybe I shouldn't be so snarky. She would be used to awe and worship from the mages, after all.

No, she finally said. *But you need my help, and in turn, you will help others when the time comes. That is why I summoned you here.*

And here I thought I came of my own will, I wanted to say, but before I could, the breeze picked up. It swirled around me, tugging my curls out of the bun I'd tied them into, and cooling my skin.

Not just my skin, I realized as I closed my eyes. It was cooling me from the inside, too, driving back the ache and calming my raw nerves. After a moment's hesitation, I bowed to the statue. "Thank you. I appreciate the relief." How did one address Resinah, anyway? Ma'am? Prophetess? I would have to consult Iannis or Fenris when I got the chance.

The flame in Resinah's hand seemed to dance a little brighter. *"You are welcome."*

"So." I raked a hand through my freed curls, looking around the temple. "Do I just come here every day for my daily dose, then?"

Soft laughter filled my head. *I am not your nursemaid, Sunaya Baine. I only offered you a reprieve. You must use that respite to gain control by yourself.*

I resisted the urge to curl my hands into fists. "How am I supposed to do that, exactly? In case you haven't noticed, I've been trying to control it for a while now. I've been running around as a teenage boy and drinking nasty potions like there's no tomorrow."

Masking your symptoms will not solve your problem.

"Then what will?" I stomped on the urge to take the empty flask in my pouch and chuck it at the statue's head. "With all due respect, your vague statements aren't exactly helpful."

Your continued rejection of your mage heritage is a large part of the problem, Resinah's voice turned cool. *If you do not want your shifter instincts to rule your body, you must learn to embrace the other half of your lineage.*

"You make it sound like there's something wrong with my shifter heritage," I protested. "I'll have you know that I've used my 'shifter instincts' to survive for most of my life."

Shifters are powerful in their own right, Resinah acknowledged, to my surprise. *Mages would not have created your race if that were not the case. But you must learn to use* both *sides of your nature. I watched you today as you were thrown out of the Enforcers Guild, and felt how stricken you were at their rejection. And I watch how you tiptoe around the shifter community, hoping they might accept you, even though you frighten them with your magic. What you have not yet understood, child, is that no one will fully accept you until you accept yourself – neither mages nor enforcers nor your fellow shifters. You must wear your unique heritage with pride and confidence.*

"That's easy for you to say," I grumbled. "I'm not sure how I'm supposed to do that with a bounty on my head, though. Strutting around, going – I'm Sunaya Baine, bring it! – isn't going to do me any favors right now."

I would never suggest that you strut around arrogantly and invite challenge, Resinah retorted dryly. *For now, you must continue to remain disguised a little longer. But be mindful of who you are disguising yourself from, and why. Are you hiding from the Resistance behind that teenage boy? Or from the world?*

Her voice faded, the breeze caressing my skin along with it, before I could answer. She had gone. Alone now, I sat on the floor of the temple and stared up at her statue, pondering the words she'd left me with and wondering if maybe, just maybe, she was right.

9

I woke to the sound of footsteps rustling in the grass and cracked an eyelid open to see who had intruded upon my space. I'd fallen asleep in the grass outside Resinah's temple, disguised as a female mage, after thinking long and hard about what she'd advised. Eventually, I'd come to the conclusion that she was right, and not just for the reasons she'd spoken of. How could I master my powers, powers that required such incredible self-control, if I remained a slave to my body? Iannis would never respect me, nor would the rest of the mage community, and I might never be given full access to my powers. Even if nothing ever came of the attraction between the Chief Mage and me, I needed to get a handle on my urges for the sake of my own future.

As though my dreams had conjured him, Iannis was right there, staring down at me. His violet eyes glowed in the darkness, reflecting the nearly full moon that shone above our heads. Desire bloomed low in my belly as I inhaled his scent... but it wasn't as bad as I expected to be. In fact, the sensation was almost normal, rather than hormonally enhanced, even when I released my illusion and assumed my real form.

Maybe there was something to this 'getting in touch with your inner mage' thing.

"You didn't come back to the Palace," he said softly as he lowered himself down on the ground next to me. "I was worried."

Pleasure glowed in my chest at the concern in his voice, and I smiled. "I was talking with Resinah," I said, gesturing toward the temple with my right hand.

Iannis arched a brow. "Talking with her? Or to her?"

"With her." I raised my own brows as his eyes widened. "Why? You got a problem with that?"

"No," he said carefully, turning to look back at the temple himself. "It's just...rare...for her to hold a conversation for any length of time."

"She mentioned that," I mused, tilting my head to look up at the clouds. "But she gave a reason for her interest."

"And what reason was that?"

"That's between me and her." I waggled my eyebrows, but despite my levity, I was serious. The conversation I'd had with Resinah had felt sacred, and I didn't think it was meant for other ears.

Iannis gave me a questioning look, but he didn't press further. "Why didn't you come back to the Palace, then, when you were done?"

I shrugged, then stretched myself out on the grass again. "I was comfortable here. I came to the temple because I needed some help controlling my heat, and after I was done talking with Resinah, I didn't feel ready to go back yet."

"I see." Iannis's eyes darkened, and he reached out to touch my cheek. "Was Resinah able to help you?"

My breath stuttered as his thumb caressed my skin, which was still sensitive – the heat was still there, after all, regardless of whether I could control it.

"She was," I said, and I was proud that my voice remained steady. "I'm reasonably sure that I'll be able to prevent myself from pouncing on every desirable male who walks by."

"Even me?" Iannis asked, grabbing my wrists. The next thing I knew, he'd rolled himself on top of me, pressing me into the soft dirt. I gasped as his hard, muscular body molded against my softer curves – even the naked kiss we'd shared in the river hadn't felt quite this intimate.

"Especially you," I whispered. "You're the very last person I should be falling into bed with right now."

"Well, I'm done with waiting. I want you," Iannis said, his voice rough with need. He bent his head so that his dark, cherry-wood hair formed a curtain around his face, blocking out the world. Warm breath fanned across my cheeks as he spoke. "I've almost lost you more times than I'd like to consider, and after I heard about the fire..." He closed his eyes, a pained look crossing his handsome, oblong face. And when he opened them again, they burned with iridescent flames. "I can't keep doing this. I can't keep taking you for granted, as if you'll always be here, waiting until I'm ready, when you could be taken from me at any time."

"W-what are you saying?" I was trembling now with the effort of beating back the hope rising in my chest. I wanted so much to believe he was ready to accept me, but I couldn't, not until the actual words came out of his mouth.

"I'm saying that I love you, Sunaya. And I want you to be mine, and only mine."

He kissed me then, a tender, passionate claiming that completely shredded my control. Hunger clawed at me, making me ravenous as I kissed him back, nipping at his lower lip and snarling at his restraint. He only laughed, a low, teasing sound as he pinned me to the ground, his hands still wrapped around my wrists. I could have bucked him off, could have broken his grip, but strangely, I didn't want to. I was okay with him having some control.

Maybe I'm not a total animal after all.

His tongue slid into my mouth, deepening the kiss, and he shifted his hips, nudging my legs apart so he could rest between them. I clamped my legs around his lean waist, pulling him tighter to me, and moaned as his arousal pressed against me, right where I needed it. He groaned low in his throat as he rocked himself into me, once, then twice, and then, suddenly, his hands were no longer wrapped around my wrists. He was moving lower, trailing kisses along my jaw, down my neck, to my collarbone...

"Yes," I moaned when he nipped the sensitive spot where my neck and shoulder met. His tongue laved across the tiny wound, sending another flash of heat through me. "Iannis..." I trailed off, forgetting what I was going to say as his hands slid beneath my shirt, pushing the fabric up as he trailed kisses along my abdomen.

An explosion shook the air, and we shot upright, twisting in the direction of the sound. My eyes widened in horror at a plume of smoke rising in the northern half of the city, far too close to the Palace.

"Bloody hell!" Iannis jumped to his feet, fury etched into the lines of his face. "Do they never stop?"

"Fuck," I muttered, pulling my shirt down as I got to my feet as well. I was starting to see flames too, licking at the night air as smoke continued to billow. What was the Resistance up to now?

"I need to go." Iannis turned back to me, and the regret in his eyes was clear as he reached for my hand. "They'll pay dearly for interrupting us – I wish there were more time."

"Go." I squeezed his hand, then grabbed his face and pulled him to me for one more kiss. It felt so good to be able to do that, to be able to reach for him without the fear of rejection shadowing me at every turn. "There are more important things to deal with right now," I added, my voice a little ragged. Inside, I felt like howling.

"Indeed." His eyes glowed with desire and frustration as he pulled away. "We're not finished here, Sunaya. I promise you that."

And then, he was gone in a rush of wind, his feet taking him faster than even I could hope to follow, as he went to save a people who seemed determined to hate him.

10

Ditching the bike completely, I shifted into beast form, then ran down the hill to catch up with Iannis and find out what was behind the explosion. It felt good to run free, my paws pounding against the pavement on the Firegate Bridge as the wind ruffled my black fur, which helped hide me under the cover of darkness.

Nevertheless, as soon as I was close to the site of the explosion, I shifted back into human form, cloaking myself in the disguise of my pimply teenage boy. Standing near the airship yard with other gawkers, I watched a group of mages fight a monstrous-looking conflagration that appeared to have already destroyed a number of airships. The fire had spread to the neighborhoods on either side of the yard, and I suspected that the explosion must have been large enough to jettison flaming debris into those sections of Maintown.

Even through the smoke and gloom stinging my eyes, I managed to pick out Iannis amongst the group of mages fighting the fire. His hands were lifted skyward, eyes closed, face tight with concentration. Though I couldn't be certain, it looked like

Iannis and the two mages next to him were standing in some kind of circle.

The air shifted, becoming thick with moisture, and I glanced up as lightning flashed across the sky. To my surprise, huge black clouds had gathered out of nowhere, blocking out the moonlight completely. Thunder boomed just a moment later, then the clouds opened up, sending down a deluge of rain.

"Shit," I muttered, ducking for cover beneath a tree planted on the sidewalk that had miraculously managed not to catch fire. But it didn't help much – I was soaked in seconds, the rain so intense I could barely see through it. Beneath the roar of the downpour, I heard the hiss of steam as the water snuffed out the fire, and shouts from the mages as well. Something about treating the wounded and canvassing the neighborhood to assess damage.

I should help, I thought miserably. *I should be out there, tending to the wounded and stopping the fire. I might not be well trained, but I have power, and I should be able to use it to help others.* But I couldn't very well go among them, using my magic as a teenage boy.

And why shouldn't you? a voice in my head murmured, one that sounded suspiciously like Resinah's. *You may not be able to appear to them as Sunaya Baine, but that doesn't mean you can't appear at all.*

Right. I dredged up an image of a female mage in my mind, then changed my illusion to match it. The rain was beginning to dissipate, now that it had done its job, so I waited until it was gone, then used my magic to dry myself so that I didn't look like a drowned rat.

Now that the downpour was no longer deafening my ears, I could hear cries and sobs from the neighborhood on my side of the airship yard. I headed in that direction at a trot, since it would look very out of character for a mage to run at my full speed, and turned left into an alley of brownstones that had seen better days. Because their structures weren't made out of wood, the houses had mostly resisted the fire, but yards had been badly burned, and smoke billowed out of broken windows from inside a couple of places.

"Sir," I called, approaching a family of four huddling outside one of the burning houses. "Are you all right? Is anyone left inside?"

The man I'd addressed turned to me, coughing badly and swaying on his feet. His face was pale and smudged with soot, and he was cradling a child in his arms. "We've got everyone out, but Alis is badly hurt," he rasped. "Do you think you can help her?"

He lifted the child, and it was then that I noticed a bad burn on her right shoulder. She was lolling in his arms, unconscious, which was probably the only reason she wasn't screaming – second-degree burns were no joke, as I had cause to know.

"Yes, I can help her," I began, but then the man erupted into a desperate coughing fit.

"Hireld!" his wife cried, grabbing him by the arm to support him, but he was too heavy. Quickly, I stepped in and took the child from his arms before he lost his grip on her and went tumbling to the ground.

"Take her," I ordered, shoving the girl into her mother's arms. "I need to see to him first."

"But Alis –"

"Mom." The son, a boy of about thirteen, spoke firmly. "Dad's inhaled a lot of smoke. He might die if she doesn't help him."

"All right." The woman took her daughter, and I knelt in the grass, pulling the man's head into my lap. My fingers against his throat told me he had a pulse, but it was weak and erratic, and I didn't know how long he would be able to hold on.

"Okay." I took a deep breath, trying to calm my nerves. I had only healed someone once before, under Fenris's direction, and it hadn't been a full healing, just enough to revive the man so he could talk to me. I had no idea if I could actually do this, but I would be damned if I would sit here and let this man die.

Closing my eyes, I placed my hands over the man's chest, and visualized my magic flowing into him. I tried to think of what Iannis had done when he'd healed my torn fingers, of how he'd formed a sort of circuit between us, drawing my pain into him as he pushed magic into me.

Suddenly, I gasped, my lungs burning, aching, full of toxic smoke. As the pain grew worse, the flow of magic from my body to his steadily increased, until I became terrified that he would drain me of everything I had. Heart thundering in my chest, I tried to pull back. But it was too late. Somehow, the man's body had latched onto the thread of my magic with a vice-like grip, and it wasn't letting go.

As I struggled to regain control, a pair of strong hands settled on my shoulders. I gasped at the sensation of another consciousness inside me – Iannis. He'd done this once before, when we'd had to defuse the bomb under the bridge, and I'd been too scared and unsure to wield the necessary magic myself.

"*Breathe,*" I heard Iannis's steadying voice say, and I exhaled, realizing I'd been holding my breath. "*Let me take care of it.*"

I took in a slow, steady breath of air, then relaxed and let him guide the magic. The pain left me, and I realized that he was taking it instead, pulling the man's wound into him as he pushed life and energy into the hurting body on the ground. Iannis had told Captain Galling that he was one of the best healers in the country, and I realized that had to mean he had an extraordinary pain threshold. How much had he already suffered during the times he had brought me back from death's door?

"Hireld!" the woman cried, a joyous sound, and I opened my eyes to see her standing above us, dark eyes filled with relief as she cradled her child. I looked down to see that Hireld's eyes were open, the color returned to his face.

"Thank you," he began, looking up at me, and then his eyes widened in fear. Before I knew what was happening, he had scrambled to his hands and knees, bowing profusely. "My Lord."

It was only then that I realized the pair of hands on my shoulders was real, and that Iannis was standing behind me. Slowly, I lifted my head to look up at him. His expression was grave, but not unkind, as he surveyed the man and his family.

"Thank you, but it's quite all right," he said as the rest of them began to bow, holding up a hand. "I did not come here for that. I came to ensure the residents here were safe and to help anyone who needed assistance."

"The child," I said, surprised at how hoarse my voice sounded. Iannis let go of my shoulders, and I stiffened my core to keep myself from swaying. Damn, but I was weak as kitten.

"Go," he told me, using mindspeak. *"I'll take care of the child. And next time, perhaps, don't attempt dangerous magic without contacting your master first."*

"Sorry," I snapped, a little annoyed at the scolding. *"I'll make sure to run off and find you the next time I come across a dying man."*

"You could have contacted me mentally," he observed as he took the child and laid her carefully across the grass. *"I was close enough, and you knew it."*

I sighed. *"Fine, fine,"* I muttered, turning away. I was too tired to argue, and besides, he was right. I *could* have called him for help. I just hadn't thought to.

"Be safe, Sunaya," he told me, his voice softer now, and I felt guilty for snapping at him. He had to be exhausted – I doubted

he'd slept since we'd arrived back at Solantha, and here he was, about to heal a little girl with a nasty burn that was going to hurt him like hell.

"*You too,*" I said, turning the corner, and then I disappeared into the shadows.

11

Furious beyond belief at the Resistance, I wanted to do nothing more than chase down the bastards who'd set fire to the airship yard and pummel them into a bloody heap. But after my impromptu healing attempt, I was running on fumes, and I was going to be good to no one if I didn't take a break.

Resigned to the fact that I needed a nap, I managed to drag myself into a small, abandoned house. After determining there were no squatters hiding in there, I dragged a blanket and pillow into a closet and crashed for a good hour. It wasn't enough to recharge me completely, especially not without food, but it was enough to give me a little boost.

The fridge in the house held nothing but sour milk and rancid beef, so I changed back into the teenage boy and went out, searching for food. Most of the market shops in Maintown had closed down, their storefronts smashed in and their innards cleaned out by desperate looters, but I eventually found a small store on the eastern section that was still open. The left side had been boarded up, and the wooden stands that had probably once held fruits and vegetables had been smashed to bits, but a beam of light cut through the door and onto the street, a glimmer of hope in the darkness.

I pushed open the door, and a bell jangled as I stepped inside. There were only a few aisles, and a row of glass refrigerators on the right wall. A quick glance told me supplies were running low – many of the shelves were empty. To my left, behind the counter, stood a man in a grocer's apron. His shoulders stiffened momentarily before he realized I was a harmless teen and relaxed. He was a stocky, balding guy with brown hair and a ruddy, tough-looking face. But the lines in his face suggested that he was more accustomed to laughing than scowling, even if he was shaped like a barrel and looked like he had no problem being intimidating when he wanted to be.

"Hey old man," I said easily, wandering up to the counter. "Got anything to eat around here?"

He gave me the beady eye. "You payin'?"

I pulled a pandanum coin from my pocket – the shifter-friendly version of silver. "Sure, if the price is right."

The man sighed, running thick, stubby fingers through what was left of his hair. "I ain't got much," he admitted, scanning the store with his mud-brown eyes. "What with the Port being closed off, and local farmers afraid to bring their wares up to town, supplies are scarce. But we've still got some tins of mystery meat."

Ugh. I resisted the urge to wrinkle my nose. "I'll take them."

"Right this way." The man led me to the third aisle and pointed to a small stack of cans on the top shelf. "That's all we've got left."

"It'll work." I plucked one of the tins off the shelf, then paused as I caught sight of the company name. Timbran's Gourmet Food. I snorted – there was nothing gourmet about mystery meat – then remembered where I'd seen the company name before. It was on the much larger cans of food Annia and I had served to the Resistance camp back in Mexia.

"Any idea where this company is located?" I asked, tapping the front of the tin.

The grocer squinted at the label. "Timbran's? They've got a factory up north, about ten miles from Turain. Why?"

I shrugged. "Just curious."

I grabbed the rest of the cans, then returned to the counter so that the grocer could bag them and ring up the sale. As he did so, I drummed my fingers on the counter, considering. Was Timbran's a clue of any kind? I had wondered how the Resistance was getting their supplies. They'd seemed to have ample food at the camp, which was surprising considering its remote location. 'Follow the money' was a phrase Roanas had often repeated to himself when he was on a case, and that applied here too. How was the Resistance being funded and supplied? Might it be possible to follow their money trail back to the source through the distributors they dealt with, like Timbran's?

Just as I was accepting my change from the grocer, the front door crashed open, and three human thugs stormed in, wielding bats.

"Give it up, old man!" shouted the one in the lead, a thickset blond with bulging biceps. He smacked his bat in his meaty palms as his two cronies split up, shoving food and supplies into large burlap sacks they'd brought in with them. "Looks like your son isn't here to help fend us off this time, is he?"

"You *scum*," the grocer roared, pulling a bat of his own from beneath the counter. He lifted it, clearly prepared to defend his store, but fear shone in his eyes, and his ruddy face had turned pale. "I'm not going to let you take my stuff!"

"Oh yeah?" The thug moved in. "And who's gonna stop us?"

I stepped between the two of them, squaring my thin, teenage-boy shoulders. "I am."

The thug laughed. "Get out of the way before you get hurt, kid." He swung at me with the bat.

I shot forward, closing the gap between us too fast for him to hit me with the business end of the bat, then grabbed both arms and pivoted, throwing him over my hip. He slapped his left hand on the ground, dispersing the blow, but I had his right arm with the bat clutched in his fist, and I brought his elbow down on my knee, bending his arm the wrong way. There was a loud crunch. He screamed, and the bat clattered to the ground.

"What the fuck?" Crony Two yelped as their leader began wailing pitifully. "Who the hell is this kid?" His half-full burlap sack had slipped from his hands, and his bat was trailing on the floor as he gaped at me.

I grinned and dropped my illusion, allowing them to see who I really was. Crony Three actually gasped, then dropped his bag and made a run for it. Before he could take more than three steps, I snatched one of my mystery meat cans and flung it at the back of his head.

He dropped like a stone.

"I'm not a kid," I said to a now-shaking Crony Two. I grabbed the bat Crony One had dropped, jumped across the row of shelves separating us, and started swinging.

***

"I REALLY APPRECIATE you beating up those hooligans," the grocer said as he snapped the reins of the cart he was driving. He'd introduced himself as Gorden Matthes after the little incident with the looters.

The dappled grey horse let out a snort, then picked up the pace, hooves clopping against the pavement as it dragged the cart behind it.

"No problem." I looked back at said hooligans, who were securely trussed up and tossed into the back of the cart. "You said this isn't the first time they've come to your shop?"

Gorden shook his head. "They've tried it once before, but, luckily, my son was there, and he's a big guy, bigger than even them. They're bullies, not used to an actual challenge, so they backed off pretty easy once they saw we meant business."

"Yeah, no kidding." I shook my head a little. Those thugs – little more than overgrown kids, really – had been ridiculously easy to beat. They were used to scaring their opponents into submission, and had little fighting experience that didn't consist of simply throwing their weight around. "So I'm guessing you're not the first store they've hit, then?"

Gorden snorted. "Not even close. There's a reason so many shops in Maintown are closed now. With the Enforcers Guild essentially deciding to go on strike, there was no one to answer our calls for help. Until you, anyway."

"That's changed now," I said, trying not to grit my teeth in anger at the selfish decision the Guild had made in Iannis's absence. "The Enforcers Guild has just agreed to police the looting and start going after criminals again." Which was, of course, why I was having him drop me off at the Guild with the thugs I'd apprehended. I fully intended on cashing in on that double bounty Iannis was offering.

"I can see that." He glanced sideways at me. "Why are you disguised like that, by the way? I don't see how you can do your job as an enforcer if you don't look like one."

I sighed a little, leaning back against the bench seat. "The Resistance is determined to kill me for getting in their way. It's not safe for me to go out in public wearing my own skin." I narrowed my eyes at him. "You're not going to rat me out, are you?"

"Nah. I've got bigger things to worry about."

I relaxed a little – the man was being truthful. "All right. I'll make sure the Guild sends extra enforcers your way to patrol, so that guys like this don't bother you again."

"Appreciate it."

Using my claws, I sliced open another can of mystery meat – I'd gone through three already – then chowed it down, doing my best to ignore the taste as we finished the journey. To my sensitive nose, the contents were no real mystery. Half mutton, half pork, with a lacing of chickpea and seasoning. Not exactly tasty, but filling enough.

I asked Gorden to pull up at the back entrance of the Guild, where criminals were usually received. Five enforcers stood guard outside the metal door, more than twice the usual number, and they eyed us with suspicion as I jumped out of the cart and went around the back of it.

"Stop right there," one of them called. He stepped away from the building, his hand on the hilt of his sword as he approached the cart. "Who are you, and what business do you have here?"

"I'm a licensed enforcer bringing in some thugs I caught in the middle of a robbery." I grabbed Crony Two by the back of his collar and hauled him upright. He groaned, cracking open a black eye to stare blearily at us, then whimpered when I dropped him back into the cart. "Mind giving me a hand with these guys and signing for the receipt?"

The enforcer's eyes narrowed. "There's no way a scrawny kid like you would be accepted into the Guild, and definitely no way you could have apprehended these guys by yourself. Where's your help, kid? It's hardly the old man driving the cart."

I hissed, baring my all-too human teeth. "I'm Sunaya Baine, you jackass, and I'm here undercover." I dropped my teenage-boy voice, and the guard's eyes widened. "Stop trying to have a pissing contest with me, and let me in."

The guard hesitated, then turned to address Gorden. "You say these are robbers?"

Gorden turned. "Yeah. They tried to loot my store. Gorden's Grocery in Maintown." His eyes narrowed. "You know the place. I've seen you in my store before."

"Umm, yeah." The enforcer scratched his head. "Your wife makes some pretty good sandwiches."

"Damn right. Now are you going to let us through, or should we just untie these bastards and let them go cause more trouble?"

"Wait a moment." The enforcer turned smartly on his heel, then went back to the door to confer with his buddies. He returned with two of them a moment later. "We'll help you get them inside."

"Thanks." I flipped down the rear gate of the cart, then jumped in and grabbed one of the thugs. I only had one pair of cuffs, so I'd had to restrain the other two with good old-fashioned rope, but it did the job well enough.

"I'll take him," one of the enforcers said firmly as I dragged the first man off the cart and forced him onto his feet.

"Okay then." I held up my hands as he grabbed the thug from me and began perp walking him into the building. The other two enforcers manhandled the remaining prisoners, and I was left with little to do but shove my hands into my pockets and follow them inside.

"Not so fast." The two enforcers who'd been holding the rear doors open closed ranks, blocking the entrance. "We can't let you through until you properly identify yourself."

"I already have," I growled. "I'm Sunaya Baine, registered member of the Enforcers Guild."

"That's all well and good, but how do we know you're not

some Resistance spy who's got good voice-acting skills?" The one on the left, a burly guy with curly, chestnut hair, scowled. "We need visual confirmation that you're one of us."

"You guys are assholes," I snarled. "You know it's me. Why won't you just let me through?"

"What, are you too afraid to show yourself?" the other guard, a blond, asked with a smirk, and I bristled. "I guess that makes sense – must have been humiliating to have your ass tossed out of here earlier today."

My cheeks flamed, and before I could think better of it, I dropped the illusion, allowing them to see my real form. "There," I growled, grabbing the blond by the collar and sticking my nose into his face. "Is that good enough for you?"

A crack rent the air, and I cried out as burning pain ripped through my right shoulder. The blond enforcer's head jerked as blood bloomed over his chest, then his knees buckled as he dropped like a stone.

A bullet wound, I realized, dazed. Someone had tried to kill me, and they got this guy instead. With a shot to the heart.

"Get inside!" the other enforcer roared, grabbing me by the arm and hauling me through the entrance. He slammed the steel doors behind him, and the sound brought reality rushing back to me.

"Gorden," I cried, turning back around. I wrenched open the door, heedless of the other enforcer's warning. Gorden was out of the cart, sprinting for the doors as fast as he could manage, eyes wide with panic. "Come on!" I screamed.

He was five feet away when he went down – a shot to the back of the head. A scream of denial tore through the night, and I realized it came from my throat. I tried to run to the fallen man, to check and see if it was a mistake, if he was still alive, but the other enforcer grabbed the door and slammed it shut, then drew the heavy bolt with shaking fingers. "Stop!" he shouted at me. "He's already dead."

I whirled around to face him, murder in my heart. "Yes, and it's *your fault*," I screeched, launching myself at him. The man reached for his sword, but he was only human, and I was too fast and too strong for him. Before he could do more than grip the hilt, I'd slammed him against the ground, my legs clamping around him so he couldn't easily get away.

"You stupid bastard," I yelled, pummeling him with my fists. He tried blocking my blows with his arms, then cried out when I started slashing at his unprotected flesh with my claws. "You killed that innocent man!" I plowed my fist into his face and heard the ridiculously satisfying crunch of his nose breaking beneath my knuckles. I was out of control, my rage burning fast and hot now that it finally had an outlet, and *damn,* it felt good.

So then, why were tears running down my face?

I paused at the sound of sobs, and I realized they were coming from me. The man beneath me was trembling with pain and fear, but so was I, guilt and anger so thick against my chest I could hardly breathe.

I'm out of control, I realized numbly. Succumbing to my volatile shifter emotions instead of using reason. Yes, this man deserved to be punished, but if I continued beating on him, I would kill him. And the Resistance had caused enough death as it was. I didn't need to coat my hands with a fellow enforcer's blood.

Sensing weakness, the enforcer bucked his hips, and in the next second, had flipped us over. The breath whooshed out of me as I landed hard on my back with all his weight bearing down on me, and I instinctively bucked as fear spiked in my chest. But between the bullet wound, the constant illusion magic, and the fighting, my strength was starting to wane. I didn't have much left in me to resist when he grabbed me by the hair and slammed my head into the concrete floor. Spots danced in my vision, but I was still conscious, so he did it again. And then, I was out.

12

I wasn't sure how long I was unconscious, but it wasn't long enough. I came awake with a splitting headache and a throbbing pain in my shoulder, then immediately rolled over and hurled mystery meat over the side of the cot I was lying on.

"I'm glad I thought to put a bucket there," Captain Galling said dryly. My eyes watered as I heaved out my guts, so I couldn't see him, but I had the impression he was sitting behind his desk, watching me humiliate myself in front of him. "I had a feeling you wouldn't be feeling so good."

"Gee, thanks," I choked out, right before my stomach heaved again. The stench was absolutely awful, especially to my shifter nose, but I had no choice but to let this take its course. I clutched the edge of the cot as I dry-heaved for a few moments more, then collapsed back down and wiped my mouth with the back of my shaking hand.

Footsteps sounded, and a shadow passed over me, blocking out the glaring light from the fixture set into the ceiling as Captain Galling bent over me. He had a glass bottle filled with water in his hand, which he held out to me.

"Drink."

I struggled up into a sitting position, then took the bottle from him. My fingers were so shaky that I nearly dropped it, but my body was so desperate for water that I managed to get it to my lips after a few seconds.

"Easy now," Captain Galling said in a gruff voice as I guzzled. "You'll make yourself sick again if you drink too fast."

I glared at him over the bottle, but slowed down, knowing he was right. When I had my fill, I set the bottle down on the floor, next to the reeking bucket, which I glared at.

Captain Galling sighed, then rose and stuck his head out the door of his office. A moment later, an enforcer came in to take the bucket away. The look on his face told me exactly how the man felt at being delegated to perform such a menial task, but he didn't say anything, just took the offending bucket by the handle and left the room.

"Anything else you need?" Captain Galling asked, pulling up one of his visitor's chairs and sitting down so that he was next to my cot. "Should I bring you some smelling salts?"

"It would be great if you could revive the civilian lying dead on the street behind the building," I sniped. "Once you do that, I think we'll be peachy."

Captain Galling scrubbed a hand over his square face. "I regret that," he said. "But you have to understand the enforcers were just doing their jobs."

"Yeah, they earned five stars for their performance today," I sneered. "Surely they could have brought me inside before asking me to show myself, couldn't they? Those fuckers *knew* I was disguised. In fact, I'm pretty damn sure at least one of them was hoping I'd be attacked." *And now he's dead, too.*

"Again, I apologize for that," Captain Galling said, his voice harder now. "And I also apologize for what happened to you in the hall earlier today, but as much as I'd like to claim otherwise, I can't control the way my men feel. If you want their respect, you're going to have to earn it. Sneaking around in disguise, wearing the face of a more popular enforcer, is hardly going to help with that. And they'll hold the death of the guard who was shot against you too."

"At this very moment, I don't give a shit about their respect," I snarled, digging my fingers into the lumpy cot. "I just want them to back the fuck off."

"Noted."

"How's your wife?" I asked casually, leaning back in my cot as I changed the subject. "Has she been cured yet?"

"Yes, she has –" Captain Galling paused, the smile freezing on his face. "How do you know about that?"

I rolled my eyes. "I'm the Chief Mage's apprentice, remember? I know a thing or two about what goes on in the Palace. And I know you agreed to haul the Guild back into line in exchange for your wife's health."

"Fine." Captain Galling growled. A vein pulsed at his temple, and his hands clenched into fists on his lap. "I'll make sure the enforcers know to give you a wide berth, and that they're not to block you in any way when you come to the Guild. But you at least have to present your enforcer bracelet. We have to maintain *some* level of security here."

"Thank you." I inclined my throbbing head. That was the best I could hope for, really.

"I'll make sure that the bounties for the thugs you brought in are credited to you as soon as possible," Captain Galling added. "The enforcers on guard duty were planning to take the reward for themselves. Which, of course, is the reason they tried to shut you out. I'll be docking their next bounties as punishment."

I wanted to be angry about that piece of information, but I

was just too damned tired and heartsick at Gorden's death, so I let it go. "Is there any way you can get a few more enforcers into Maintown? I promised..." A lump swelled in my throat, and I forced back tears. "I promised that I would see about sending some guys out there to police the thugs."

Captain Galling's dark blue eyes softened briefly. "I'll see what I can do, but we're stretched pretty thin now that Privacy Guard is refusing to work with us."

His remark reminded me of the strange lack of guards outside the Palace, and I frowned. I had thought perhaps Iannis had decided to get rid of them for some reason, but I hadn't realized they were no longer working with the Enforcers Guild either.

"What the hell is up with that?" I demanded. "Why is Privacy Guard refusing to help?"

"They've issued a statement that they're suspending all activity pending the outcome of the 'insurrection', as they put it," Captain Galling said tightly. "Because of that, we now have to look after our own prisoners and guard the building as well. We could have managed if we still had our previous numbers, but since a lot of us have left, it's slim pickings around here."

"I'm sorry," I said, and I meant it. I didn't envy Captain Galling's job right now – he had too much to do, and too little manpower to do it with. The fact that Privacy Guard was refusing to lift a finger was just another straw on an overburdened camel's back – and just what were they up to, anyway? Why were they standing back from the fight, when they should be taking advantage of the opportunity to make good money? Was the owner of the company allied with the Resistance somehow?

Something else to look into, I thought, adding it to the list.

"Don't be sorry," Captain Galling said, rising from his seat. "Be effective. You seem to be pretty good at nosing your way into the heart of things, Baine, so put that nose of yours to good use and find out who's behind this. I'm sick and tired of all this fighting, and the last thing I need to do is drop dead at the business end of a Resistance rifle after my wife's just been healed." He shook his head, laughing bitterly. "That would be a cruel dose of irony, wouldn't it?"

I smiled sadly. "I have a feeling that a lot of that's been going around."

CAPTAIN GALLING ARRANGED transport back to the Palace, which was a damn good thing because I was healing way too slowly for my liking. My shoulder had been bandaged up when I'd been unconscious, and it wasn't bleeding, but it still ached like hell, and my headache was taking a long time to dissipate. I needed to raid the kitchen, and then I needed a few good hours of sleep.

You could see about finding Iannis, a voice in my head suggested as I trudged up the Palace steps. *He'll want to know you're safe, and he'd probably be happy to heal you.*

The idea lifted my spirits momentarily, and a quick consultation with my *serapha* charm told me that he was in the West Wing, maybe even in his rooms. But then I remembered he'd been up for close to forty-eight hours, and that he'd used his magic to bring down a rainstorm and heal who knew how many injured civilians. Iannis was powerful, but even he had limits. He probably needed a recharge by now.

The kitchen staff was gone at this time of night, the lights turned off and the ovens shut down, so I raided the pantry, loading up on dried meat, cheese, and bread. After all, it wasn't as if I had anything to fear since there were no Privacy Guard employees in the Palace to try and jump me anymore. They'd done that the last time I raided the pantry, on my first night here, and nearly killed me. Of course, I doubted they'd have the balls to do it again now that I was an official apprentice, but still. I'd made sure to stay away from the kitchens when they were closed after that incident, until now.

I hauled my load to the little table in the corner and started scarfing it down, heedless of manners since there was no one around. I was halfway through a round of cheese when I heard footsteps on the stairwell. I paused, my senses going on high alert. Then I relaxed as I recognized the scent.

"Fenris," I called. "Come to share a midnight snack with me?"

"Something like that," he said, smiling as he emerged from the darkness. I'd turned on the lights, and his yellow wolf-shifter eyes squinted for a moment as they adjusted. As he stood there, I took a moment to study him. Fenris looked well enough, his dark hair and beard shining from a recent shower, but there were smudges of fatigue beneath his unusually heavy-lidded eyes. As usual, he was dressed in one of his old-fashioned tunics, this one a dark grey, but *un*usually, he had a short sword strapped to his waist.

"Can you even use that thing?" I asked as he approached the table.

Fenris smiled faintly and switched to mindspeak. "*Mages have been known to engage in combative sports for pleasure, such as fencing. This blade isn't the same thing as a rapier, but I think I can manage it if I have to.*"

I shook my head as he took a seat across from me. "*It's still hard to believe you're actually a mage,*" I muttered, matching his discretion by keeping the conversation silent. You never knew who might be lurking in a corner of this huge building, listening to conversations that were none of their damned business.

He frowned. "*I was a mage,*" he corrected. "*Now I am a shifter.*"

"*With some mage abilities*," I pointed out, arching a brow.

He sighed, picking up a crust of brown bread. "Perhaps I do not truly understand what I am," he admitted out loud. "But I do know I am not who I once was."

Same here, I thought as I polished off the rest of the cheese in my hand. As I swallowed my last bite, my shoulder began to itch, and I realized my regenerative abilities were revving up. Hot and uncomfortable, I shrugged off the jacket Captain Galling had lent me, draping it across the back of the chair. Oh well, at least it was my healing abilities causing this discomfort rather than the heat, which had temporarily abated beneath the stress of my wounds.

"Sunaya!" Fenris's eyes widened as he caught sight of my bandaged shoulder. "I thought I'd smelled blood, but I didn't realize it was more than a scratch. What happened?"

"Someone took a shot at me outside the Enforcers Guild," I said darkly. I recounted the story for him, starting with my apprehension of the thugs and ending with being knocked out by the enforcer I almost killed.

"It's no wonder Iannis asked me to wait up for you," Fenris said, his dark eyes glittering with fury. "Danger really does seem to stalk you wherever you go." He pushed up from the table, and his chair made a screeching sound against the concrete floor. "Let me take a look at your wounds. *I didn't use much magic today, so I'm sure I can heal you,*" he added in mindspeak.

"Don't bother." I held up a hand. Fenris's magical reserves were limited, and I didn't want him wasting them on me. "I'm healing well enough on my own, now that I've eaten. I just need some sleep, then I'll be good as new." It wasn't a lie – I was regenerating well enough that my heat was starting to kick in again, responding to Fenris's proximity. I bit down on the inside of my cheek, hoping the pain would distract me from the surge of hormones.

Fenris's nostrils flared as he caught my scent, and understanding lit his eyes. "Very well," he said, reluctantly returning to his seat. He eyed the rapidly diminishing pile of food. "I imagine you should be going to bed soon."

"Soon," I agreed, ignoring the dirty flashes the word 'bed' conjured in my mind. "But first, I want an update. How are things going on your end?"

"It depends on who you ask," Fenris said ruefully. "But overall, not terribly considering that we no longer have Privacy Guard to help with the defense. We've warded off the entire Mages Quarter from anyone without magic. Doing so poses a problem for our human employees since they can no longer leave or enter, but it also makes this area the safest section in Solantha. I can tell you that the mages are much less troubled about going out and fending off Resistance attacks, knowing that their families are safe behind the wards."

"Yeah, about that," I said, remembering my decision to look into Privacy Guard. "Do you know who the hell owns Privacy Guard, anyway? I can't help but think that their refusal to assist means their owner is involved with the Resistance somehow."

"Yes, I also find their behavior highly suspicious," Fenris agreed. "I will ask the appropriate department to investigate the company's origins. In hindsight, it was a mistake to rely on a single private company to such an extent, and I will advise Iannis not to do so again. We will need to look into other private security companies in the future."

"Or hire your own staff," I suggested. "There are plenty of unemployed humans and shifters in the city who would probably thank you for it, even now. Not everybody who's stayed behind is a Resistance supporter. Come to think of it, there are probably some lower-ranked mages you could employ as guards too."

"That's a good idea," Fenris said, nodding slowly.

We both turned at the sound of footsteps on the stairs, and I scowled as Cirin Garidano, the Finance Secretary, walked in. "What the hell is this?" I snapped irritably. "Did I put out a memo that I was hosting a party down here tonight?" Talking to Fenris was one thing, but I wasn't interested in an audience. Especially a male one.

Down, girl. The Finance Secretary was good-looking, but he was a little *too* similar to Iannis for my liking. Even if I was able to throw my conscience to the wayside, and even if Cirin was interested, I wouldn't be able to help but think of Iannis anyway.

"You aren't the only ones who get hungry in the middle of the night," Cirin said dryly. He sauntered over to the table, plucked a length of summer sausage from the pile, then deftly unwrapped it with his long fingers. "I believe I've just as much right to this food as you," he added when I bared my fangs at him.

"Fine. Well, if you're going to intrude on my dinner, the least you can do is be helpful." I kicked out a chair with my foot, gesturing for him to sit. As he did so, I blinked in surprise as I caught a whiff of smoke clinging to his clothes. "Were you out helping with the defense tonight?"

"Yes, then I had to go back to my office to take care of a few things, so I didn't get a chance eat until now. The kitchen staff had a buffet set out in the dining hall for us, which I missed, so I decided to come here instead."

"Oh." I pouted a little at that – it would have been nice to have a cooked meal. "I guess it's gotta be tough, doing Finance Secretary stuff while helping with the defense."

Cirin shrugged. "Lord Iannis ordered all the more powerful mages in the Guild to scale back their normal duties until the emergency is over. I'm hardly the only one juggling paperwork with magical defense."

"Thank Magorah I don't have to deal with that," I muttered around a mouthful of bread.

The conversation turned back toward the rising crime in the streets. I told Cirin and Fenris about the swelling prisoner population and the problems the Enforcers Guild was having due to being shorthanded.

"Many of the looters were honest citizens up until recently," I said, waving a crust of bread in the air as I spoke. "I'm not going to deny that a good portion of them are assholes, like the thugs I apprehended earlier today, but a lot of them are just desperate. It doesn't seem right that they should have to endure the punishments we normally dole out for theft."

Fenris sighed. "We can hardly maintain any level of order if we allow them to roam free," he said. "Doing so will just tell the citizens that we condone this sort of behavior, and it will embolden the looters while making the victims feel less safe."

"Indeed," Cirin agreed. "And considering that our reputation is suffering every day this goes on, we need to demonstrate to the citizens that we are reasserting control and not abandoning them."

A wave of exhaustion hit me then, and I leaned back in my chair. My body was trying to force me into shutdown mode, so it could use the food I'd eaten to finish healing.

"I'm going to get some sleep," I said with a yawn as I stood up. "Will you tell the Chief Mage, when you see him, that I need to speak with him?" I asked Fenris, knowing he would likely run into Iannis before me.

"Is *speaking* really the right term?" Fenris asked, giving me a knowing look. I blushed a little, surprised he'd even gone there considering how reserved he normally was.

"What does that mean?" Cirin asked with a frown.

"Never mind," I said, then hurried from the kitchen, bidding them goodnight and leaving them to deal with the leftovers. "Good night."

I headed up to my room, hoping for a restful night's sleep for once, instead of the hot and heavy dreams that usually came with heat. Resinah's advice about getting in touch with my mage half was obviously the key to controlling my heat, but whether I'd be able to do it within the darkness of my sleeping mind was another story entirely.

13

"Sunaya!" Fenris's voice shook me awake as he knocked on my door. "Sunaya, are you awake yet?"

Groaning, I sat up and glanced at the clock on my bedside. Eleven in the morning. Damn. I'd slept longer than I'd intended. I'd gone to bed around midnight last night, and because I'd been so exhausted, my sleep had been dreamless, the heat kept at bay by my body's need to recover.

But now that I was awake, I was hyper-aware of the fact that I was sitting up naked in bed and that only a single wooden door stood between a virile male and me. Warmth rushed through my body, and I threw off the sheets, my skin too hot and sensitive to bear them.

"Just a second," I called. "I'm not decent."

Instead of hurrying across the room to grab some clothing, I stood in the center of the room, away from the windows, and took deep, calming breaths. Instinctively, I fell back into a breathing pattern my mentor Roanas had taught me, the one he used to clear his mind and focus.

You're a mage, I told myself firmly, willing the thought to stick in my brain. I turned my focus inward, toward the pulsing ball of magic that always stood at my center. Warmth spread through me as I touched it, but not the aching, uncomfortable warmth of the heat – this sensation was soothing and energizing at the same time. As it filled me, my surging hormones receded.

Opening my eyes, I let out a relieved breath. No, I'd never forget that I was a shifter, but Resinah had been right. I needed to constantly reaffirm my identity as a mage if I wanted to stay in control. That was why my teenage-boy illusion had been so helpful – I'd been using my magic. Overall, the heat hadn't been nearly as bad as it normally was – when a shifter female went into heat, she was usually reduced to little more than a wild animal, consumed by the need to mate, and couldn't function without a steady supply of sex for the entire week. Yet, somehow, even when I wasn't using illusion magic, I'd managed to keep my head. It had to have something to do with the fact that Iannis had unlocked most of my magic.

Feeling more grounded, I went into the closet, then paused in surprise at the sight of several pairs of pants and shirts hanging inside, as well as a bathrobe. They only filled up a fraction of the large space, but I was damn sure they hadn't been there yesterday.

Moving in closer, I recognized the tops and pants as the same ones the Palace had provided for me the first time I'd come here, as a prisoner. As far as clothing went, it was pretty generic – a few pairs of jeans and some monochromatic shirts – but it would do until I had the time and resources to buy a wardrobe.

Obviously, Iannis had thought to have someone put clothing in here for me. The idea that he'd remembered my needs despite his insane schedule made me smile, and I reached for a green top, wondering if it would bring out the color in my eyes.

"Are you going to leave me standing out here all day?" Fenris demanded, and I jumped at the sound of his muffled voice coming through the doorway.

"Sorry!" I called, snagging the fluffy robe off its hanger. I shrugged it on, then made sure it was tightly belted and covering up as much as possible before I opened the door to admit Fenris.

"About time." He brushed past me, looking unusually agitated, and shut the door behind him. "What took you so long?"

"I'm not a morning person." I tried not to snap the words – clearly, something was troubling him. "What's this all about?" I glanced down toward the paper tucked beneath his arm.

"Our old friend, the Herald, is at it again," Fenris growled, pulling the paper from beneath his arm and handing it to me.

I unfolded it, then bared my teeth at the headline stamped across the front page. THE RESISTANCE PREVAILS! MAGES GUILD TAKES HUGE BLOW AT LOSS OF SOLANTHA AIRSHIP YARD, it read, and beneath was a photograph of the flaming airship yard, obviously taken last night, as it was hard to see much more than shadows and fire. *Full story on page 13.*

"Don't bother," Fenris snarled as I flipped open to page thirteen. "It's all bullshit propaganda, slanted to make it look like the Mages Guild is a bunch of bumbling idiots and that the Resistance's well-executed, organized attacks are turning the tide."

"Yeah, but I need to see it for myself." I read the article anyway – it wasn't that long, no more than two pages – and by the time I was done, I was shredding the edges of the paper with my claws. "They don't even mention the civilian casualties," I growled, crumpling up the paper and tossing it in the trash like the piece of garbage it was.

"I thought this sort of thing would have ended once Yantz was removed as chief editor, but whoever replaced him must also be working for the Resistance," Fenris said, his yellow eyes burning with frustration. "Considering how much influence this paper has over the humans in Solantha, we cannot allow them to continue to spew such hostile propaganda."

I arched a brow. "Are you saying you want to take a field trip to the Herald?"

"I am." He looked me up and down, no doubt taking in my lack of clothing and the rat's nest on top of my head. "When will you be ready to leave?"

MUCH AS I wanted to rush out the door and chase down this new lead, I was way overdue for a shower, and I didn't want to show up at the Herald looking like a crazy homeless person. So I grabbed a quick bath, got my hands on a hairbrush, and shimmied myself into a pair of jeans and a top that fit a little *too* loosely. The strenuous trek through Coazi territory had caused me to lose a few inches, not to mention all the recent healing I'd undergone. I was definitely going to need to find the time to eat more.

Just as I was about to leave, I remembered the *gulaya* I'd borrowed from the library, which was still in the pocket of the pants I'd worn yesterday. I quickly retrieved it, then strung it on my necklace so that it rested next to the *serapha* charm. Since the *serapha* couldn't be removed by force, this would ensure that the *gulaya* would remain safe as well.

My stomach grumbled as I headed out with Fenris, and I wished I'd thought to stock up on snacks from the kitchens. Unfortunately, Fenris would likely have a fit if I suggested running by the kitchen for some food now, so I swallowed my tongue and followed him out to the side entrance instead. I blinked in surprise at the sight of two sleek, black steamcars with the Canalo Mages Guild emblem painted in gold on their side, puffing out clouds of smoke as they waited for us.

"Seriously," I complained under my breath as Fenris and I approached the second car. "How is it that you rate *multiple* steamcars, but I can't even get one?" I might have been a mere apprentice, but as far as the rest of the world knew, Fenris was only a shifter. Yes, he was a close friend of Iannis, and sometimes even acted as a direct messenger for him. But I still didn't understand why Cirin had gotten him a steamcar instead of me.

"I cleared it with Iannis this morning," Fenris said dryly. "After going over the morning paper over breakfast, he decreed that the Herald needs to be shut down, and told me to take you, the Legal Secretary –" he pointed to the car behind ours – "and a few other mages from his department as backup. And before you ask," he added as the driver came around to open the front door, "no, you can't sit up front. You need to stay in the back, out of sight, where it's safe."

"Tyrant," I grumbled as Fenris got into the front seat, but I acquiesced, climbing into the backseat when the driver opened the door for me. As I settled in, strapping the seatbelt on, I noticed the windows had some kind of coating that darkened them. I was grateful because it meant I couldn't be easily spotted from the street. Fenris was right – I did need to stay out of sight as much as possible, and this would give me a chance to travel through the city as myself while remaining relatively safe. That was a damn good thing, because I couldn't very well show up at the Herald looking like a pimply teenage boy. I was acting as Sunaya Baine, enforcer extraordinaire.

Besides, my teenage-boy cover was blown after last night. I made a mental note to pick a different disguise the next time I went out, because I was certain the Resistance would have spread the word to keep a look out for that persona by now. Hopefully, they didn't kill any innocent teenage boys by mistake. I winced a little at that thought. Maybe I should have picked something a little less vulnerable for my disguise.

You can't second-guess every damn decision you make, I told myself. *The Resistance is going to kill people no matter what you do, until you bring them down.*

Despite the fact that it was lunch hour, traffic was almost non-existent, especially once we crossed into Maintown. That wasn't surprising – with most of the restaurants closed down, there was nowhere to go for lunch even if people did want to brave the dangerous streets. One would have thought that Maintown would be one of the safer parts of the city – after all, the Resistance was supposedly fighting for human and shifter rights. But aside from the more affluent section on the coast, which I noticed was mostly intact and heavily guarded by private mercenaries, the bulk of Maintown had been hit just as hard as the rest of the city.

It only took us ten minutes before we pulled into the lot surrounding the Herald's white, circular building. I wasn't terribly surprised to see two men dressed in mercenary leathers guarding the revolving door, and even less surprised that I recognized them from the Enforcers Guild. These deserters had to do *something* for work after they left the Guild, and their being there was additional evidence that the Herald was firmly pro-Resistance.

The guards stiffened as we disembarked from the vehicles, hands going to the hilts of their swords. I bared my teeth at that – were they seriously going to fight us for entry? – but before I could take a step forward, Fenris grabbed my arm.

"Let the Mages Guild do their job," he said. "We are here under their authority."

I grumbled a bit at that, but allowed the Legal Secretary and his entourage to take the lead. Like Iannis and Cirin, the Secretary was a tall, lean man with long hair pulled into a low tail, and I wondered if 'tall, lean, and long-haired' were job requirements for high-ranking positions in the guild.

Council members excluded, of course, I thought with a sneer as I recalled Omonas ar'Candar, the fat, pompous councilman who had successfully blocked me from being allowed to join Iannis's rescue team.

I racked my brain for the Legal Secretary's name and came up empty – he was new to the position. The last one, a frail, ancient-looking fellow, had nearly been killed by the Resistance when Iannis's delegation had been kidnapped on their way to the capital. Upon his return to Solantha, he had, understandably, retired from office, and now we had this new, much younger guy filling his shoes.

Well, at least he doesn't look feeble, I thought as the mage came to a stop in front of the door. He looked commanding enough in his dark red robes, and his blond hair was pulled back tight, leaving his stern face unframed.

"Step aside," he ordered the former enforcers, who had closed ranks and were blocking the door. "We are here on official business."

"What sort of business?" sneered the deserter on the right, a burly guy with dyed-blue hair. I rolled my eyes at his eyebrow and lip piercings. What kind of enforcer actually had those, much less wore them on the job? It was like asking for trouble in a fight. "You can't just come in here without stating your intentions."

"My *intentions* are to shut down this miserable excuse for a newspaper," the Legal Secretary snapped. He pulled a sheet of paper from the sleeve of his robe and held it up so the men could read it. "I have a decree, signed by Lord Iannis, stating as much."

The other deserter, a leaner guy with white hair, snatched the decree and scanned it. "This looks like a bunch of bullshit," he growled.

The Legal Secretary lifted his hand, and yellow energy

crackled at his fingertips. "Would you like to test me?" he asked pleasantly as the air grew thick, charged with tension and magic.

The two deserters exchanged a long look, then silently moved aside. The Legal Secretary and his mages passed through the revolving doors, and Fenris and I quickly followed behind. I didn't miss the dirty looks the men sent me as I passed, or the way their fingers twitched against their sword hilts – no doubt they were thinking that if they delivered my head to the Resistance, they would get a handsome reward for it.

The same curly-haired brunette I'd met last time sat behind the circular, white reception desk in the center of the gleaming lobby. Her oval face turned pale, but she stiffened her slim shoulders and lifted her chin as we approached.

"Inform your CEO that the Legal Secretary of the Mages Guild is here to speak to him," the Legal Secretary commanded.

"I'm sorry," she said coolly, "but the CEO is not in the building at this time."

"Very well, get me his second-in-command then."

"The deputy CEO is not here either," she said, still in that same cool monotone.

"Are there *any* senior staff in the building?" the Legal Secretary asked, a hint of annoyance creeping into his voice. "Or is everyone out to lunch?"

"I am under no obligation to answer that question," she said in a voice like ice, and it was then that I realized she was expecting us.

"The CEO knew we were coming," I said aloud. The Legal Secretary turned to face me, a look of censure on his face – clearly, he wasn't happy with me speaking out of turn. But I plowed on. "Someone at the Palace must have tipped him off. I bet you he and his senior staff gathered any important papers and evidence and are already long gone."

The Legal Secretary stared at me for a moment, then whirled back to the receptionist. "Where are your printing presses?"

"I am under no obligation –"

"Silence, foolish girl," he said in a tone a thousand times icier than hers. Her eyes widened with fear, and she pressed her lips together. "I'm certain it would not take me long to find the presses myself, but I want you to tell me. If you don't, I will have you arrested for obstruction, and will send you to Prison Isle. A pretty woman like you will have a grand time with the hardened criminals there."

"D-downstairs," the receptionist said in a shaking voice, and I almost felt sorry for her. That was, until the memory of Gorden's crumpled body seeping blood in the back alley of the Enforcers Guild flashed in my mind's eye, as well as all the wounded civilians from the airship yard attack.

No, this girl didn't merit any sympathy. She was aiding cold-blooded killers and deserved whatever was coming to her.

The receptionist gave us directions on how to access the basement – through either the elevator or a stairwell around the corner. The Legal Secretary opted for the stairs, taking Fenris and one of his mages down there so they could disable the presses and send the remaining staff home. I went upstairs with the other two mages to scour the offices and check if the CEO or his staff had been careless enough to leave anything incriminating behind.

Nearly an hour later, I met the others back in the reception hall. "We found nothing," I told the Legal Secretary, doing my best to keep the frustration out of my voice. "I don't know how much lead time they had, but it was enough that they managed to take every single shred of useful paperwork they had. They could be burning it or dumping it in the bay right now, for all we know," I added in disgust.

"That is unfortunate," the Legal Secretary acknowledged,

"but our primary purpose in coming here was to shut down the Herald, and we've done that. We've broken various components in their printing presses to ensure they cannot simply start back up when we've left, and have told all the staff to leave and not come back." He turned his head to give the receptionist a beady-eyed stare. "That includes you, Miss."

The brunette sniffed, then rose from her chair, her things already gathered, and left the building with her head held high. I eyed her as she joined the continuous stream of humans filing out through the main lobby, and was half-tempted to arrest her just for being a bitch. Not to mention the whole 'aiding and abetting terrorists' thing. But we didn't have the space to hold every single person who was allied with the Resistance, and unless we found out she was actually engaging in criminal activity I couldn't justify apprehending her.

"As soon as the rest of the humans have cleared out of here, we should return to the Palace," the Legal Secretary announced as more humans passed us. Quite a few of them gave us dirty looks, but many more had stricken, hopeless expressions on their faces, and my heart twisted with sympathy. "Our work here is done."

"No, it's not," I said.

The Legal Secretary's eyes turned frosty. "Excuse me?"

"Those humans." I pointed to the thinning crowd. "You need to see about putting them back to work somehow. Surely the Mages Guild can afford to set aside some gold for rebuilding projects."

"It hardly makes sense to rebuild when the city is still under-going attacks, Miss Baine," the Legal Secretary said coldly. "Besides, it is no concern of mine what these humans do now. They should not have worked for a company with such questionable morals and loyalties."

"Are you fucking serious?" I shouted, stepping forward into

the Legal Secretary's personal space. I wanted to slap the shit out of him, but physical altercations with mages, especially ones who were well trained, weren't a smart idea. "These people don't have a clue! Whatever their bosses were up to, the rest are just trying to keep their heads down and put food on their families' tables." I took a deep breath, meeting his uncomprehending and outraged eyes. "As a mage, you wouldn't know of their troubles, but food is scarce, and they're not even certain they'll have homes to return to at the end of the day. This is *not* their fault, and by sending them home today, jobless, all you're doing is reinforcing the idea that the Mages Guild is evil." Fenris looked almost as outraged as the mages, but I ploughed on, determined to have my say. Was there no way I could make them see what was so obvious to me? "The Herald fed their families, and the *Mages Guild* just put them out of work. Who do you think they're going to blame for their hungry children? Because I can tell you right now, it's not the Resistance. You're creating more enemies every day by refusing to acknowledge the needs of the people."

"Miss Baine may have a point," one of the other mages said quietly, and the Legal Secretary looked at him in surprise. "Idle hands may easily be turned to destructive pursuits. If we don't find a way to keep the population occupied, they will likely join the revolt."

The Legal Secretary sighed, then turned back to look at me. "This is hardly my department," he said stiffly, "but I will speak to the Chief Mage, and perhaps he can figure out what to do next."

"Great." I'd be checking in with Iannis myself on this, but for now, I had something more important to do. "Do you have any idea where I might be able to get a ride?" I asked, turning to Fenris.

He frowned. "Why? Where are you planning on going?"

I told him about the tin company I'd run across in the

grocery store, and its possible connection to the Resistance. "I'm tired of running around in circles on this," I told him. "It's about time we start pulling on threads, and this is the only real one I've got."

"I'll come with you," Fenris decided. "We'll return to the Palace for some food, since I know you're starving, and I'll arrange transportation."

"Great," I said, and that was when the windows exploded.

14

"Get down!" I screamed, grabbing Fenris by the collar. I threw us both to the ground, heedless of the glass sprayed all across the floor, and began crawling for the dubious safety of the reception desk. More windows exploded under the onslaught of gunfire, raining glass everywhere, and my ears rang from the deafening noise.

I heard the mages, who had ducked for cover as well, simultaneously speak a series of Words. The burnt-sugar scent of magic laced the air, and the hair along my arms stood as I felt energy ripple through the room. I peeked over the top of the desk just in time to see a blue force field ripple into existence, spreading across the front wall, and I sighed in relief as I watched a bullet ricochet off it.

"This won't hold long," the Legal Secretary warned as he got to his feet. "We need to neutralize the threat outdoors if we want to get back to the Palace safely."

"Yeah, no shit." I rose and peered through the blue shield so I could get a look at our attackers. The two deserters were standing outside, along with eight other men with the Resistance's red bands around their arms. And all of them were carrying rifles. "Is there any way to disable their guns?" I asked as I watched several of our enemies split off from the group, running around to the back of the building. "They're not that much of a threat without them." *Not against us, anyway,* I thought as I eyed the Legal Secretary. "I'm hoping you can use your magic for more than defense?"

"All mages are trained in the basics of magical combat," the Legal Secretary said stiffly. "I have not had much cause to use it up until very recently, but I daresay I won't prove entirely useless."

"Great." I glanced at Fenris. "You should change," I suggested. "You'll be way more effective as a wolf if you have to fight."

Fenris bared his teeth. "I don't like the idea of having to sit back –" he began.

"You're no good against a bunch of guys with guns," I said sharply, switching to mindspeak. *"I took a bullet yesterday, and it hurt like hell and took a long time to heal. I don't think we can survive a whole lot of them, especially if we get shot in the heart or the head."*

"I'll just use my magic in wolf-form, then," Fenris snapped. *"As long as I'm subtle about it, no one will notice."*

I sighed. *"Fine. Just don't die."*

Fenris crouched down behind the desk, and I turned away from the glow of bright, white light as he began to change. "Come on," I told the Legal Secretary. "Let's head them off from the back."

We split up, as there were two corridors that wrapped around each end of the building, and left the other mages to hold the shield at the front. I sprinted for the rear exit, fairly certain they would come through there, then skidded to a halt as a door flew open, and two men charged in. Guess they'd broken in through whatever room lay beyond. They were big, and the corridor was narrow, so they fumbled to aim their guns.

I took advantage of their slowness, blasting them both with balls of flame. The stench of burning human hair and flesh filled the air, along with their screams as the fire slammed into them, and I ducked as one of their guns went off, narrowly avoiding a bullet. They both dropped to the ground, trying to extinguish the blue flames by rolling around, and I blasted them again, then kicked them back through the door and shut it on them.

Footsteps sounded, hard and heavy against the tile. My nose told me the runner was human, so I whipped a chakram out and flung it. The large, metallic circle whizzed through the air as it spun around the curved hall, and I heard a loud gurgle as it struck flesh. My ears told me there was no one else around the corner, so I peeked around and watched as the blue-haired ex-enforcer dropped to his knees with my chakram sticking out of his throat, blood pouring from the wound and gushing all over his chest. He toppled sideways as his last breath left him, and I stepped forward and yanked the chakram from his throat.

"I see you've got things under control," Fenris said dryly as he came around the corner, in his wolf form, as I had suggested. I was wiping my bloody chakram on the dead man's clothing, and I straightened to look at Fenris, twirling the circular blade around my finger. *"Good thing too, as the two men who'd stayed out front have shot holes into the engines of our steamcars."*

"Lovely," I muttered. "Do the phones still work in this place? I think we're going to need to call for transportation."

"Indeed," Fenris said. *"It is neither expedient nor safe to try and return home on foot or by use of public conveyance."*

By unspoken agreement, we trotted to the rear of the building to make sure there was no one else lurking. The Legal Secretary was already waiting there, a dead mercenary at his feet, and my eyes widened as I noticed he was clutching a bloody shoulder.

"You got hit," I exclaimed, closing the distance. "How bad is it?"

The Legal Secretary waved me off with his free hand, a gesture that caused him to wince. "The bullet only grazed me," he said, briefly lifting his hand so I could see the wound. True to his word, it looked like the bullet had only ripped through cloth and a few layers of skin, rather than puncturing muscle. "Painful, but survivable. How many did you take out?"

"Three."

"I've done the same," he said, and I couldn't help but be impressed. Guess the Mages Guild wasn't just filled with useless bureaucrats after all. "Now there's just the two in the front to deal with."

"How do you suggest we take them out?" I asked. "I guess we could sneak around from the back."

To my surprise, the Legal Secretary gave me a small grin. "I think between the two of us, we can do better than that."

In the end, the solution turned out to be surprisingly simple. We took the stairs up to the second floor, then opened magical fire on the two remaining men from above. It was quick and efficient, and anybody watching them get struck down by a combination of magical lightning and fire would be scared shitless.

Yeah, Elnos was right. Humans might be a bit scarier when they were toting guns, but they were still no match for magical warfare. The thought made me more certain than ever that the only way to get the mages to change their ways was through reason, not violence.

By Magorah, I thought, shaking my head a little. Who would have thought that Sunaya Baine would be advocating the use of words instead of fists? And they said people couldn't change.

The phone lines were still working, so we were able to call and arrange transport back to the Palace, in the form of more black steamcars. An entire fleet of them, in fact, filled with more mages to act as a guard for us. Even so, the ride back was silent and tension filled, and I braced myself for another attack from the Resistance. I didn't relax until we were safely behind the warded protection of the Mages Quarter.

I half-expected Iannis to be waiting for us – after all, his apprentice and his closest friend had nearly been killed – but he was tied up in yet another meeting. Trying not to look too disappointed, I headed down to the kitchens with Fenris, who had turned back to human as soon as we'd arrived, to grab some lunch. They had prepared some kind of creamy pasta with chicken, and I wolfed down a mountain of the dish, refueling and drowning my disappointment in food. Yes, it was childish, but I wanted to see Iannis again. He'd left me on Hawk Hill with the promise that we'd finish what we started, and here I was, having to deal with the heat all by myself. Besides, I wanted to talk to him about mobilizing the jobless shifters and humans in order to keep them from defecting to the Resistance.

"Come to the side entrance," Fenris called. He'd finished eating long before me and had gone to arrange transport. *"We're ready to go check on that factory."*

Fenris was waiting for me there, but he held up a hand as I made for the double doors. "Hang on," he said. "We can't go outdoors without a disguise. It's entirely possible the Resistance has shifters watching us from the air."

"All right." I crossed my arms. "I was thinking we'd come as tax inspectors from the Finance Secretary's office. Does that work for you?"

"Yes," Fenris said, a slightly amused expression crossing his face. "Perhaps we should have brought the Finance Secretary himself along."

"Yes, I'm sure he'd just love to stop what he's doing to come on a field trip with us," I said dryly, then placed my hands on his broad shoulders. In short order, I'd turned him into a reedy mage with dark hair and spectacles, dressed in dark blue robes, and myself into a severe-looking strawberry blonde in pale pink. Both of us had the Mages Guild emblem stitched onto our breasts, and we were sporting clipboards, so I was sure we'd appear to be very official.

"What are the chances we're going to get attacked again?" I wondered as we descended the steps and headed for the steamcar awaiting us.

"We can't rule out the possibility," Fenris acknowledged. "To be on the safe side, I had the car warded against bombs and bullets. It's not foolproof – there's little we can do if they blow up the bridge while we're on it, for example, but the car should be relatively safe to travel in. Besides, we won't be going as Sunaya and Fenris. We are Zane and Tanita from the Mages Guild."

I groaned at the name Fenris had chosen, but before I could complain, he went around to the driver's side of the car.

I stared. "Wait a minute. You're driving?"

"There is little point in endangering a driver," he called as he shut the door, and I yanked mine open so I could hear what he said next. "And before you ask, no. You can't drive on the way back."

"How the hell do you get off on saying that?" I demanded. "I didn't even know you *could* drive."

"I've been practicing new skills," Fenris said lightly as he put the vehicle into gear.

Half an hour later, my fingers were twitching with the need to grab Fenris by his collar and shake him. "Do you think you could go *any* slower?"

Fenris raised an eyebrow. "I'm going at the suggested speed

limit for non-residential roads," he said, pointing to the dashboard.

"There's a reason it's a suggestion," I retorted with a growl. "At the rate you're dawdling, the factory will be closed by the time we arrive. Get moving, or I'm tossing you into the backseat and taking over."

Fenris scowled, but he increased the speed until we were going at a clip that would actually get us there at a decent time. Timbran's Gourmet Foods was located about forty minutes north of Turain, according to the map I was looking at – still a good hour and a half from here – so I settled into the passenger's seat for a nap. After all, the car was warded, and there was little I could do unless we were actually under attack.

Please, please, don't let there be another attack. The last thing I needed was to be stranded on a road many miles away from Solantha and any sort of shelter.

"Sunaya." Fenris's voice woke me, and I sat up, startled. I felt like I'd barely fallen asleep, but as I looked around, I realized that Fenris was taking us down a winding dirt road that led to a factory building just a few hundred yards ahead. It was situated right at the water's edge – which made sense, since many of their shipments and supplies probably came and went by boat. "We're here."

"Great." I slapped my cheeks to force myself into alertness. "Don't forget, *I'm* taking the lead on this one," I warned. After all, this was all my idea.

"If you insist," Fenris said mildly.

As he parked the steamcar, it occurred to me how anomalous it was for Fenris to be as easygoing as he was. After all, just a few years ago, he'd been Polar ar'Tollis, Chief Mage of Nebara – a mage who had defied the Federation by helping a group of humans escape a death sentence. Clearly, he'd not only been a leader, but he'd also been willing to completely disregard the Federation's authority in favor of his own.

And paid the price for it, I reminded myself as I looked at him. The one photograph I'd seen of Polar ar'Tollis had depicted a tall, fair-headed mage not unlike the Legal Secretary. Fenris had not only had to change his identity on every level, but his appearance as well. Perhaps the knowledge that his actions had cost him life as he'd known it had taken him down a few notches.

"Is there a particular reason you're staring at me?" Fenris asked as he killed the engine.

I thought about brushing off the question, but we had a minute, so I answered it instead. "I just wonder if you regret your actions," I said. "The actions that forced you to go into hiding and transform yourself into a shifter," I clarified when Fenris arched a brow.

Fenris sighed, leaning back in his seat and staring out the windshield. "There are times when I wonder whether it was truly the right decision." A faraway look entered his currently dark brown eyes. "I do wonder if it might have been better to let that family die, and use my position to lobby for changes to some of the outdated laws that continue to make lives difficult for Northia's non-mage citizens." He shook his head, laughing softly. "But then I remember that if the case had not come to my attention, if the injustice of their situation had not caused me to take action, I may very well have gone on governing as I was, indifferent to the plight of my subjects."

His expression grew serious as he turned to face me again. "No, I may have paid a steep price for my actions, but on the whole, I prefer Fenris, the man I've become, to the late Polar ar'Tollis. And besides, I am needed here at Iannis's side, at *your* side too, and right now, I can't think of a better place to be."

I smiled, tears stinging the corners of my eyes, and threw my arms around Fenris to hide them. "You're such a sap," I told him.

Fenris laughed, returning the embrace. "I'm not the only one," he said, seeing through me.

"Seriously though, I'm glad you're here. I don't know what I would have done if you hadn't been there when I first came to the Palace." Fenris's calming nature and willingness to act as a go-between for Iannis and me had been crucial to bringing us together as master and apprentice... and maybe something more. "I might even be dead," I added softly.

"Don't be silly," Fenris chided. "You're far too resourceful to die. I've watched you escape death too many times to count in the short time we've known each other. I don't know if it's luck or intelligence that keeps you alive, but you defy death on a regular basis."

"Maybe someone's watching out for me," I said with a grin, pulling back. I took a moment to compose myself, settling my face into stern lines again, then reached for the door. "Now let's get inside and scare these poor people into telling us what they know."

15

"Right this way," the manager babbled as he led us down a dimly lit concrete hall in the factory. It had been pleasantly easy to intimidate the security guard into calling his boss, who came down and immediately began blustering and threatening us for trespassing. But once Fenris had produced a document that demanded access to Timbran's tax records – an illusion, of course, but a human couldn't tell that – the manager had crumbled, fear entering his grey-green eyes at the thought of being dragged back to Solantha and tossed onto Prison Isle for failing to cooperate.

"I assure you, we keep meticulous accounting records," the manager continued, shouting over the noise of the factory machines. I forced myself to stop breathing through my nose – the stench of old food and meat that I sincerely hoped was not making it into tin cans, was turning my stomach. "And, of course, the head of our finance department is up to snuff on tax codes. She would *never* make a mistake."

"Of course not," I said smoothly, injecting a slightly patronizing undertone into my voice. "But we have to make these surprise visits every once in a while, or else businesses would become complacent and try to work around the codes."

"Yes, yes, I understand." The manager led us into a large, utilitarian office space. Vertical filing cabinets and stacks of bankers boxes lined the walls. The two desks in the room, while neatly organized, had large stacks of paper on them, and boxes were stacked on the floor next to them.

"If you had come a few hours earlier, I could have had Verna show you the records." The manager's eyes darted around the room worriedly. "But, unfortunately, she's gone for the day, as she gets in very early. I'll do my best to find what you're looking for." He scooped a hand through his thinning hair, then turned to look at us again. "What did you say you were looking for again?"

"Let's start with shipping records, from the past six months," I supplied helpfully.

The man's high forehead crinkled. "What exactly do you need the shipping records for?" he asked.

"*You're not interested in our reasons for looking at the shipment records,*" Fenris said, magic resonating in his voice. I'd witnessed him use this talent only once before, to make a pair of Coazi forget they'd seen us, and I held my breath, hoping it would work. Fenris had said it was less effective on the strong-willed. "*You want to show us what we need to know quickly, so you can get back to work.*"

"Right!" the manager's face cleared, and he turned on his heel. "I know exactly where the shipping records are. Come this way."

I gave Fenris an arch look as we followed the manager over to the opposite corner, where he immediately started opening cabinet drawers. "*I'd hate to think what would have happened if that didn't work. Our cover would have been blown for sure.*"

"*I am a fairly good judge of character,*" Fenris said, sounding a little offended that I would doubt him. *"I've rarely been wrong about suitable subjects for suggestion magic."*

Suggestion magic. That was what Iannis had called it too, during that time when he had used it to break into the house where the sick Federation Minister had been held against his will. That would be such a useful talent to have...

"Here we are." The manager pulled out a logbook, then turned and handed it to us. It was a little beat up, and the leather binding had seen better days, but the handwriting on the pages was clear and neat.

"Thank you. We'll be just a moment," I told the manager before turning around and placing the book on the desk nearest us. Fenris and I bent our heads together to look over the pages, and I quickly flipped through the last few months, scanning the records with ease. I'd developed an eye for paperwork after weeks of doing grunt work for the Mages Guild, and though I never thought I'd be thanking them for putting me through that hellish torture, I had to admit it was paying off now.

"Here. And here. And here again," I told Fenris, pointing to certain shipments that caught my eye. *"These must be the ones who are going to the Resistance."*

"Ah, yes, I see." Fenris's eyes narrowed as he nodded in agreement. *"These shipments are much larger than any of their other customers, and unlike the other recipients, there is no shipping address listed here."* The records only showed that the merchandise was picked up by boat, but not where it was delivered to, and that the bills were promptly paid by a company called Supplysafe.

"Do you know where Supplysafe is located?" I asked over my shoulder.

"W-what?" the manager stuttered, clearly unprepared for the question.

I turned around to face him. "Supplysafe. According to these shipment records, they're currently your biggest customer. Where are they located?"

"I'm not sure. Gaston, I think," the manager said, referring to a distant town on the East Coast. "We don't know very much about them."

I arched a brow. "I noticed. You don't list an address for them on your shipments. Isn't that unusual?"

"Yes, it is," the manager mumbled, rubbing the back of his neck as he looked at the ground. But then, he pulled himself together and looked straight at me. "But as you mentioned, Inspector, they're currently our best customer, and business had slowed down in the past year. With the quantities they order and their willingness to pay promptly, it didn't seem wise to push them when they neglected to provide a delivery address. The extra income from their business has allowed us to purchase several additional steam-canning machines, and for the first time in years, we're looking at expanding again." He folded his arms and gave us a beady eye, as if the explanation could justify his apparent willingness to look the other way. "There aren't very many businesses that can say that in these troubling times."

"Indeed," I said sharply, and he flinched. "Your records say that the shipments go out by boat. Where are your captains told to bring the freight?"

"They aren't," the manager admitted. "Supplysafe sends their own boats to pick up the shipments. Like I said, they're a great customer."

Fantastic, I grumbled to myself. "How did Timbran's first come into contact with them?" I demanded. "Surely a representative must have gotten in touch with you, or vice versa."

"All our business with Supplysafe has been via letter and messenger," the manager explained. "And the messengers work for courier companies, as far as I can tell."

"So you've never met the owners?"

"Never." The manager frowned. "What did you say this was about again?"

I bit back a sigh as Fenris took control of the conversation, using his suggestion magic to steer the manager's suspicions away. We asked him a few more questions, but the only other information we managed to get out of him was the billing address Supplysafe had given them, and the account numbers used to pay the bills. My eyebrows went up as I noticed the account belonged to Sandin Federal Bank. There was no way that was a coincidence. If I could find a link between Sandin and Supplysafe – aside from their initials – we might be that much closer to discovering the Benefactor's identity.

"My nose isn't as well trained as yours," Fenris said once we were outside and headed back to our vehicle, "but as far as I could tell, the man seemed truthful. Do you concur?"

"I do," I said as I got into the steamcar. "If there's more to this story – and I'm sure there is – the manager doesn't know about it. The Benefactor has not only done a great job of covering his tracks, he's also ensured that the people he deals with can't give much away, since they know next to nothing themselves."

"Will you consult with the Finance Secretary, then, regarding the Sandin Federal connection?" Fenris asked as he started the steamcar and guided us back down to the dirt road. "I imagine he could be quite helpful in this matter."

"First chance I get," I decided, settling into my seat for the ride. "Now hurry up and get us back."

∾

SOMEWHERE ALONG THE drive back home, Fenris developed a lead foot. We got back to the Palace in half the time it had taken us to get to Timbran's, which was a good thing because I was getting antsy to move on with the investigation. Fenris, it turned out, had matters of his own to deal with, so I left him to take care of returning the steamcar, and headed toward the Mages Guild to enlist the Finance Secretary's help.

Unfortunately, Cirin wasn't in his office, and I didn't think he'd appreciate it if I enlisted one of the few over-loaded staff he had left to help me, without his permission. Annoyed, I went to see if I could speak to Iannis, but Dira informed me he was out again, dealing with the prisoner crisis. Damn. These problems were stacking themselves on top of each other, and I *knew* if I could just get a few moments to talk to Iannis, my suggestions might help him figure out a solution.

If we could keep our hands off each other, that was.

Shoving my hands into my pockets, I headed back out of the Guild offices, trying to figure out what to do next. My feet took me in the direction of the West Wing, and the next thing I knew, I was standing outside the library. Hmm. Libraries were supposed to be good resources of information, right? Maybe there was something in there that could help me.

"Good afternoon, Miss Baine," Janta said, pushing up her spectacles as I entered. She was dressed in set of daisy-yellow robes today, her silver hair braided into a coil and wrapped around her head. Once again, she was all alone. "Is there some-thing I can help you find today?"

"Maybe." I dragged a hand through my hair, wondering how to phrase my request. "Umm, is there a way to find out who the owners of a company in another state are?"

Janta smiled. "But of course. The library has a nation-wide company directory, and updates are published biannually. It's never entirely up to date, but close enough."

"Really?" I grinned, surprised and pleased. "Do you think it'll have companies listed that are located in remote towns? Like, say, a company called Supplysafe in Gaston?"

"That may be a tough one," the librarian admitted as she rose from her seat. "But we'll see. Give me just one moment."

She bustled away to, leaving me alone at the front desk for a few moments. I drummed my finger against the wooden surface as I waited, trying not to get carried away by the hope dancing around in my chest. It seemed like an eternity before Janta came back – although it was probably only a few minutes – but when she emerged from between the shelves, she was carrying a large, heavy-looking book.

"Here, come around to my side of the desk," she said kindly, pushing aside some papers so she could set the tome down. "We'll have a look at this together."

I did as she asked, snagging a chair from one of the tables and bringing it over so I could sit next to her. Janta opened the book to a certain section, then scanned the directory with a slender finger, drawing my attention to her silver-painted nails. She murmured softly as she read the names aloud.

"Supplysafe," she finally said, raising her volume to an audible level again. "It says here they are a subsidiary of something called the Bellington Trust."

I bit back a groan. "I don't like the sound of that." The last thing I needed was to go through a bunch of different companies, only to hit another dead end.

"Now, now." Janta gave me small smile. "Don't be so impatient, Miss Baine. We'll get to the bottom of this."

Using the alphabetic index, we found the entry for the Bellington Trust, which was based in Dara rather than Gaston. Janta's research skills managed to unearth the interesting fact that the trust was also a majority owner of Privacy Guard. Moreover, it had its fingers in dozens of rather important pies, including the recently disbanded Sandin Federal Bank.

"Wow." I sat back in my chair nearly an hour later, glancing over the growing pile of record books we'd amassed. "I can't believe you managed to find all this, Janta. You're amazing." For the first time, I felt like I was finally getting somewhere with this. I wondered if maybe after this was all over, I could enlist Jana's help in finding my father. I knew Iannis wasn't keen on the idea of me searching for him, but I wanted to know the truth, dammit, and ten years was far too long to wait.

The librarian shrugged off my compliment, but still seemed pleased. I was definitely getting better at reading mages. "I can find out more," she promised. "I have a colleague in Dara whom I can consult regarding the Bellington Trust. She may be able to help us establish the identity of the owners." A slight frown creased her brow. "It may take a while, though, because the few lines in the Palace that can be used for out-of-state calls have been reserved for emergencies."

"Don't worry, Mrs. Urama," I said, rising from my seat, filled with new optimism. "Finding the identity of the Benefactor is a major part of the current emergency, and might just be the most important task aside from fending off the Resistance attacks. I'll speak to the Chief Mage today, and get you cleared to make your phone call."

And with that in mind, I swept from the room, determined to locate Iannis and get my long-overdue audience.

16

A quick consultation of my *serapha* charm told me that Iannis was back in the Palace, so I followed the tug in my chest, hoping I might find him alone for once. Unfortunately, said tug led me back into the Mages Guild, and Dira flagged me down as soon as I stepped into the lobby.

"The Chief Mage is a holding meeting, and it's starting right now," she told me. "He requires your presence in the conference room immediately."

I couldn't find it in me to be annoyed that I wasn't getting my private audience – I was curious what this conference was about, and why I was being summoned to it. Thanking the receptionist, I made my way to the conference room, which was next door to Director Chen's office.

"Miss Baine," Iannis greeted me with a nod as I walked in. "Please, come join us." I caught just the briefest flash of pleasure in his eyes before he retreated behind his stoic mask, and I had to bite back a smile. He was at the head of the conference table... right between Director Chen and Fenris, who was attending in human form for once. The urge to smile quickly disappeared as

I noticed just how close Chen leaned in toward Iannis – they were practically rubbing elbows.

I glanced dubiously at the only seat available –to the left of the very bottom of the table, furthest from the Chief Mage. Iannis opened his mouth to speak again, but I cut him off. "This will do great," I said cheerfully, pulling out the chair and giving Secretary Bosal, who was occupying the foot of the table, a wide smile. "It's nice to see you again, Secretary."

"And you as well," Bosal said, inclining his head courteously. I'd helped rescue him from the Resistance camp along with the other delegates not long ago, and as a result, he was friendlier to me than most of the other mages. The Finance Secretary was sitting on this end too, and though he and I weren't exactly friends, I was reasonably sure we were in the same camp.

The discussion was pretty interesting at first, as the senior mages reported how the conflict against the Resistance was developing. A few key Resistance members had been captured, and were being kept apart from the looters and other riff-raff in a special cell on Prison Isle with extra security. Privacy Guard was still on strike, and they all agreed to boycott the company in future. I mentioned that I was investigating the company's ownership, and that there might be ties to the Benefactor through something called the Bellington Trust in Dara. Iannis seemed pleased to hear it, and readily agreed to authorize Janta's further investigations into the matter.

As the discussion turned back to the prisoners, I wondered if my cousin Rylan was amongst them, and added that to the increasing list of topics to discuss with Iannis in private. I didn't like the thought of Rylan stuck on Prison Isle, but at least it would mean he wasn't causing any more trouble, or in major danger for the moment.

Since most adult mages had volunteered to help with the defense and counterattacks, there was a severe manpower shortage in the Mages Quarter. Mages were having trouble coping with the menial chores that were usually delegated to human servants. Some of the apprentice mages were helping out with cooking and cleaning and bitterly grumbling about it, but the better-trained ones had been drafted to set wards and taking care of other tasks related to defense. Everyone agreed that this could not go on for much longer.

"We have been lucky with our food supplies thus far in the Mages Quarter," the Finance Secretary said, "but I fear we've only enough for a few more days until we run out."

"That should be sufficient," Iannis assured him. "The situation will be resolved by then. The Resistance is beginning to lose ground now that we've captured some of their higher-ranking officers. The loss of leadership is affecting their morale, as well as the fact that they have not been able to get the entire population on their side, as they apparently hoped for. The enforcers returning to their jobs are also making a difference, and as mentioned earlier, Miss Baine and Fenris have made some strides in the investigation of the Benefactor's identity." He inclined his head at me, and I kept my face blank, determined not to light up like a silly schoolgirl at his acknowledgement. But I did nod back – it would be rude not to respond to the praise.

The discussion moved on, and though the mages were still deeply unsettled by the unexpected emergency, they seemed to be happy with Iannis's leadership, and confident they would triumph now that he was back.

An aide sidled in and whispered in Iannis's ear. Despite the distance, my sharp ears caught the words "Minister" and "emergency."

"Please excuse me," Iannis said, "I have an urgent matter to attend to. Director Chen will continue to chair the meeting in my stead." His eyes met mine for the briefest of moments before he swept from the room, and I fought against a smile as I caught just a hint of warmth in them.

"Let's resume," Director Chen said in her clear, smooth voice as the door shut in Iannis's wake. "Are there any other suggestions for dealing with the Resistance, or pertinent information that has not been voiced yet?"

"To further demoralize the enemy, we should take a few of the captured officers and set an example with public executions," one of the mages declared. "It will make the citizens think twice about defecting to the other side."

"That would be a terrible mistake," I protested, and all eyes turned toward me. Director Chen pressed her lips together, and the mage who had spoken reddened, but I ignored their reactions. "Haven't you guys learned from your mistakes yet? The council's heavy-handed measures are what got us into this mess in the first place. More violence isn't the answer."

"Then what do you suggest we do?" the mage snapped. "Sit back and let the Resistance take the city? They are not shy about using violence against us – surely you, of all people, can't be suggesting that we show weakness and leniency to them? Or are your loyalties divided, since so many of the Resistance are shifters?"

"That was out of line, Secretary Corwin," Fenris said. "The Chief Mage has complete confidence in Miss Baine."

"His apprentice may be loyal, but hardly objective, when she has one foot in either camp," another mage objected. "How could she be? Anyway, I support Corwin's proposal about public executions. These renegades understand no other language. *Not* to punish them with utmost severity would send the wrong message."

"It is certainly an interesting proposal," Director Chen said to the last speaker. "I have concerns about the timing, however."

By Magorah. Was she fucking serious? I couldn't believe Director Chen was going along with this bullshit.

"*No,*" I said firmly, drawing all eyes toward my end of the table. "Obviously, we have to fight back – I'm not an idiot. But if you execute the prisoners while emotions are running so high, you'll make them martyrs, and that will only rally their successors and bring even more people to their side out of sympathy. Sentence them to labor in the mines – it's a better deterrent anyway – and find a different way to discourage the citizens from joining the Resistance. Maybe you could even start by convincing them why they should side with *you* in the first place," I added with a sneer. "Why would they show the slightest loyalty to mages, the way you have been treating them all this time?"

"Preposterous!" the execution-happy mage roared, and the other mages at the table began to add their arguments as well. The words 'ignorant', 'naïve', and 'ungrateful' were thrown around, and to my frustration, Director Chen did nothing to stop them. In fact, she was listening attentively to their asinine arguments. I tried to subdue the anger bubbling in my chest, but it was hopeless. It was obvious the mages didn't understand why they needed to care about the views of stupid humans and shifters. In their eyes, the shorter-lived races were unable to understand their own best interests, and it would be a waste of time and sign of weakness for the Mages Guild to explain itself.

"This arrogant attitude toward humans and shifters is exactly the reason why we are in this current mess!" I shouted at them, but that only led to further argument. When the hell was Iannis coming back?

"*Why don't you say something?*" I challenged Fenris with mindspeak.

"*It would be useless – I'm a shifter in their eyes. And I half agree with them,"* he responded, to my frustration. *"Leave it to Iannis to deal with this."*

"Enough," Director Chen said at last, raising her voice so she could be heard above the others. "This is a conference room, not a public house!" She turned her dark gaze in my direction, and I stiffened as I realized she blamed the controversy on *me*. "We'll have a civilized discussion, or no discussion at all."

"It's obvious to me that it's impossible to have a civilized discussion with you lot," I snarled, shoving up from my chair. "Enjoy trying to solve the city's problems with your heads up your asses. It's not like I know anything about what the people actually want and what they might respond to."

I shoved away from the table, then spun on my heel and stormed from the room. I was a fool to come to this meeting, to think they might be prepared to hear reason from the one person present who understood the other side's grievances. Iannis might have wanted me there, but the rest of the mages were unwilling to listen to any outsider. It was becoming more and more obvious to me that there was no place for me in the Chief Mage's life – that I would never be able to see eye to eye with these arrogant jerks who called themselves mages.

17

I left the Palace in the disguise of a brawny, but otherwise non-descript human male, with the intention of heading to Maintown. Apprehending more looters seemed like a good way to burn off some anger, and besides, I'd promised Gorden I would see to it that more enforcers were sent to his area. If that meant I was the enforcer being sent, then so be it. As a bulky male, I would look a lot less strange beating up criminals than I would as a woman or a teenager.

It took me a good hour to walk through the Mages Quarter and across the warded boundary into Rowanville, and the walk helped me blow off some steam and gave me room to think. Was there a way for me to mobilize the citizens myself, without the aid of the Mages Guild? It was becoming apparent to me that even if the Enforcers Guild was still resentful of me, and there were more than a few people around who were happy to take a shot at me on the Resistance's behalf, there were others who had shown themselves to be allies. There was Forin, the human who lived in my old apartment building, and then Nimos Barakan, a son of the Tiger Clan. Lakin might even be able to help – he had to be released by now, along with my aunt Mafiela's family. They were probably conferring even now about what to do next.

Right. The Jaguar Clan. What side did they stand on? Mafiela owed me for rescuing her granddaughter, Mika, from the Shifter Royale. That had been fun, particularly since Mafiela had ignored my warning about a possible kidnapper, and her daughter Melantha had then blamed me for Mika's kidnapping. In fact, she'd come to my apartment and tried to kick my ass, and I'd had to threaten her with magical fire to get her away from me.

I know, I know. My loving family environment was a big part of why I had such a charming personality. But Mafiela had begrudgingly sent me a thank-you card after Mika's rescue, so maybe if I went to see her and asked for her help on this, she'd actually invite me into the house for a real discussion instead of making me wait on the front porch.

Yeah, or she'll just try to rip your face off again.

Okay, so maybe I didn't have the mental fortitude to attempt a civilized conversation with my aunt just yet. But I could start by talking to Lakin, at the very least, and besides, I needed to make sure he was all right after his ordeal. Once I was done here in Maintown, I'd pop over to Shiftertown and see what kind of reception I got. Hopefully, Lakin wasn't so angry at the Mages Guild that he'd refuse to work with me.

The sound of shouts and crying pulled me from my thoughts, and I looked around, trying to determine the source. There was nothing happening on the street I was walking on – I was in a residential area, all the shutters closed, all the doors locked, not a single person enjoying the summer night on their front porch – so I followed the direction of the noise, heading west. A couple of blocks later, I found myself across the street from a hospital. A large, horse-drawn cart had just pulled up in front of the two-story building, and as I crossed the street to get a better look, I saw wounded men and women being loaded onto stretchers and rushed inside. They seemed to be suffering from burns, cuts, and broken limbs.

"Hey, you there!" Someone tapped me on the shoulder, and I turned, startled to see it was a thirty-something civilian male, sweaty and dressed in a stained shirt and jeans. "Come, help us get these patients in! The hospital is short-handed. It has asked all able-bodied Maintown civilians to pull together and help. You look strong enough."

"Uh, sure." Since I wasn't dressed as an enforcer, I couldn't very well tell the guy I was on patrol, so I let him pull me forward and introduce me to the two hospital staff who were directing the transport of all these patients. We grabbed a stretcher, and I winced as they loaded an unconscious woman with a badly burned face onto it.

"What happened to all these people?" I asked the man as we carried the woman inside.

He looked at me as if I were crazy. "A battle broke out between the Resistance and the Mages at the Maintown-Shifter-town border. It was all over the radio. Didn't you hear?"

"No, sorry," I muttered. "I've been a little busy." Obviously, this battle was a very recent development, since it hadn't been mentioned at the meeting.

We carried the woman into a large room filled with beds. The stench of burnt flesh, blood, and other bodily odors and fluids filled the air, along with moans and cries coming from the other rooms. We deposited her as gently as we could onto the last available bed in the room, then went back out to grab the next victim. I hoped there were more beds in other rooms, because, otherwise, these poor patients were going to have to lie in stretchers on the floor as they waited for treatment.

It turned out that this wasn't the first cart of patients to be dropped off, and nor was it the last. I helped unload three more carts, taking the wounded to different rooms depending on how the staff directed us. All the victims had major injuries – apparently, the ones who only suffered minor burns or scrapes were simply sent home with instructions for care, and told to come to the hospital if they needed supplies – but some were much worse off than others. The man with the broken arm, for example, was deemed much less severe than the woman bleeding out from a gash across her abdomen. As I watched the nurses triage them, I couldn't help but feel grateful for my shifter abilities – these poor humans would take weeks or months to heal from their injuries, and some might never regain the mobility they'd once enjoyed.

I was impressed with how calm the hospital staff managed to remain in the face of such suffering, assessing each individual's injuries and sending them off to the right department, and refusing to flinch or back down when some people thought their cases were more urgent than they actually were. They had a difficult job, and one I wasn't sure I'd be able to manage with my temperament. Bedside manners weren't really my thing.

Between unloading and delivering the wounded, I also helped bring food to recovering patients and overworked hospital staff. Repeatedly, I was asked to help hold a patient down so a broken limb could be set, or to assist in a minor surgery. As I stood by surgical tables, cleaning used tools and implements and passing over new ones, all while listening to whimpers and screams and trying to ignore the stinging antiseptic smell, I wondered why Iannis hadn't thought to send a mage healer over to help treat the wounded. When I mentioned as much, both the doctor and a civilian volunteer standing nearby gave me withering looks.

"Haven't the mages caused enough damage already?" the doctor snapped as she leaned over the abdomen of the patient she was stitching up. "We just want them to stay out of our lives.

We don't need them here in this hospital, barking orders and making things worse."

I swallowed the argument that rose to my lips, knowing it wouldn't do me any good to defend the mages, and kept my head down. I couldn't bring myself to leave these people – they might be refusing assistance from the Mages Guild, but they needed all the help they could get.

"All right," the female doctor I'd been helping said, wiping her sweaty brow as she turned away from her last patient of the night. "It looks like we've done what we can for now. You ought to head home, and the rest of you too," she said, raising her voice so the civilian volunteers could hear her. "Well done, everybody – we really needed and appreciate your help today."

"No problem," I said, relieved it was over. Yeah, I'd wanted to help, but hospital work wasn't for the weak, and after all these hours of relentless labor, I was beyond exhausted. I filed out with the rest of the volunteers into the main waiting room, then bit my lip as I glanced at the big clock on the wall. Nine o'clock was two hours past curfew time, and anyone seen on the streets who wasn't an enforcer or a mage was subject to arrest. Yeah, I was technically both, but I'd just adopted this new disguise, and I didn't want to lose it just yet by being forced to reveal myself.

Dammit, why couldn't I have been born a bird shifter? My life would be so much easier if I could just fly places.

"Hey." The guy who'd commandeered me into helping out clapped a hand on my shoulder. "Why don't you come join us for a drink?" I turned to see him standing with two other guys, all of whom I'd worked with at some point in the evening. "After the day we've had, we could all use a chance to wind down."

"Sure," I said easily – a cool drink would be very welcome, and besides, there was no place else to go. "Where we headed?"

"Branson's, of course." The man gave me a strange look, as

though he couldn't understand why I was so clueless. "Where else?"

'Branson's' turned out to be an underground beer cellar just a block away. It was located in a back alley, behind a thick wooden door with a sliding grate for a peephole. The man who'd invited me rapped on the door, and my sensitive ears picked up on a pattern that must be a sort of code.

The grate slid open, revealing a pair of dark, suspicious eyes. "Password?"

"Humanity."

The grate slid shut, and a series of locks clicked before the door swung open. The bouncer, a big fellow dressed in a flannel shirt and jeans, gave us all a long once-over. Once he was satisfied we were all humans, he stepped aside and allowed us to descend the long, steep staircase into the cellar.

To my surprise, the place was packed. It was a large cellar, with enough space to fit at least three hundred people. There were so many wooden tables that the servers barely had enough room to squeeze by with their trays, and a bar at the back. Somehow, we managed to grab a table right behind the stairs – not the greatest spot for people watching, but it allowed us some privacy and shielded us somewhat from the loud buzz of conversation.

We all ordered beers and pretzels, as well as an assortment of plain food, and then the man who invited me leaned back in his chair and looked at me. "So, what's your name?" he asked, and though his tone was friendly enough, there was just a hint of suspicion in his eyes. "I don't think I've seen you around town."

"Brandt Urson," I replied, the name coming easily to my lips as I'd already decided on it hours before. "I live in Rowanville."

"Rowanville!" Another man, this one steel-haired and pot-bellied, spat. "So you're one of those fools who think we can co-exist with the others."

"Maybe I am, maybe I'm not." I lifted my chin, speaking coolly. "Or maybe I had a good job over there. What's it to ya?"

The man who'd invited me laid a hand on Potbelly's beefy shoulder. "Now, Jemin. Let's not jump down each other's throats. We haven't even made introductions yet."

Jemin grumbled a little, but he relented. "I'm Jemin Fillbaker," he said.

"Fiden Trumbel," the third, a lean, curly-headed blond chimed in. He had blue eyes and the kind of earnest baby face that made you think pure souls might really be a thing. "Nice to meet you."

"I'm Manson Grandish," the first man said, "and yes, we appreciate your help, especially since you're not a Maintown citizen."

"It's no problem," I said as the beer arrived. "I would have done the same for anybody. I was on my way back from checking on my grandmother, and she taught me that everybody deserves to be treated with the same level of respect, no matter what race or background you come from. Beneath it all, everyone's worth the same."

Jemin scoffed, and Manson leaned forward on the table, his expression growing serious. "Do you really believe that?" he asked. "That we're all the same?"

I picked up my beer, took a long drink, and pretended to savor it as I considered my answer. It was warm, but the brew was decent enough. "I don't believe we're the same," I finally said as I put my mug down. "That's impossible. We all have different personalities, different levels of intelligence, different abilities, et cetera. But underneath all that, as a whole, we're not that different, right? Mages came from humans, and so did shifters."

"Very true," Manson nodded, then took a sip from his beer. "In fact, you might say we're the original race, right? The master pattern of creation, while the others are just later aberrations?"

"I suppose," I allowed as alarm bells started ringing in my head.

"Maybe you might even say that we've got more right to own this world than any of the other races, including the mages who have had their boots on our throats for thousands of years?"

I shrugged at that. "As far as power is concerned, I think the phrase 'might makes right' still stands. And since the mages have all the might, I don't foresee humans taking power anytime soon." Just who the hell was I talking to, anyway? Were these guys members of the Resistance?

"How can you say that?" Jemin demanded, slamming his mug down on the table. "Didn't you see the morning paper? The Resistance is more than holding its own against the Mages Guild. They might even win, at the rate things are going."

"Right?" Fiden chimed in, his blue eyes glowing with excitement. "What do you think is going to happen when the Resistance wins? What kind of government do you think we'll have, once the mages are out of the way?"

I managed not to roll my eyes at the sheer stupidity of these men. "Even if the Resistance *does* manage to prevail here in Solantha, that wouldn't last long. Mages from other parts of the Federation would come here to turn the tide – in fact, they might be on their way right now," I added, though I had no idea if that were true. "Mages from other countries could even come to join the fight. There's no way mages across the world would allow a victory from humans to stand – it sets a dangerous precedent for them."

"What you say sounds very reasonable," Manson said easily, leaning back in his chair, "but I don't think you have the full picture. Our time is coming, Brandt. In fact, it's a lot closer than you think. Soon, mages and shifters will be gone not just from the Northia Federation, but also from all of Recca, the world over. Humans will be able to take our place once again as the strongest species on this planet, as we were for thousands of years before the mages arose."

"That's... interesting," I said, struggling to hide my outrage. So these guys didn't just think that mages should be gone – they wanted to get rid of shifters too? I had half a mind to flip the table and storm out of here, but another part of me told me to stay put and see what else I could learn. It seemed like there was some kind of plan among the humans I was missing out on. Besides, the guys were friendly enough, and I was still too pissed about the meeting at the Mages Guild to return to the Palace. "I'd love to know what inspires all this confidence. It would be great if the human race could be on top again."

"Maybe you will," Manson said, lifting his glass to me. "But enough about politics for now. Let's kick back and relax!" He downed his beer in one go, and the others did the same.

I spent another hour drinking, eating, and talking with the guys. When the vast quantities of beer consumed, coupled with the late hour, made them too tired and incoherent to continue, Manson signaled for a server and told her we wanted a room for the night. There was some grumbling when she told them that the usual price had doubled due to the curfew, but we all pitched in a bronze coin. The woman led us behind the bar, down a hall, and into a sparse room with six cots. Two men were already snoring in them, I noticed, and I made sure to take the cot on the opposite side of the room, so that my back wasn't facing any of the men. Hopefully, my new companions didn't snore too much, because unlike them, I was completely sober. My mind was working overtime and not ready to switch off, despite my exhaustion.

As I settled into the less-than-fresh bedding, my mind turned to Iannis. Would he care that I wasn't back at the Palace by now, and if so, was there any chance he would come looking for me? Surely he knew by now that I'd stormed out of the meeting in disgust – Fenris would have told him. My logical mind hoped he wouldn't, because having the Chief Mage show up at a human-only bar to retrieve me would blow my cover for sure, and it would destroy any chance to learn more about the plan these humans were hatching. But the emotional part of me, the one that still wanted to get closer to Iannis, wished he would come and find me. He'd told me he loved me, hadn't he? That he wanted to make me his?

And yet, despite his words, despite the hot kisses and erotic caresses, he'd sat me on the farthest end of the table from him at that meeting. And as much as I wanted to believe he was different, Iannis *was* the chief of the mages who had earned the hatred of the whole city, and who were now considering executing citizens in order to set an example. For all I knew, he'd given that asinine mage the go-ahead after returning to the meeting, and tomorrow morning, those prisoners would be rounded up and brought to the city for a public execution.

Come on. Iannis wouldn't actually do that, or at least he wouldn't make the decision so hastily. You know better.

Even so, in the face of such prejudice, such stupidity, how could I blame the humans for wanting to take control? How could I even blame them for thinking the mages were stupid and disorganized enough that the Resistance stood a chance?

Something needs to be done about this, I thought, rolling over and trying to get comfortable. Someone needed to stand up, someone all three races would be willing to listen to, and talk sense into the people before we succeeded in tearing what was left of Solantha apart. But damned if I knew who.

18

"Hey. Brandt. Wake up."

I cracked open a gritty eye at the sound of the unfamiliar voice. A big, dark-haired man stood over me, looking more than a little scruffy, and it took my sleep-deprived mind a moment to remember that this was Manson, the human who'd invited me out for drinks last night after volunteering at the hospital. And that *I* was Brandt. Between my worries, the loud snores and unpleasant smells, and the occasional magical explosion in the distance, it had been tough to fall asleep last night.

Even when I'd managed to shut my eyes, I'd been plagued by a repeating loop of Gorden being shot down in the back alley of the Enforcers Guild. In the nightmare, he would raise his head from the pool of blood, look me in the eye with his dead gaze, and tell me over and over that it was my fault. That his sons would no longer have a father. That his wife would no longer have a man to support her. That his store would close, and his employees would be jobless.

And all because of me.

"Hey!" Manson shook my shoulder again. "Don't just lie there staring up at me. That's creepy as fuck."

"What's going on?" I asked, sitting up and rubbing the sleep from my eyes. Thank Magorah my illusion had held through the night, or I'd be in serious trouble. "We under attack or something?"

"No," Manson said with a chuckle. "We're going to a special service at the Maintown Temple. We thought you might like to come along. You'll find it a very pleasant upgrade from that dingy little Ur-God shrine in Rowanville."

"Oh. Umm, sure." I gave him a smile, trying to look pleased about that. "Yeah, I haven't visited the Maintown Temple since I was a teenager." The Ur-God was the human version of Magorah and the Creator. Except, according to humans who worshipped the Ur-God, He had only wanted to create humans. To them, mages were an unfortunate accident caused by the Ur-God's rebellious assistants, who were subsequently kicked out of the Ur-God's domain in punishment and banished to Recca. Absurd, but then again, the Mages probably considered the shifters' belief in Magorah and our legends about ancestral spirits to be absurd as well.

We used the establishment's barebones bathroom to clean up as best as we could, then grabbed a few sandwiches before heading to the temple. It was located in the heart of Maintown, and though I'd passed by it a time or two when I'd come down here on enforcer business, it wasn't until I was up close that I realized how large it was. A broad granite structure with roses and vines carved into its outer walls, it was easily three times the size of the Shiftertown temple, and it seemed ridiculously extravagant to me. We shifters didn't need such large temples – we mostly preferred to worship Magorah on special days, such as the Solstice, and many of our celebrations were held outdoors.

The inside of the Maintown temple was just as fancy, with elaborate carvings of important human figures decorating the walls, and a large, colorful fresco on the ceiling depicting humans frolicking in the Flowery Fields. As I'd learned in school long ago, the Flowery Fields were the place humans hoped to go to after death, if they had been good and followed the Ur-God tenets during their lives. If they had been evil, they were sent to the Pit instead, where they languished for all eternity. This doctrine was very different from shifter beliefs. We believed that when we died, we had the choice between becoming good or bad spirits, depending on how we had lived our lives, or reincarnating as shifters again, or as another life form.

The main hall of the temple was huge, easily twice the size and four times the height of Branson's beer cellar, with plenty of seating. Even so, it was standing room only this morning, with people crowding the aisles and the back of the room. I watched as temple staff dressed in white tunics with pale gold edging gently guided people out of the center aisle, so that a clear exit path would remain.

"You weren't kidding about this being a special service," I murmured to Manson as we found a spot in the corner to stand in. "Or is it normally this packed?"

"Not always, but Father Monor Calmias is delivering today's sermon. Surely you've heard of him?"

I shook my head.

"Then you're in for a treat! He's a famous preacher who travels across the Federation, and it's a great honor whenever he visits our temple."

From the hushed, but excited, conversation that buzzed in the air, the crowd seemed to concur with this assessment. The humans were commenting on how inspirational Father Calmias's last sermon had been, and how they'd begun to see the light at the end of the tunnel ever since he first started speaking a few years ago. According to them, his radio sermons were the highlight of their weekends, and sometimes, they were the only thing to get them through the following week.

A hush fell over the room, and I looked up to see a man enter the stage from a door hidden in the velvet curtains that lined the back walls of the hall. Like the other temple staff, he was dressed in a gold-and-white tunic, but his had a cowl hanging down his shoulders and a sort of cape that trailed to the floor. He also wore a tall hat perched atop his silver hair, with a golden rose – the symbol that represented the Flowery Fields – stitched onto the front. Without the costume, he would have looked like your average grandpa, with the lines in his face and his kind blue eyes, but as he stood behind the podium and surveyed us, he looked grand indeed.

So this is the famous Father Calmias.

"My children," he said in booming voice, lifting his hands and beginning some kind of prayer. When everyone else began chanting along with him, I hurriedly tried to mouth the words, hoping my 'buddies' wouldn't notice. Judging by the words, which talked about our status as the Ur-God's favored children, and that we would always be safe in the shelter of his arms so long as we followed his tenets, and so on, I gathered this was a basic opening prayer that all humans were supposed to know by heart.

Of course, if I'd *known* I was going to be infiltrating an Ur-God temple, I would have researched this ritual beforehand. But this had been sprung on me before I'd even gotten out of bed, and I was woefully unprepared.

Thankfully, Manson and his friends seemed too caught up in the spell of the moment to notice that I wasn't actually saying the words aloud. A quick glance told me their eyes were glued to the preacher, so I mimicked them, not wanting to draw unwanted attention by being the only human darting my eyes around. The last thing I needed was for someone to come up and question me. Judging by how tight-knit these people seemed, if I mentioned my non-existent grandmother, they'd start asking nosy questions about her name and what neighborhood she lived in.

Once the opening prayer was finished, those in the congregation who were lucky enough to have garnered seats parked their behinds, and a reverent hush settled over the chapel. "My children," Father Calmias said again. "I have spent much time in prayer lately, communing with the Ur-God in this sacred space, and he has given me fateful tidings to share with you. He knows that despite your faith in him, many of you are troubled by the recent wave of death and destruction, and wishes for me to assure you that all you see around you is part of His plan. Indeed, be of good cheer, for we are well on our way to achieving His plan for us, to re-establish humanity's undisputed supremacy over this world. Have faith that He will let nothing stand in our way. Recca will be wiped clean of mages and shifters, as well as the stains they have left behind on our world. The Ur-god and we, his Children, *will* rule again!"

The congregation let out a series of whoops and cheers, and Father Calmias paused to let them have their moment. I slid my hands into my pants pockets to keep from clenching them or showing my claws, and focused on mimicking the reverent expressions that everyone else wore, instead of gaping in shock at the crazy preacher. Wiping the world clean of mages and shifters? I'd thought Manson was exaggerating last night, but apparently, he was completely serious. These humans really did want to wipe us off the face of the planet.

After the crowd had settled down, Father Calmias went on to explain that our temporary alliance with the shifters was necessary in order to get rid of the mages, who were the primary

enemy – after all, shifters were only a nasty by-blow, an unfortunate product of evil spell craft that would have never come to be,
if not for the mages. As soon as the mages were eliminated, the
shifters would be taken care of.

He ended this uplifting sermon by urging the congregation
not to give in to the mages' insidious propaganda – the mages
would try to tempt them back to their side with promises of
food, gold, and jobs, but that was only a smokescreen to entice
them into continued slavery. He told them to stay the course,
that all freedom had a price, and that their faith and persistence
would be rewarded very, very soon.

The entire congregation got to their feet with claps and
cheers, praising the Ur-God and Father Calmias. I clapped and
cheered too, but on the inside, I was sick to my stomach. Who
was this preacher, with his powerful voice and charismatic
personality, who was so blatantly urging the human population
to support the Resistance? Was the Mages Guild aware the Ur-
God Temple was promoting such a destructive, despicable
doctrine? Presumably, this wasn't the only temple in Canalo, or
even the Federation, that was being fed this self-serving bullshit
– Manson had said that Father Calmias was a famous preacher
who traveled all over the Federation. Why had I never heard of
this before?

I wanted to go up to Father Calmias and question him, to try
and determine his probable ties to the Resistance, and maybe
even the Benefactor. Unfortunately, the crowd of fervent
worshipers who had gathered around him was too thick to pene-
trate without looking suspicious, so I followed the rest of the
people instead, who were exiting the main hall through two side
entrances.

It turned out that these side entrances led to two large rooms
where the congregation could talk and socialize. The temple
staff were circulating, sporting aprons over their white uniforms

and carrying trays in their hands, and they served us coffee and refreshments. Grabbing a tall glass of iced tea from a passing staff member, I sipped it carefully as I walked around, listening to the snippets of conversation from the parishioners.

"I told you," a woman was saying to her husband. They were a well-to-do couple, the woman dressed in a pale green dress and pearls, her husband in a suit. "I told you there was a reason behind the Resistance's alliance with the shifter population. They're not compromising our beliefs; they're following the Ur-God's clever plan."

"I still don't like the fact that our son is forced to fight side by side with shifters," the husband said in a low tone. "They're too emotional, too easily distracted. What if those mangy creatures decide to revolt? They're a slave race, created to serve the mages, and I could easily see the Mages Guild figuring out some way to make them turn on us. Maybe that's been the plan all along, and they're just waiting for the right time to flip some kind of switch."

"Don't be ridiculous," his wife chided. "There's no switch. If there were, the mages would have used it long ago, considering how much trouble shifters cause in society. Personally, I think we would have been better off if they had never been freed."

I forced myself to move on before I dumped my glass of tea down the back of the woman's dress. I couldn't decide who sounded more asinine – she or her husband – and it truly didn't matter. All of these people were brainwashed, stupid sheep who were being guided to the edge of a cliff by a charlatan, and who would gladly throw themselves off it for the sake of a misguided cause.

"I do wish Father Calmias would give us more details about the secret weapons," I heard a man complain. He was leaning back against the wall, dressed in a suit that had seen better days, as he conversed with the burly bouncer from the beer cellar last night. "I mean, I'm faithful, no question, and I trust the Ur-God's plan, but we could be of more help if we were given more details about what's coming."

"No, it makes perfects sense," the bouncer said as he munched on a raisin cookie. "If we don't know all the details, they can't be tortured out of us by the Mages Guild. The Ur-God and Father Calmias are just trying to protect us. Trust me, my brother sends me messages from his camp every once in a while, and he assures me that the one secret weapon he knows about will ensure our victory, one-hundred percent."

A chill went down my spine at that. Was it only bluster, or did the Resistance truly have some 'secret weapon' that could make them so confident of their chances to overthrow the mage regime? Either they were still in denial or ignorant about how powerful the mages truly were, or they had got their hands on something truly cataclysmic. It wasn't good, no matter which way I looked at it.

I wandered around for a few more minutes, listening to conversations, but I didn't hear anything else that was useful. I did spot a couple of former enforcers present, and I couldn't help but feel a pang of disappointment. Sure, I didn't get along with most of the human enforcers, but I'd worked with one or two of these very guys from time to time, and I'd believed we were on the same team. Now they were being led to believe that both halves of my heritage were evil, and it disheartened me that people could be so easily swayed. What use were concepts like loyalty and decency if they could be steamrolled over by false promises and grandiose plans that anyone with a working brain could see were completely insane?

"Hey." Manson's voice came over my shoulder, and I turned to see him standing behind me. "You okay, Brandt? I noticed you've been wandering around, looking a little lost."

"Yeah," I said, affecting a yawn. "I'm good. I just didn't sleep well on that cot last night, and my girlfriend's probably worried about me. The sermon was great, but I really should see about getting back home."

"Aww, that's too bad," Manson said, and he looked genuinely disappointed. "I thought maybe we could talk about the sermon for a bit."

"Oh, it was a revelation," I assured him. "I definitely see why you think we have a good chance, and Father Calmias has given me hope. But I've got to get back to my girl. I don't want her wandering the streets looking for me, not during times like these. Some of those looters are shifters," I added, though it pained me to do so.

"Yeah, you're right," Manson agreed, his expression darkening. "We've got to keep our women and children safe from those animals." He clapped me on the shoulder. "Travel safe, and feel free to look me up the next time you come visit your grandmother, okay?"

"Will do," I agreed, then made a quick exit. I wasn't sure how long I could keep up this charade, but at least the experience had confirmed one thing. I needed to get the mages and shifters on the same team, before the Resistance managed to destroy us all.

19

Tired of skulking around town on foot, I filched a steambike parked in a side alley outside the temple, using my magic to light a spark since I didn't have the key. As I shot into the street, distant shouts told me my theft had not gone unnoticed, but I simply put on another burst of speed as I rounded a corner, refusing to feel guilty. If these people had no compunction about killing off the entire mage and shifter population, I wasn't going to lose any sleep over stealing a steambike from them.

Besides, it felt damn good to have some steampower rolling beneath my thighs again.

I kept up my breakneck pace until I crossed the border into Shiftertown, then took it down a notch. The last time I came to Shiftertown I'd been in a hurry, almost blinded by heat, and since the Cat's Meow was close to the Rowanville border I hadn't seen much of the town itself. Now that I was traveling at a slower pace, I took in the sights around me, and they weren't pretty. Burnt houses, rubble in the streets, shops boarded up, and windows shuttered. The amount of visible damage decreased the further I went into Shiftertown, and I figured that the battles between the Resistance and the mages never made it too far past the borders. Still, though the houses showed less wear and tear here, tension was thick in the air, and I could feel eyes following me from all around. No doubt many of those tracking me were Resistance members, holed up for the day as they planned their next move. I was especially grateful for my human disguise under these circumstances.

Even so, I was a stranger around here, and it would only be a matter of time before I was stopped. I stuck to back alleys and deserted sections, taking a roundabout way to Boon Lakin's house. Between him and Aunt Mafiela, he was more likely to listen to me, and more importantly, believe me. I really needed to talk to someone who wouldn't dismiss me as crazy right off the bat.

I arrived outside Lakin's small, one-bedroom home after some twenty minutes, then parked my stolen steambike at the curb. The curtains in the living room window fluttered briefly as I strode up the path, telling me that my arrival had not gone unnoticed.

"I'm not taking visitors right now," Lakin called as I knocked on the door.

"Oh, for Magorah's sake, Boon, open up," I called, using my real voice. "It's me!"

There was a long pause, followed by the sound of footsteps. Lakin flung open the door, staring at me in disbelief. "Sunaya? Is that really you?"

"Don't I look stunning?" I asked, fluffing my illusion's short hair sarcastically and batting my eyelashes. "Seriously Lakin, let me in."

"I'm not sure that's a good idea –" Lakin protested as I pushed past him, dropping my illusion as I stepped into the small entrance that connected the kitchen and the living room.

"You!" an accusing voice shouted, and I started at the sight of two shifter males, bird shifters judging by their slender frames and hawkish noses, sitting on the couch. They were wearing red Resistance bands on their upper arms, though they wore shirts and jeans instead of uniform khakis. One of them jumped up, and I ducked as he flung a trio of throwing knives at my head.

"What the fuck!" I shouted, returning fire with one of the chakrams in my pouch. It embedded itself in the wall above Lakin's couch as the shifter twisted away, but I didn't care – the projectile was just a distraction. I took a flying leap at the guy, and he let out an honest-to-Magorah squawk as I brought him crashing down to the ground.

"That's *enough*," Lakin roared just as I yanked one of my crescent knives from the holster on my thigh. He grabbed me by the back of my collar like an unruly cub and yanked me off the shifter. "This is my house, not a battleground," he seethed, glaring at the two Resistance soldiers. "You will behave. All of you."

"She is on the Resistance *kill* list," the first shifter screeched, jabbing a long finger in my direction as the second shifter scrambled to his feet again. "You cannot expect us to sit here and do nothing!"

"Then I refuse to negotiate with you," Lakin said coldly. "Get out of my house."

The two bird shifters shared a long look, and I knew they were having a mindspeak conversation. Eventually, they turned back to Lakin as one. "We will agree not to harm the traitor Sunaya Baine, so long as we are under your roof. That promise expires as soon as we leave your property."

"Right," I sneered, getting to my feet. "Because the Resistance is such an honorable group."

"Shut up, Sunaya," Lakin snapped without even looking at me. I blinked, astonished at the aggression in his tone – he'd never spoken to me like that. But then I noticed the way his nostrils flared and how his color was up, and I remembered my heat. Yeah, it was mostly under control, but my body was still giving off pheromones that any red-blooded male would scent from a mile off. The other two shifters weren't affected because they were birds, a completely different species of animal that couldn't procreate with me. But Lakin was a jaguar shifter just like me, and he and I could definitely make some cubs if we set our minds to it.

You are not *making cubs with Lakin,* I told myself as the heat surged within my veins, setting off that hungry ache in my lower belly. I'd already put that thought to bed a long time ago, the moment I'd realized Lakin would never truly be able to accept me. Yes, he liked me, but he was afraid of my magic. As Resinah had pointed out, accepting my mage heritage was key to controlling myself, and thus mastering my powers. If Boon knew how I felt, he would *try* to overcome his fear of my magic, but it would always be a part of him. And I couldn't live beneath the shadow of that fear, not if I wanted to gain full control over my powers.

"Can you send her away so we can finish our discussion?" the second shifter asked, shooting me an annoyed look. "We were here first, and her intrusion is very rude, regardless of who she is."

Lakin sighed. "I'd like to know what she's here for, first," he admitted, finally turning his yellow-orange gaze my way. The hunger in them was unmistakable, but for the moment, perhaps because of the witnesses, curiosity seemed to be trumping animalistic need. "I'm assuming you didn't just come here to say hi."

"Well, I did want to check on you," I said, retreating to the recliner – a new piece of furniture that hadn't been there the last time I was here. "But really, I came to bring important news about the Resistance's plans for shifters. And actually, it's news I think you'll want to hear too," I added, glancing at the Resistance soldiers.

Shifter One scoffed. "What plans could *you* possibly know about, that we don't already?"

I crossed my arms over my chest and arched a brow. "How about their plan to dispose of you all – all shifters, I mean – as soon as they've defeated the mages?"

Both of the soldiers' faces turned bright red at that. "Impossible," the second shifter spat. "You're lying!" But his nostrils flared, and I knew he scented no lie or subterfuge from me.

"I'm *not* lying, and you'd be stupid not to listen to me," I growled, then launched into my story. I told them about the three human males I'd met in Maintown last night, about their confidence that the human race would prevail over the others, and the disturbing sermon at the Ur-God temple. By the time I was done, all the hunger had drained out of Lakin's expression, and even the two bird shifters looked troubled.

"That doesn't make any sense," Shifter One protested. "How could the Resistance have been planning such a betrayal the entire time, while keeping us all in the dark? There are shifters higher up in the ranks, including your own cousin Rylan Baine. Surely, someone would have found out. You're just misinformed!"

"I don't know, Gyron," Shifter Two said slowly. "I've noticed over the past year that only humans have been getting promotions. Don't you remember how Tifon was passed over for captain in favor of that bumbling human idiot?"

"That's true," Gyron hissed, his eyes narrowing. "And right after that, he was sent off on a dangerous mission to the East that ended up getting him killed." He straightened then, remembering himself. "But that still doesn't mean she's not lying, Urion! She works for the mages, remember?"

"I don't 'work' for the mages," I growled, drawing their attention back to me. "I'm an enforcer, see?" I held up my wrist so they could see my bracelet. "And in case you've forgotten, I've lived most of my life as a shifter. I haven't switched sides just because I can use magic now."

"Pah! The Enforcers Guild is funded by the Mages Guild, is it not?" Gyron accused. "How are you any different?"

"The Enforcers Guild is funded by the tax payers," I pointed out. "Yes, those funds are paid out by the Mages Guild, and yes, we have to listen to them if they give us orders, but until all this bullshit with the Resistance started, they mostly left us to take care of the crime in this city on our own." I decided to leave out the fact that Captain Galling had gotten lazy without someone leaning on him for results, and had allowed the Main Crew to become a bloated mass that cared more about the bounties than about solving actual cases. "Like you, I spent most of my life hating the mages and everything they stand for, but now that I've had experience on both sides of this line, I can tell you one thing." I leaned forward, pinning the two shifters with as much intensity as I could muster. "If we don't get our shit together and learn how to co-exist, we're not going to be around for very long. The humans will play on our differences to make us tear each other apart, and then they're going to sit on a throne made of mage and shifter bones and laugh while we rot in a mass grave somewhere."

There was a long silence as the bird shifters sat on the couch, staring at me in shock. Finally, Lakin cleared his throat, drawing my attention to him – he'd remained standing by the door since there was no chair for him to sit in.

"Sunaya, I know you're being truthful...but is it really as bad as you say?" He sounded a little pained. "Were all the humans at the Maintown temple truly on board with this?"

"They were practically rubbing their hands with glee," I confirmed. "Trust me, Lakin, they've been having this message drummed into them for a long time. I'm not saying all humans are our enemies, but the ones who attended the sermon today have definitely been brainwashed into thinking that shifters and mages are evil, and that the only way they can live peaceful lives is to get rid of us. They think the Resistance is carrying out a mandate from the Ur-God, and they're eager to provide whatever support they can to make sure that mandate is carried out."

Gyron finally sighed, relaxing his shoulders. "Much as I hate to admit it, we can't ignore the information you have provided. It bears further looking into, and we will discuss it with the other shifters in our platoon, in private."

"Be sure that you do, because the best chance you've got of surviving is to get out of the Resistance while there's still time. Losing their shifter soldiers will hamper the Resistance enough to delay their genocidal plans, at the very least." A thought occurred to me then, and I asked, "Have either of you heard of a person known as the Benefactor?"

Gyron shook his head, but a flash of recognition lit Urion's bright blue eyes. "I've heard whispers," he said. "Mostly from the captains or other higher ups. All I really know is that he's our main funder."

"Yeah, that's you and everybody else." I sighed, dragging a hand through my hair. Dammit, but how could the person who was financing the entire Resistance be unknown to them? Why didn't these morons care that their strings were being pulled by some unknown party, for sinister purposes? They were putting their lives on the line without even knowing for whom and for what.

"This news makes our earlier discussion moot," Lakin told the bird shifters. "No way am I going to openly wear those red armbands, or persuade the clans to fight at your side. At least not until we have followed up on Sunaya's warning."

So that was why they'd sought Lakin out. It wasn't too

surprising they would go through him – after all, Mafiela hated the Resistance and would refuse to listen to a word if they showed up on her doorstep. On the other hand, even though Lakin was new to the community, he served the shifters in all the clans, and was fast becoming well acquainted with them. He would be a good ally for the Resistance to have.

"I guess," Gyron said glumly. "We'll get confirmation from a reliable source, and be in touch when we know one way or the other."

The two bird shifters said their goodbyes to Lakin, ignoring me completely. Once they had departed, Lakin shut and locked the door, then leaned against it with a sigh and stared at me from beneath hooded eyes.

"You sure do know how to have a good time," he said, sounding tired.

I grinned at him. "You know me. I always bring the fun stuff." But my grin faded a little as I took in the bags under his eyes and how thin he was. "Are you all right?" I wanted to give him a hug, but right then, closing the distance was a bad idea, so I stayed in my chair.

"Better now that I'm out of that hellhole," he said, crossing over to the couch and plopping down on it. I focused very hard on maintaining my control as I caught a whiff of his enticing scent. "I tell you, Prison Isle is no joke. I'm glad they have a separate section of the prison just for shifters, and that I haven't been around long enough as the Shiftertown Inspector to have put many shifters in there yet. Otherwise, I'm not sure I would have survived."

I winced. "I'm really sorry you had to endure that," I said, and I meant it. I'd been to Prison Isle a time or two to question prisoners, and the place was fucking grim. The prison guards were lower-level mages specially trained in combat magic, and they were not afraid to use force against anyone who stepped out of line. Since non-violent offenders usually just got sentenced to work in the mines as punishment, Prison Isle was full of hardened, bloodthirsty characters, and the guards were generally content to sit back and let disputes sort themselves out. If you didn't make the right sort of allies, chances of surviving your sentence were slim to none. The mages only stepped in if things were getting too violent, if the violence was being directed toward them, or if the situation threatened prison security. Otherwise, almost anything went.

Another thing I was going to have to speak to Iannis about.

"It's not your fault," Lakin said. "There was nothing you could have done to stop it, and if you hadn't brought the Chief Mage back, I would still be languishing in a cell right now." He scooped a hand through his sandy hair, making it stand on end, and his eyes glittered as he looked me up and down. "I'm glad to see you're back," he said softly.

"I'm glad to be back."

The sexual tension in the room thickened, and I cleared my throat, desperate to steer the conversation away from the dangerous attraction between us. "You're not going to join up with the Resistance, right? Even if those guys do come back and try to recruit you again?"

Lakin shook his head. "My duty is to the clans, to Solantha's Shiftertown. Since the clans are divided on the issue, that makes it easier not to take sides, which is my natural inclination anyway."

"Good." I hesitated. "If my aunt Mafiela decided to throw her allegiance in with the Resistance, would you go along? You are technically a Baine Clan member."

Lakin let out a half-laugh. "Chieftain Baine would sooner eat her firstborn than join the Resistance," he said. "We had a brief meeting shortly after being released, and while she was furious at the Mages Guild and intends to demand restitution, she is just as angry at the Resistance. Especially at Rylan, as she feels that he should have protected the clan through his influence, and instead, Mika got roped into the Shifter Royale."

"Right." Although I doubted Mika's kidnapping was Rylan's fault, or even that he knew about it, I wasn't exactly happy about his loyalties either. He'd already made it clear that the Resistance's aims were more important than his family.

"Could you meet with Mafiela again and relay the information about the Resistance's plans for the shifters?" I asked. "She's probably more inclined to believe it than the other clans, and she'd call a council meeting for sure to discuss it."

"I can try that," Lakin said cautiously. "Of course, she will ask where I obtained the information."

"You can tell her I was the one who told you." I raised my chin a little. "And if she wants to speak to me directly, I'll meet with her. Hell, if she wants me to speak to the council, or the entire town, I'll do it. The shifter community needs to know."

Lakin smiled a little. "As entertaining as that would be to watch, I expect Chieftain Baine will choose to have as little involvement from you as possible. There are many shifters in the community who are grateful for your part in unmasking the Shifter Royale, but more than half of those people have left the city, and the ones who remained tend to favor the Resistance. They will certainly hold your mage heritage against you when trying to decide whether or not your claims are truthful. Some may even try to kill you on sight, like those soldiers."

I sighed. "I guess it's better that I remain in disguise, then," I said, and I couldn't help but feel a little disappointed. What use was my growing popularity amongst the shifter community if my supporters weren't even here?

Lakin's expression softened with sympathy. "I'll send word to you after I've met with the Chieftain, and if we do end up calling a town meeting after she meets with the council, I'll let you know when. We can decide at that point whether it would be more helpful or counterproductive for you to attend and testify to what you learned."

"Thanks," I said, flashing him a grateful smile. "I really appreciate all the help you've given me," I added, getting to my feet.

"Is there anything else I can help you with?" Lakin growled, getting to his feet as well. The hunger in his yellow-orange eyes swirled to the forefront, and the next thing I knew, his hands were on my hips, nostrils flared as he sniffed at me.

My internal temperature shot up at the contact, and the tingling in my lower belly started up again. It would be so easy to give in, to just lean into him and claim the sweet, sweet relief he was offering.

But instead, I gently but firmly pushed him away. "Sorry, Lakin, but I don't need any help. I'm doing a little experiment with abstinence right now," I added with a grin.

"Abstinence?" Lakin's eyebrows shot up, and he looked at me as though I'd lost my mind. "While you're in *heat*? Is that even possible? You're crazy, Sunaya Baine."

"That's what they tell me," I said over my shoulder as I walked out the door, cloaking myself in illusion once more. I sighed a little, both in relief and disappointment, as the heat receded. I wasn't actually trying to be celibate during this time, but at the rate things were going, I just might end up going through heat without having sex once.

The question was, could I hold onto my control the entire time, as Resinah had suggested was possible? Or was I going to lose my mind after all?

20

Since there was nothing left for me to do in Shiftertown, I hopped onto my stolen steambike and sped back to Solantha Palace. Yes, I was still a little angry with the Mages Guild, but I needed to tell Iannis what was going on. Besides, even though the meeting he'd invited me to had ended badly for me, at least I *had* been invited. If somebody had told me two months ago that I was going to be present at a meeting in the Mages Guild to discuss war strategy, I would have laughed in their face. Yes, there was still progress to be made, but there was no doubt I'd made leaps and bounds already in my relationship with the Mages Guild.

I parked my stolen bike outside the side entrance of the Palace, then hurried to the Mages Guild to see if I could catch Iannis. Unfortunately, my luck in that area was still shitty as ever.

"Lord Iannis is out dealing with the rebellion," Dira informed me primly. "There has been another outbreak of fighting at the Port, near the Fish Market, I believe."

"How long has he been gone?" I demanded.

"Since early this morning. As I'm sure you understand, it is impossible to tell when he'll be back. He'll return as soon as possible, since he has urgent Palace and Federal business to attend to, but dealing with the Resistance is of primary importance."

"Obviously," I muttered, trying not to sound too irritated. Truthfully, it was admirable that Iannis was out in the trenches – he could easily claim that as the Chief Mage, he was better suited behind the lines, but instead, he was making use of his formidable powers and directing the mages in person. It was also a shrewd political strategy – by choosing to be on the front lines instead of cowering behind the warded walls of the Palace, he was rallying the mages and showing the citizens that he cared enough about the city of Solantha to defend it with his own two hands.

Still, I wished he *would* sit back and do a little more delegating. How the hell was I going to get him to implement any of my plans, if he was always out fighting in the streets?

"The Chief Mage asked for me to tell you to remain here when you returned," Dira said, breaking my train of thought. "He was concerned when he couldn't locate you in the Palace this morning, and he wants to speak with you." Dira's face was expressionless as she delivered the message, but I wasn't entirely sure she approved. Not that her approval meant shit to me.

"Is that right?" I asked casually, as if my heart wasn't doing a little happy dance in my chest. Maybe Iannis really did miss me as much as I missed him. "Well, I guess it's a good thing I need to speak to him. Tell him I'm right here in the Guild when he comes back."

Not that she actually needs to, I thought to myself as I headed down the hallway leading to the Guild offices. Iannis would be able to locate me any time with his *serapha* charm. But that was not for Dira to know.

I entered Iannis's office, grabbed a piece of paper and a pen, and scribbled out a note with the salient details of what I'd learned at the Ur-God sermon this morning, as well as my meeting with Lakin. I sealed my report in an envelope and left it on his blotter, then headed down to the kitchens to refuel.

The scents of cheese, pasta, and sausage had my stomach rumbling in anticipation long before I trotted down the steps to the kitchen. My mouth instantly started watering as I caught sight of a huge pot of crumbled sausage and tomato sauce bubbling away, and my stomach let out the loudest growl the kitchen staff had probably ever heard.

Mrs. Tandry, the head chef, turned in the direction of the sound, propping her hands on her hips and giving me a friendly scowl. "Don't you come nosing around these pots!" she warned, wagging a wooden spoon at me. "You go sit down right there, and I'll serve you."

"Yes ma'am," I said sheepishly, but as she turned away, a horrible thought popped into my mind. Mrs. Tandry was human, as was all the kitchen staff. Most humans believed in the Ur-God to some degree, and I couldn't imagine this stout, middle-aged woman as an atheist. Did that mean she believed the same things as the humans I'd met at the temple? That shifters and mages needed to be wiped from the face of Recca, and only humans had the right to exist? In light of that, was it really wise to have any human servants in the Palace at all? It was already obvious that somebody within the Palace walls was feeding intelligence to the Resistance...who was to say it wasn't Mrs. Tandry or one of her staff? Could any of the humans be trusted?

Stop that, I told myself sternly as I took a seat. This was exactly what the Resistance wanted...for the races to mistrust and hate each other so it would be easy to tear society apart and take what was left for themselves. I couldn't allow fear to cloud my judgment, and everything I'd seen from Mrs. Tandry so far indicated that her loyalty was to the Palace.

Still, when she bustled over with a plate piled high with ravioli and tomato-sausage sauce, I couldn't help but ask if she'd ever heard of Father Calmias, and what she thought of his sermons.

"Oh, I don't listen to that madman," she insisted, waving her hand away. "He's a very good speaker, and clearly devout, but anyone with a brain can hear that his hatred of mages is excessive and has warped his message."

"Yeah, that's what I thought, but he was speaking at the Ur-God temple in Maintown, and the crowds there were just eating up his words. I was there in disguise," I added when she gave me a surprised look.

"Well, that may be so, but it doesn't mean that all of us, or even most of us, buy into Father Calmias's teachings," Mrs. Tandry said with a sniff. "That temple is the largest and best funded in Maintown, but it only became so in the last couple of years. There are other smaller temples, both in Maintown and Rowanville, that represent different denominations. The one I used to go to every Sunday, before the wards went up, teaches that the Ur-God promotes acceptance across all races, and that his plan was to move us toward a society where we could all work in harmony."

I frowned a little. "You've been working at the Palace for years, haven't you?" I asked, and she nodded. "Hasn't that ideal been shaken even just a little bit by the fact the mages don't seem inclined to agree with your interpretation of the Ur-God's plan?"

Mrs. Tandry smiled. "I've been here for thirty years," she said, "and in that time, the Mages Guild has slowly moved toward the Ur-God's ideals without being fully aware of it. The change sped up when Lord Iannis took control, and even more so when you came into our lives." Her expression turned serious. "I didn't trust you in the beginning, Miss Baine, but now I understand that the Ur-God sent you to us. You're crucial to making His plan a success, and if there is anything I can do to help, you have but to ask."

I stared at her, stunned. The way she was talking, it was almost as if she viewed me as a savior or something! If there was one thing I was sure of, it was that I wanted no part of the Ur-God's plans, benign or otherwise. But before I could protest, she gave me a serene smile, then returned to her work. I turned back to my cooling food and tried to enjoy my meal, but the weight of responsibility on my shoulders suddenly seemed very heavy. How many other humans in the Palace had similar thoughts about me? Was this what my human neighbor had thought when he'd helped me escape from the apartment building? He'd said I was a hero, and that I needed to be free to do my hero thing. That sounded awesome, in theory, but I didn't want to be looked up at as a hero. Heroes were objects of admiration, but they were also targets.

Maybe that's why you're being targeted by the Resistance, a snide voice in my head suggested. *And why you attract trouble wherever you go.*

Scowling, I shoved that voice into a box, locked it, and threw away the key. I didn't need my own sense of sarcasm turning against me, thank you very much. Tired now, I finished my meal and made tracks toward Iannis's office. I might as well wait for him there, I reasoned, maybe take a nap on his couch.

But my feet took me straight past the Mages Guild, and the next thing I knew, I was outside the library again. *Right,* I thought as I pushed open the door. I meant to check in with Janta anyway, to see if she had any new information for me.

"Miss Baine!" Janta's eyes lit up behind her spectacles, and she rose. Today, she was dressed in a peach-colored robe with tiny daisies sewn along the collar and sleeve hems. "I was hoping you would come by soon. I was able to gain access to a long-distance line, and I've had word from my colleague in Dara."

"Oh yeah?" The fog of exhaustion lifted from my brain as excitement filled my veins. "What did they say? Did you find out who owns the Bellington Trust?"

"Indeed I have." Janta picked up a piece of paper from her desk and handed it to me. I read the name on it, and felt the pieces of the puzzle finally fall into place.

The beneficiaries of the trust were Curian Vanderheim and his wife, Thorgana Mills.

"By Magorah," I muttered, re-reading the names once, twice, then three times to make sure I hadn't made a mistake. "The Vanderheims! I just saw them at the ball in Dara, only days ago."

"Everyone knows them, or knows of them," Janta said. "Mrs. Mills is in the social news all the time. But I confess, I am surprised. Are you sure it is not just a coincidence? Ownership is not proof of wrongdoing, in itself."

"No, it's definitely not a coincidence." The more I considered the matter, the more certain I felt that we were on the right track. "Thorgana inherited Mills Media and Entertainment, which the Herald is a subsidiary of. The very same Herald we just had to shut down, and where that serial killer Yantz was the chief editor."

Energy thrummed through my veins as the pieces began to fall in place in front of my eyes, and I drummed my fingers on the desk as I thought aloud. "Her husband is one of those wealthy, but otherwise unremarkable, businessmen who you tend to overlook. The perfect disguise for a criminal. I could absolutely see him pulling the strings behind the Resistance without drawing attention to himself. Since Thorgana doesn't give a shit about Mills Media, she wouldn't care if her husband occasionally decided to dip his toes into it."

"She does seem to be rather enamored with her parties and fashion clubs," Janta said, the slightest hint of censure in her tone. "I would not be surprised at all to find out that she has her husband talk to her managers in her stead. Undoubtedly, that's one of the reasons he married her. Who wouldn't want access to a powerful media empire?"

"Damn. Damn!" I paced back and forth in front of Janta's desk, agitated now that I realized the truth had been right under our noses. "I've been to Thorgana's mansion here several times! I took on extra work as a bodyguard in the beginning of my enforcer career, standing by to make sure no jealous socialites tried to mess up her hair during those soirees she used to host. I never really liked her, but I never once saw anything to suggest they were supporters of the Resistance."

"Well, I doubt they would advertise the fact," Janta pointed out. "Besides, isn't the mansion they own here a mere vacation home? As far as I understand, their main residence is in Dara, where the Bellington Trust is incorporated."

"Of course," I muttered. "The perfect location for spinning a web. Still, if I'm right, there's a good chance we'll find something incriminating in their house. I mean, it's clear the Benefactor has chosen Solantha as the center stage to launch the rebellion from. I should head over there right now, see if I can search the place."

"By yourself?" Janta asked, sounding concerned. "I'm not certain that's wise, Miss Baine."

I opened my mouth to argue, then sighed, remembering previous occasions when I'd gone off half-cocked and lived to regret it. "No, no, you're right." I forced myself to stop pacing, taking some deep breaths to push my heart rate down to a manageable level. I was getting all ramped up now, out for blood, but with a price on my head, the worst thing I could possibly do was start up a manhunt against the leader of the Resistance on my own. I needed to bring reinforcements, and most of all, I *needed* to talk to Iannis.

"Thanks for the information, Janta," I told her. "I owe you big time."

Janta shook her head. "I'm simply doing my duty to Canalo, and research is my passion," she said firmly. "If there is any other information you need that would be helpful in thwarting the Resistance, don't hesitate to ask. You can even come to my house if you want and wake me up in the middle of the night. Solantha is my home, and I don't want to see it overthrown by these violent rebels. We all must do what we can to defend it."

I thanked her again, then headed back to Iannis's office as I'd originally planned. My blood was still buzzing when I shut the door behind me, but one look at the comfy couch in front of the fire was all it took to bring the exhaustion back. After kicking my boots off, I stretched out on the thick cushions, fully prepared to make up for the horrendous night of sleep in that beer cellar. I'd better get some rest while I could – I had a feeling that once Iannis heard my news and we decided on a plan of action, it would be a long while before I found the time to sleep again.

21

"Are you absolutely certain of this?" Iannis demanded, his fingers clutched around the note I'd scribbled almost three hours ago. He and Fenris had returned from a skirmish to find me sleeping on the couch. When Iannis had insisted on a report detailing my whereabouts and actions for the last fourteen hours, I'd simply lifted a finger and pointed to the envelope I'd left on his desk.

"Is there a reason I'd be lying about it?" I asked, leaning back in the visitor's chair. He frowned as the two front legs came off the ground, clearly not happy with my abuse of his furniture, but loath to sidetrack the conversation.

"I'm not doubting the truthfulness of your words, Sunaya," he said, using my name since only Fenris was around to witness it. "But this...the very idea that the humans would even *dare* to think they could get away with such horrific treachery..." He seemed to be struggling to find words, a truly rare moment for him. "Let us simply say that if anyone else had come to me with this information, I would have laughed them out the door. It's utter insanity."

"And just what do you think the Resistance represents, if not just that?" I pointed out. "They've already gotten it into their inflated heads that they can overthrow the mage regime with nothing but guns and brawn. Why not get rid of shifters too?"

"Indeed," Fenris remarked dryly. He stood over Iannis's shoulder, scanning my note again with narrowed eyes. "Grooming the human population to fall in line with their beliefs is a smart plan," he conceded. "This ensures the Resistance has a large support base to rely on. They can't hope to succeed if the civilian population does not support their aims."

"There's more," I said before Iannis could comment on Fenris's observation. Both men turned to me, eyebrows raised as though they couldn't believe there could possibly be more to this outlandish picture I was painting. "I found this out after I wrote the note, so I didn't add it in there. But I'm almost certain that Thorgana Mills's husband, Curian Vanderheim, is the Benefactor."

"*What?*" Fenris stared at me. "That mindless fool? Why would you think so?"

"It sounds unlikely indeed," Iannis agreed with him. He was frowning. "Why him, of all people?"

I took them through the line of investigation I'd pursued with the help of Janta in the library, starting with Supplysafe and ending with the discovery that the Bellington Trust was owned by Thorgana and her husband. "Thorgana owns the largest media company in the Northia Federation," I reminded them. "It would have been easy for her husband to convince not just the Herald, but their other news outlets throughout the Federation, to spread Resistance propaganda. Remember that not too long ago, the Herald was printing stories specifically angled to pit humans and shifters against one another."

"Well, we always knew the Benefactor had to be immensely rich," Fenris said, considering. "Vanderheim certainly fits the bill in that respect."

"He also supported the faction who wanted to get rid of the Minister at the Convention," I reminded Iannis.

Iannis was silent for a minute, thinking it over. Finally, he gave a decisive nod. "Yes, it does seem plausible – at the very least, he must be a trusted associate, if not the Benefactor himself. Well done, Sunaya. I'm impressed you've managed to uncover so much useful information in such a short amount of time." His eyes shone with appreciation as he studied me, and I felt a blush creep in my cheeks as my body reacted. "We should certainly go to the Vanderheim mansion and search the property, as you suggest. I will send a scout ahead to see if anyone is home."

It didn't take much time to get an answer – half an hour later, a messenger rushed into the office to inform us that Thorgana Mills was in residence, along with a few staff members.

"Based on past experiences with Mrs. Mills, I doubt she will give us too much trouble," Iannis said as we headed to the Mages Guild to mobilize a task force. "But we should bring reinforcements, even so."

It didn't take Iannis long to gather the people he needed – the Legal Secretary, to inform Thorgana of the raid and the purpose behind it, two apprentices to help us conduct the search of the house, and two large, mean-looking mages I recognized as former enforcers who had retreated to the Mages Guild after the insurrection had started. The latter were equipped with manacles to arrest Thorgana or any of the staff as accessories, depending on what we found.

Excitement and nerves buzzed in my veins as we climbed into the steamcars waiting for us outside – Iannis and I sat in the back of one, while Fenris rode in front with the driver. I *knew* I was right, that Thorgana's husband had to be the one behind all this, but as we headed toward the coastal section of Maintown, where the wealthiest humans resided, a sliver of doubt crept in.

What if Janta's contact in Dara had been wrong, or worse, had deliberately misled us? It would be completely humiliating for us to show up and conduct a raid, only to find out that Thorgana and her husband had nothing to do with the Resistance. Worse, since Thorgana owned Mills Media and Entertainment, news of such a mistake would be plastered all over the country. The papers and radio would run with two stories – one, that the Mages Guild was losing its touch, going after harmless socialites, and two, that the Chief Mage of Canalo's judgment was being severely impaired by his *hybrid apprentice.*

"Relax," Iannis murmured, quietly enough so that only I, and perhaps Fenris, could hear. His hand found its way across the backseat and squeezed mine gently. "I trust you."

A rush of warmth made my fingers tingle and my cheeks glow, and I squeezed his hand in return. It meant so much to me, those three simple words. Trust was rare and precious, and if Iannis was willing to put his reputation on the line on my say-so, perhaps we did have a future together.

Hell yes, my body seemed to say in response to that, and the heat spread through me like wildfire. My breath quickened as tingles and aches made themselves known again, and my skin suddenly felt too tight against my flesh. Iannis's eyes darkened as he looked me up and down, his grip on my hand tightening, and I knew his body was unconsciously reacting to mine.

Fenris cleared his throat loudly then, obviously scenting my arousal. More heat flushed my cheeks, this time with embarrassment, and I quickly let go of Iannis's hand and scooted closer to the door.

Distance, I thought, leaning my cheek against the cool glass window and taking deep, calming breaths. I desperately needed distance.

I could sense Iannis's disappointment, but he said nothing more, allowing me my space as I wrestled my unruly body back under control. By the time my heart rate had steadied, we were turning into a long gravel drive that wound its way up a steep, grassy hill. A large limestone mansion sat on top, overlooking the city from the front and the coastline from the back. An iron fence, taller than even Iannis, surrounded the grounds.

We rolled to a stop outside the gates. A guard was sitting in the small booth, and he spoke to the driver of the steamcar in front of us. I watched as the back window of the car rolled down, revealing the Legal Secretary's face, and whatever he said to the guard made the man's face go white. Nodding hurriedly, he rushed back into the booth and pulled a lever. There was a loud buzz as the gate swung open. As we drove inside, I saw the guard had picked up the phone and was hurriedly speaking into it.

"She'll be expecting us," Iannis murmured as we approached the house.

We descended from the vehicles on the broad front drive, the Legal Secretary taking the lead with the two enforcer mages. I watched curiously to see if they would try to handle this mission tactfully, or with force. I had my answer when the Legal Secretary gestured to the two enforcer mages to step forward. The one on the left blasted the huge, arched wooden door with what looked like a concentrated ball of air. The door splintered as it fell backward, landing in the hallway with a loud crash, and the enforcers walked over it as they led the way into the house.

Talk about making an entrance, I thought as we followed them inside, the apprentices bringing up the rear. The foyer was as huge as I remembered it from Thorgana's receptions, with orange-veined marble floors and a long, arched ceiling. The tall arrangement of lilies and gladiolus that presumably belonged atop the large mahogany table in the center of the room had toppled over, scattering the floor with shards of expensive pottery and white blossoms that were fast growing limp in the spreading puddle of water.

A shriek of fury echoed through the mansion, and Thorgana Mills herself rushed down the carpeted staircase at the end of the hall. She was dressed in a white velvet robe, her pale blonde hair in curlers, and judging by the state of her face, had been halfway done with her evening makeup. Even so, she looked younger than the forty-eight years she admitted to.

"What is the meaning of this?" Thorgana demanded imperiously, her normally pale, perfect skin blotchy with outrage. She skidded to a stop behind the table, mindful of the broken pottery with her thin silk slippers, and crossed her arms over her chest as she glared at the Legal Secretary. "Who has given you the right to come into my home and damage my property?"

"I'm afraid I did," Iannis said firmly, stepping forward into her line of sight. Thorgana's eyes widened as her gaze snapped to him. "You see, Mrs. Mills, we've come across some compelling evidence that your husband has been financing the Resistance, and that he is known in certain circles as the Benefactor."

Thorgana swayed for a moment, and the non-painted half of her face grew noticeably paler. But after a moment, she let out a scornful laugh, pressing a hand to her chest. "Ridiculous! Curian, a criminal mastermind? Lord Iannis, you are absurdly mistaken about that."

"You might not be aware of his activities," Iannis suggested. "We may know more after searching the house."

Mrs. Mills shook her head contemptuously. "Curian's wealth is not nearly large enough to finance the Resistance, even in part. You are, as they say, barking up the wrong tree. He will expect your apology for this."

It was my turn to step forward. "You're telling the truth," I said, surprised. Thorgana pressed her lips together at the sight of me, looking down her straight nose imperiously. My own nose told me she hadn't lied, and yet something told me she was hiding something.

Iannis and Fenris looked at me questioningly, no doubt wondering if I had made a mistake after all, and the Legal Secretary frowned. But Mrs. Mills' smile turned into a small, secretive gloat, and at that moment, something clicked.

"So your husband isn't the Benefactor, and his purse alone isn't enough to finance the Resistance," I acknowledged as more pieces fell into place. "But *yours* is, isn't it?"

"What do my finances have to do with any of this?" Thorgana demanded. Her expression grew more strained, and her right hand clutched at the pendant dangling from her white-gold necklace.

Iannis exchanged a quick look with Fenris. "That would explain a great deal," Iannis observed, his eyes narrowing on Mrs. Mills. She recoiled beneath his gaze, face growing even whiter. I could see the swift calculation behind her cold blue eyes – she must be wondering if further denials would be worthwhile. I expected fear to be rolling off her in waves, but she smelled more of fury and determination than anxiety. Did she have something up her sleeve? I tensed instinctively.

"Man, I've been so stupid. You completely took me in with that airhead socialite act." I shook my head at my own obtuseness. "At first, I thought your husband was using your money and connections. After all, that's his right, and as an airhead socialite who doesn't give a hoot about finances, who would you be to stand in his way?" Thorgana's eyes narrowed at the insult, and I grinned – she'd built up the airhead persona precisely to draw attention away from herself, so she couldn't very well refute it now. "But no, now I'm realizing that it's not the case at all. *You're* the Benefactor, aren't you? You've been pulling the Resistance's strings with your perfectly manicured hands all along."

Thorgana shrugged her elegant shoulders. "You've clearly taken leave of your senses, Miss Baine." Her blue eyes appealed to Iannis after passing over Fenris with faint contempt. "Surely you will not lend any credence to the ravings of an inexperienced young shifter, Lord Iannis? People like us don't get involved in such sordid matters. You must know better."

"Mrs. Mills is definitely lying," Fenris said, staring at the woman with disgust. "I, for one, believe Sunaya is right."

"I know." Iannis gestured to one of the enforcer mages waiting in the background. "Secure Mrs. Mills. She is under arrest."

"You will regret your decision in hell!" Thorgana spat, ripping the pendant from her neck. It was a glass pendant, and a chill ran down my spine as I caught sight of a red, smoky substance within it. Leaping forward, I tried to grab it from her, but she threw it to the ground as hard as she could just as I slammed her against the wall.

"*Ul'fraith!*" Iannis shouted, and I turned my head to see a strange, yellow bubble form around the reddish smoke, enclosing it completely. It pulsed, then flared brightly, and I shielded my face as a shockwave rippled through the space.

"Get *off* me," Thorgana spat, shoving me away. To my surprise, I stumbled backward – I hadn't expected her to be that strong. She made a dash for the exit, but the two enforcer mages grabbed her before she could make it more than three steps.

"I do not know what that was," Iannis said coldly as Thorgana struggled to break free, "but I strongly suspect you just tried to kill us all, Mrs. Mills. You will be tried and convicted of attempting to kill multiple members of the Mages Guild, in addition to the mountain of other charges the Legal Secretary will file against you."

"You can't prove that," Thorgana cried. "You can't prove any of it! I'm just the wife of a businessman!"

"Oh, we will prove it," I hissed, meeting her malice-filled

gaze. "And I'll make sure your victims are avenged, even if I have to do it with my own two hands."

It was a chore for the enforcers to get Thorgana into cuffs – she struggled mightily against the two large men, using strength that a small human woman, especially a socialite, shouldn't possess. A theory popped into my mind about the reason behind that, but I filed it away for later consideration. I was still wrapping my mind around the fact that this puny socialite was the Benefactor. Had she acted alone, or in concert with her husband? For all I knew, she had a whole team of co-conspirators. Now that we finally had her in custody, I hoped we'd be able to clear up this mystery. But judging by the ice-cold hatred in her gaze as she passed me, it might not be easy to get her to talk.

"Let's search this place thoroughly," Iannis commanded.

Fenris and the enforcer mages left to escort Thorgana back to the Palace, where she would be held and interrogated, while Iannis and I split up with the apprentices to search the house. Iannis took his team to the upper floor, which I knew from my previous stays held the majority of the rooms, and I left the apprentices to search the ground floor while I descended a set of stairs toward the back that led down to the cellar.

The mansion's cellar proved to be a veritable warren of underground rooms, mostly used for storage. One room, for example, held bulging bags and cases of dry goods – enough rice, flour, sugar, and beans to ride out a siege. Another was filled with racks of dusty wine bottles and other types of liquor.

I examined a bottle of red that was thirty-two years old, according to the label. I gave it a slight shake, but only heard the slosh of liquid, nothing hidden inside. The booze always flowed freely at Thorgana's parties, so it figured she kept her wine cellar well stocked. Perhaps she took advantage of the inebriated guests. I'd seen her collect donations from sloshed attendees on more than one occasion, usually exorbitant amounts meant to support some kind of humanitarian cause. Had that money really been going to the Resistance?

She probably managed to obtain more resources than just gold, I reflected as I left the wine cellar and moved across the hall to the last room. This one was filled with stacks of boxes. Judging by the variety of shapes and sizes, they could hold anything from dinner plates to pieces of furniture.

As I moved toward the nearest stack, my ears picked up a rustling sound. I froze, listening again. The slight noise, which would not have been noticeable to human ears, was coming from the brick wall on my right.

There shouldn't be anything behind that except dirt. I pressed my ear to the wall and caught the distinctive sound of something scraping against concrete. I took a step back and surveyed the wall. There was probably a loose brick that had to be pulled, or a lever cunningly hidden somewhere in this room.

"Fuck it," I muttered, lifting my hands. I didn't know the Words for the spell I wanted, so I simply channeled my magic into my hands and visualized a huge, incredibly dense ball of air into existence. Sort of like the one the mage enforcer had used on the front door, but much deadlier.

I let it fly, then immediately dashed behind a tower of boxes to avoid the resultant explosion. The sound of the air ball ripping through the brick was deafening. I clapped my hands over my ringing ears and leaned into the boxes to keep them from toppling over as chunks of brick slammed into them.

"What the hell was that?" a familiar voice shouted, and I grinned. Here was all the proof of Thorgana's guilt we could have asked for: she was harboring Petros Yantz, the former editor-in-chief of the Herald. The man who was directly responsible for the silver murders that had claimed my mentor Roanas as a victim. Yantz and I were going to have a really nice talk right now. One that was going to involve broken bones.

Drawing my crescent knives, I stepped from behind the boxes and through the jagged hole I'd blown through the wall. A large, concrete room lay beyond, a hidden sanctuary that had been fashioned into an apartment with a kitchenette and table, and two beds in the back. Yantz stood panting by the table, dusty with debris from the wall. His tall frame was a lot thinner than I last remembered, and there were shadows in his gaunt face. Good. The bastard was suffering.

"Happy to see me?" I asked, advancing on him, then froze as I caught the scent of another man – or rather, mage, I realized as I inhaled a whiff of magic.

"You again!" Argon Chartis spat, hobbling out from the corner behind Yantz. He was leaning very heavily on a cane, and I caught a glimpse of a wooden leg peeking out beneath his robes. His dark green eyes blazed with fury, and fear sparked in my chest as he raised a hand and shouted several Words. I lifted my hands in defense as he hit me with a blast of sickly green magic, but my arms froze in place as the energy rippled over me. My heart rate skyrocketed as I tried and failed to open my mouth, tried and failed to reach for my magic, tried and failed to do *anything* at all.

"Foolish hybrid," Chartis sneered at me. "Coming down here all by yourself. If you'd brought a more experienced mage as backup, you might have stood a chance."

"Thankfully, she's as stupid as she is impulsive," Yantz said, yanking a dagger from a sheath on his belt. Panic shot through me as it caught the dim light emanating from the single bulb in the ceiling, and I realized the knife was made of silver. The sick gleam in Yantz's eyes told me that if he had his way, this wasn't going to be a quick knife to the heart – he was hoping to torture me, and he was going to enjoy the hell out of it. And without my vocal chords, nobody would hear a thing.

"Iannis!" I screamed, trying desperately to reach him with mindspeak.

"Sunaya?" I felt his startled reaction, and I knew he was coming to me. At least Yantz would not have time for any torture, but not even Iannis could navigate that confusing cellar as fast as a silver knife could cut my throat. A knife that was swinging toward me even now.

But in the instant before it could connect, something hot seared my chest, right below the center of my collarbone. Yantz's eyes widened as orange light exploded from me, washing the room in a strange glow.

"No!" Chartis shouted as the room began spinning around me. My stomach pitched with nausea as the colors and shapes melded together in a blur, and I wished desperately I could close my eyes. Frozen, I watched as the blur of colors lightened around me, catching hints of brilliant green and clear blue. What the hell was happening? Was this an unintended side effect of Chartis's spell?

But as my surroundings gradually came to a halt, things started to become clear. Literally. The colorful blur gave way to miles of clear blue ocean, a long stretch of powdery white sand, and dark green fronds waving from the tree line to my left. A warm, salty ocean breeze caressed my skin, and strange calls from tropical birds pierced the open air.

Somehow, some way, I'd teleported to another place. And it sure as hell wasn't anywhere near Solantha.

22

It took nearly an hour for Chartis's immobilization spell to wear off, and it was easily one of the most uncomfortable hours of my life. I was forced to stand there with the hot sun beating down on my head, and the salty ocean breeze stripping the moisture from my lips and skin. A crab crawled across my feet as it headed for the safety of the water. Poop from a seabird landed on my hair as it flew past, mocking me with its shrill caw.

Paradise.

As I stood immobile in the sand, my thoughts immediately circled back to Iannis. What was going on back in Solantha? Had Iannis apprehended Chartis and Yantz? I wondered what his reaction had been to my disappearance. He must have questioned Chartis and Yantz about it...if he'd caught them. And his *serapha* charm would tell him that I was far away now.

Iannis wasn't the only one I was worried about. How were Comenius and Elania holding up under the rebellion? Were they still safe behind the walls of Comenius's shop and the barricaded Witches' End? And had Com gotten any word from Elnos as to how he and Annia were doing on their rescue mission? I hadn't been able to spare much thought for them in the past few days, but now that I was standing here with nothing else to do but think, I realized Comenius should have heard from them by now.

When the spell finally wore off, the first thing I did was strip down and dive into the water. Yes, it was salt water and didn't do a damn thing for my parched throat, but I was hot as hell and itching to wash the bird crap off me. Unfortunately, the water was too warm to be called refreshing, but when I stalked out a few minutes later, the ocean breeze coupled with my soaked skin helped cool me off.

How the fuck did I get here?

I stared out at the gentle waves breaking against the shoreline, contemplating that question. Instinctively, I reached up to touch my *serapha* charm, and as I did, my fingers brushed against a second charm.

The *gulaya.*

I looked down to see the *gulaya* sitting innocuously atop my chest. Damn. It must have activated in response to the mortal danger I'd been in, then transported me to this place. On the one hand, that was great, because I was safe from torture and death by Yantz's silver knife. But on the other hand, I was in the middle of nowhere, too far away from the battle to be of any use. I consulted my *serapha* charm, curious to know just how far Iannis was from me. Unfortunately, it could only give me a general sense of direction and distance, and it told me that Iannis was much farther away than he'd been when I'd gone searching for him.

Needing to do something other than stand on a deserted beach and ask myself questions I had no answer to, I put my clothes back on, then changed into beast form. White light engulfed my body as it stretched and changed shape, and a few moments later, I was a black panther standing on the sandy white beach. My pitch-dark fur did absolutely nothing to keep the heat off my back, so I headed for the trees, seeking shade and water. The small critters scurrying around in the undergrowth went quiet as I passed, remaining that way for a long time after I left – I might be a new species to this place, wherever it was, but I was still a predator. I caught glimpses of snakes, weasels, and porcupines down on the ground, and above, orange-and-black primates with shaggy hair and thick, long tails clung to branches and watched me with fear and suspicion.

My nose and ears led me to a spring a good two miles into the dense vegetation, and I drank greedily, then rolled around in the cool water for a bit. Ahhh, bliss. In animal form, my human worries felt much less urgent – as a beast, all I cared about was slaking my immediate needs.

Once I was satisfied, however, I remembered that I needed to figure out where the hell I was. A quick climb up a tall, long-limbed tree with thick, dark green leaves told me what I needed to know. Clinging to the trunk, I swiveled my head, taking in the miles and miles of sparkling blue sea that stretched in all directions, broken only by a tiny land mass off in the distance.

I was on a fucking island. And unless I was very much mistaken, there was no sign of civilization here.

Climbing down the tree, I began to explore the forest, wondering if there might not be indigenous people living among them. I needed to get the lay of the land, find out exactly what I was up against. If there were people around, maybe they had some kind of boat or canoe that I could commandeer.

And then what? I scoffed at myself. *You don't know the first thing about sailing, and even if you did, you have no idea where to go.*

Yeah, okay. Maybe that was true, but I'd cross that bridge if and when I came to it.

I padded back out to the beach again, still in panther form, and did a walk around the island. My little stroll turned up no boats, canoes, or fishing contraptions of any kind, and the only footprints I came across were my own, when after some two hours, I finally came back to where I started.

Upon re-entering the forest, I immediately forgot all about searching for human life when the appetizing scent of blood hit my nostrils. Wild boar. I stalked the scent to a small clearing about a mile away, where I found the wounded boar drinking from a stream. Quills sticking out from its right rear leg told me it had recently lost a tangle with a porcupine, but that wasn't a deterrent – I simply attacked from the left instead. The boar squealed when I pounced from the trees, gathering its legs beneath it and trying to make a run for the safety of the undergrowth, but it was in pain, and I was much faster. It didn't take long to bring it down.

Two hours later, after my impromptu meal and a long nap, I resumed my search, heading deeper and deeper into the forest. Aside from a confrontation with a large snake, I ran across absolutely nothing of interest until the terrain suddenly grew steeper, and the scent of bat droppings thickened the air.

Following the pungent scent, I climbed what I rapidly realized was a hill, probably near the center of the island, and came to a cave hidden in the hillside by dense foliage. I was deliberating whether or not the cave was worth exploring when the wind shifted, strengthening the scent of the bat poop.

But it also brought just the faintest whiff of magic.

Okay, now I have *to go inside,* I thought. Magic was the absolute last thing I expected to encounter on a deserted island. I crept into the darkness of the cave with caution, going slow so I could give my eyes time to adjust to the darkness. About thirty yards in, the cave floor dropped off steeply, and my nose and ears told me the bats' lair was down this way. But to my left, there was a small tunnel, and as I drew closer to it, the scent of magic grew stronger.

I crept along the narrow shaft for a good hundred yards before it opened up again into a wider space. There was absolutely no light there, so I shifted back into human form, then conjured a ball of fire.

My jaw dropped as I held my impromptu flashlight aloft. I'd just found somebody's hidey-hole. There was an ancient-looking wooden desk and a chair in one corner, a small cot with bedding, a carved chest, and a shelf filled with old, leather-bound books. The air was cool and dry, quite unlike the humid air outside, and surprisingly, there was no dust or bat guano at all. Excitement filled me, temporarily banishing my worries as I wondered who had lived here on this island, and whether the contents of this strange chamber could help me find a way off it.

Carefully, I started pulling books off the shelf, taking care not to crack their leather bindings further or damage their fragile pages. Janta would have been proud of me. Unfortunately, most of the books seemed to be advanced magical tomes written in Loranian, but a smaller book filled with cramped writing turned out to be a diary of the mage who'd called this place home. The yellowed pages told me his name had been Messindor, and that he was a pirate hailing from the far southeast. This cave was one of several hiding places he kept across the world, mostly on islands close to or south of the equator. Judging by the gaps in entry dates, he only updated the diary when he was in residence here every other year or so.

"Three hundred years," I muttered, staring at the date of the final entry. This pirate mage had last entered this cave close to three-hundred years ago. That, or he'd gotten tired of journaling. It was unlikely that he was still alive, but perhaps he had grown weary of piracy and retired to a more hospitable isle than this one before meeting his end.

With nothing more of relevance to learn from the diary, I searched the desk drawers. I found some old coins, a congealed inkwell and a few quills, and a couple of pieces of parchment in one. Another held several rolled-up maps, which I laid across the table, using the coins as paperweights. One of the maps was of the Coracciao, a group of tropical islands south of the Northia Continent. There was a group of dots on the map that were a little way off from the main cluster of islands, closer to the Southia Continent, and a red arrow was pointing to one of the islands, possibly indicating my location.

Okay, so I wasn't so far from civilization that my location wasn't on a map. But I *was* far enough away that most people looking at said map would have a hard time even finding the island I was standing on.

The second map was of the island itself, with exes marked in different spots. I imagined these were the locations of various caches Messindor had scattered all over the island, in case he couldn't get back to the main one he had here. It would help pass the time to track them down. I kept it on the desk while I rolled the other map up and put it away.

In the last drawer, I found various magical charms and amulets, including yet another *gulaya,* bigger than the one that had brought me here. I picked up the star-shaped charm and sniffed it, but could only detect a hint of magic – it was no longer charged. Oh well. I had no idea where this one would take me even if it did work, and I didn't have the means to charge it myself.

The wooden chest was possibly the most perplexing thing in the room. It was beautifully crafted, with a variety of runes carved into the dark wood, but there was no way to open it. I could see the seam where the lid met the container, but it was impossible to fit even the tiniest sliver of fingernail beneath it, and there was no visible lock. I considered smashing the chest, but I didn't want to harm the contents, and besides, it smelled strongly enough of magic that I feared some kind of magical retaliation if I did so.

With nothing else to do, I curled up on the cot and tried to sleep. The bedding was remarkably well preserved, as was everything else in this room aside from the dried ink. The scent of magic clinging to the air made me wonder whether the mage had set some sort of preservation spell on this chamber to hold everything in a magical stasis, so that time or the elements could not harm his possessions. That would be a useful spell, especially for a pirate who had to stash treasure and supplies in all manner of places. I decided I would ask Iannis to teach it to me, if I saw him again.

When I saw him again, I reminded myself firmly. Iannis would come to rescue me. He had to.

My eyelids closed as sleep found me, but instead of dark, dreamless sleep, the heat assailed me, fire creeping in my veins, phantom caresses sliding across my skin. Memories of Iannis swirled in my mind, of his hands on my naked skin, his deceptively wicked mouth on my lips, his seductive sandalwood scent invading my space. His presence forced all thought out of my head, leaving only my desire for him.

"I want you to be mine, and only mine," Iannis whispered darkly into my ear. His tongue flicked out to caress my earlobe, and I shuddered as more intense heat lashed me. But when I reached for him, my hands only met empty air, and I found myself back in the cot, my clothes on the floor and my limbs tangled in a sweaty blanket. Frustrated, I ripped off the sheet and made my way out of the room and down the tunnel.

Standing at the cave entrance, I allowed the cooler night air to caress my naked skin. The touch was both a curse and a blessing, as it took the edge off my overheated skin and reminded me of the real, physical touch I desperately craved. The full moon was finally here, taunting me with its bright, shiny roundness as it hung over the sea. For whatever reason, the light of the moon increased a shifter's power; we were stronger and able to shift more quickly during the full moon. But when a female shifter was in heat, the full moon only amplified her desperate need.

Remember your heritage, Resinah's voice whispered as the breeze picked up, swirling around me. *You are not merely the sum of your parts, Sunaya Baine. Whole, you have the potential to be stronger than both your shifter and mage ancestors.*

I sighed in relief as Resinah's cooling breeze drew the heat out of me, and with it, the fog of lust clouding my mind. *Whole,* I thought, looking at the full moon. I had the capability of being stronger than a mage or a shifter, if I could figure out how to combine my two halves into a whole. That was something I could try to work on while I was stuck on this lonely island.

I only hoped that Iannis would come to find me, as I'd found him, and that when he arrived, my sanity wouldn't be splintered into a thousand pieces.

23

"I am going absolutely bat-shit crazy," I muttered, swinging from one tree branch to another like the damned howler monkeys that were chittering away in the branches across from me. Unlike them, I wasn't doing this because I was trying to get anywhere. After a whole week on the island, I was literally bored out of my fucking mind, and with little else to do, I was mimicking the wildlife while figuring out new ways to train my muscles.

It turned out that the local animal population was a lot less scared of me when I was in human form. I thought they still sensed the predator in me, because a lot of them stayed away, but the howler monkeys had grown used to me to the point that they didn't even run away when I tried to climb into their trees. Of course, some of the animals had good reason to fear me, especially the white-tailed deer – whenever I got hungry, I'd simply change into beast form and go hunting, and deer and the wild pigs were on the top of my menu list. I'd also tried fresh fish and lobster while swimming in the ocean as a panther, but they were harder to catch, and I had to eat a lot more of them to satiate myself.

During the first couple of days, I'd gone around the island with the map I'd found, locating Messindor's ancient caches. Some of them were tougher to find than others, and each of them held something different. One had a pair of pistols, a small sack of gunpowder, and a box of blackened bullets that I scalded my fingers on before I realized they were silver. Another location turned out to be a cellar dug into the ground and filled with glass jugs of booze, no longer drinkable. But in a third one, I'd found a clay jar filled with gold that was heavy enough to pay my food and rent for the next few years.

Not that money was a concern for me right now. Or booze. Or guns. Most of the stuff I unearthed was fairly useless to a person in my position, but I did take the gold back to Messindor's cave dwelling. If I ever got off this forsaken island, it would definitely come in handy.

As I swung my body from one tree to the next, a howler monkey took offense to my encroachment of his territory, and it lobbed a bright red fruit at my head. I ducked barely in time, then shot him a glare as he chittered angrily at me. Looking up, I saw a female in the branch above me, holding tightly onto the baby monkey wrapped around her chest, and sighed. The guy didn't want me disturbing his family.

Dropping down to the ground, I made my way to the beach and took up my usual spot beneath a shady tree just at the edge of the forest. The sun was halfway through its descent to the horizon now, and soon would be setting on my seventh day on this island. I always sat out here for a few hours in the very early morning, and then again in the later afternoon, to keep a lookout in case any ships passed by that I could signal. None had as yet, and it was hard not to feel as if the entire world had forgotten my existence. I'd stopped checking on the *serapha* charm after my fourth day on the island. It was too disheartening not to see any change in the distance between Iannis and me, even though I knew he had to be coming. Maybe the charm just didn't register change in distance outside a certain radius.

I wished I had some sort of scrying glass, or that I knew how to make one, so I could see what was happening in Solantha. How was the shifter community faring? Had they heeded my advice and withdrawn their support for the Resistance? Or had the ones who'd been released from prison decided to take up arms against the Mages Guild in retaliation for the injustice committed against them? Had the Mages Guild confirmed definitively that Thorgana was the Benefactor, and had they gotten anything useful out of her? And what about Chartis and Yantz? Were they finally in custody, or had they escaped yet again?

I wanted to think everything was going well, but I couldn't help but worry that things were out of hand. What else could be taking Iannis so long to come find me? The city must still be in danger, or he would be here already. After all, he'd said he loved me. He'd said he wanted me to be his.

Stop that, I snapped at myself as tears smarted at my eyes. There was no point speculating as to the reasons behind Iannis's absence. He'd proven his faith in me when he'd organized the raid on Thorgana's mansion based on my say-so, and I needed to have faith in him. He would come. I believed that with every fiber of my being.

I just wished he'd hurry the hell up.

I wasn't sure how long I stared at the horizon, but my vision eventually blurred, and I fell asleep. It wasn't a deep sleep – I never allowed myself to fall asleep completely while I was out in the open – but more like a trance, allowing my mind to drift while keeping my ears and nose alert for any threatening changes in my environment.

Sometime later, the sound of footsteps on wet sand caught my attention, and a familiar sandalwood scent followed close behind the sound. My eyes popped open, and I squinted against the brilliant orange-and-gold sunset as my heart began to pump hard and fast. Could it be?

A tall, broad-shouldered figure, backlit by the sun, was walking toward me, his long hair rippling in the wind. He was dressed in a loose, button-up shirt and shorts rather than his usual robes, but his addictive, masculine scent was unmistakable, and my heart leapt in my chest. Beyond, I could make out a small sailing boat at anchor in the bay.

"Iannis," I whispered, stumbling to my feet. He picked up the pace as I rushed to meet him, and the next thing I knew, I was in his arms. He lifted me off my feet and swung me around, kissing me until I forgot I was on a deserted island, forgot I was anywhere but in his arms. He tasted like the sea, but also like Iannis, and I greedily clutched at his broad shoulders, wrapping my legs around his hips as I pressed my body tight against his.

"You came," I gasped against his mouth between ravenous kisses. "You finally came."

"Of course I came for you." He pulled back a little to meet my gaze. His hands tangled in my hair, and he cupped the sides of my head as he searched my eyes. "Did you doubt I would?"

"No," I said honestly, and I kissed him again, clawing at his shirt. "What the hell are you wearing?" I muttered as I fumbled with the buttons.

"Sailing attire," he growled as he lowered us to the sandy beach. "I can't wear mage robes for every activity, you know."

His shirt was half-undone now, and I slid a palm up the expanse of his chest, marveling at the warm, silken touch of skin poured over hard muscle. Man, but he was sexy as hell, with his dark, cherry-wood hair tangling in the wind and his gorgeous violet eyes burning with desire. The brilliant sunset backlit his form, making him look like some kind of god glowing with celestial flame.

"Did you really sail all the way here?" I asked, popping another button open on his shirt.

Iannis grinned. "That would have taken too long. I used an airship for most of the distance. When I realized you were on a deserted island, I hired the boat for the last bit. It seemed worth the small delay for the added privacy."

"I imagine the *serapha* told you where to go, but what happened after I was whisked away? Did you realize what had happened to me?"

His expression darkened. "Not right away. When I rushed downstairs and there was no trace of you – only that murderer, Yantz – I feared the worst."

"Only Yantz? Argon Chartis was not there?"

"No, he managed to sneak away again. We only learned what had happened from interrogating Yantz, and by that time, of course, Argon was long gone. Janta, from the library, came to me with a tale about an old *gulaya* ... but how did you know it was still active?"

"The scent of magic," I explained. "It seemed worth trying, at least."

"I'm glad it did work, and it saved your hide. And even more glad we exchanged the *serapha* charms, to guide me to you."

I nodded in agreement and slowly, teasingly, popped another button on his shirt.

Iannis arched a brow. "You're awfully relaxed for someone who is in heat," he commented, leaning forward and nipping at my lower lip.

I grinned. "The heat's been over for several days now. Somehow, I managed to survive without you."

He winced. "I am sorry I was not there when you needed me, Sunaya."

"Don't be sorry." I brushed my thumb across one of his high

cheekbones, drinking in the sight of his face. "You came as soon as you could. And I'm just happy you're here now."

"Well then," he said, eyes drifting up and down my naked body – my leather pants had been ruined by the elements and my top was shredded, so I'd spent the majority of the past week running around naked. "Are you saying that you really want me? That this –" he brushed his thumb across my nipple, and I gasped, "isn't just a side effect of your shifter heritage?"

You are more than just the sum of your parts.

I wrapped my arms around Iannis's neck, drawing him flush against me. "I've always wanted you," I murmured against his mouth, then I kissed him again.

Iannis swept his tongue inside my mouth, and I moaned as the dark, exotic taste of him filled me. Desire burned low in my belly, and a pulsing ache spread through my body with each stroke of his tongue against mine, each brush of his fingers against my tingling skin. Impatient, I used my claws to shred the shirt from his body, and he laughed, rising up a little so he could shrug off the tattered garment.

"More," I demanded, grabbing the waistband of his shorts. I was about to rip them off as well, but he closed a hand over mine.

"Slow," he murmured, stroking his thumb over my knuckles. Somehow, he managed to infuse so much sensual promise in that one word that my knees went weak, and I was glad I was already on the ground.

"Slow," I agreed, and he released his hand. Rising to my knees, I pressed my bare torso against his, savoring every ridge of muscle as I kissed him long and deep. My fingers worked gently at the buckle on his belt, easing it free, and then the button on his shorts came next. By the time I gripped the button with my thumb and forefinger, we were vibrating with anticipation.

I unbuttoned his shorts slowly, feeling every inch of his arousal as my knuckles slid against the fabric. His shaft sprang into my waiting hand, and I grinned against his mouth as he growled in approval.

"No underwear?" I teased, skimming my finger along his length.

"I never wear any," he muttered, trailing hot kisses across my jaw. His teeth clamped down on my earlobe, and I instinctively squeezed him.

"Yes," he groaned in my ear, hips rocking forward. A thrill shot through me at the sound of raw need in his voice, and I gave him what he wanted, stroking him until his shoulders gleamed with sweat in the moonlight and his chest heaved.

"Enough." His voice was rough as he pulled my hands away, and I let out a surprised yelp as he reached around and collected my breasts into his big hands. I moaned as my sensitive nipples rasped against his palm.

"You're extraordinary," he murmured, eyes on mine even as he used his skilled hands to tease my breasts. He seemed to be drinking in every detail of my face. "I don't think the Creator could have crafted a more beautiful and spirited woman if he tried."

My face flushed at that. "Now you're being ridiculous."

He laughed. "Of everything I've said and done in the past few weeks, *this* is what you find ridiculous?" He let go of my right breast to stroke my cheek with the backs of his fingers. "The fact that you're stunning?"

I grinned a little. "No, you've said plenty of things that are ridiculous," I said to him, sliding my hands down the back of his shorts and squeezing his ass. "It's just hard to believe that someone who's lived as long as you have has never met a better-looking woman than me."

"I've met many beautiful women in my lifetime," Iannis admitted. "But none of them were *you.*"

He ducked his head, and I gasped as he took one of my nipples between his teeth. Electricity zinged through my veins as he teased the taut, sensitive bud with his teeth and tongue, and I scraped my nails up his back and dug them so hard into his shoulders that I was certain there would be gouge marks in his flesh in the morning. But my response only seemed to encourage him, and he slipped one hand down my flank, his long fingers finding that aching place between my legs.

"Iannis!" My eyes flew wide as he slid a finger inside me. My legs turned to jelly as my sensitive, aching flesh pulsed in response to his touch. Sensing weakness, he took advantage of the opening and pushed me onto my back, then claimed my mouth in a searing kiss as he slid a second finger inside me. I arched against him as his fingers found that sweet spot inside me, and he massaged it until I was a hot, writhing mess, moaning incoherently as my hips strained against his hand. I desperately needed release, but his palm was just a little too far away for me to get the right angle. He was teasing me, the bastard, drawing it out, and I wasn't sure if I loved him or hated him for it.

"Please," I finally begged. "I want you inside me."

"Do you?" His voice echoed in my mind, and I gasped as he slipped inside me again, the same way he'd done back in Maintown when he'd helped me heal that human. The sensation of his soul brushing against mine sent a thrill through my body, and I was suddenly awash in Iannis's desire for me. I could feel how hungry he was, how his body ached to be joined to mine. But even more important was his desire to please me, to watch me tremble and gasp, and to know he was the cause of every sound of pleasure that sprang from my lips.

His fingers slid against my sweet spot again, and the scent of magic teased my nostrils. I cried out as an explosion of exquisite sensation filled me, clinging to him tightly as whatever he did triggered the most intense orgasm I'd ever experienced. I was utterly alive, ever single fiber of my body lit with glorious flame as pleasure rippled through me.

Gasping, I went limp in his arms as the wave finally receded. I shivered as he trailed hot kisses up my neck and across my jaw again, my body still aching for more despite the release.

"What...what the hell was that?" I managed as he nibbled on my earlobe, fingers still working inside me.

"Magic," he said, his lips curving against my skin as he sensed my shock. "What, it never occurred to you that a mage could use his power to enhance his woman's pleasure?"

"Sex and spellcraft don't usually go together in my mind," I said breathlessly, arching my hips against his hand.

Iannis chuckled, his violet eyes glittering as he pulled back to look at me. "They will by the time I'm done here tonight."

I gasped as his power filled me again, bracing myself for another explosion. Instead, he only enhanced my need, increasing the tingles running through my veins, the heat flushing my skin, the swollen ache between my thighs until I writhed beneath his fingers, mindless with need. He held me at the brink of orgasm for a long time, then released me just when I was on the verge of punching him. My cries of pleasure echoed in the night as pleasure ripped through me again, leaving me breathless and shaking.

"Now," he growled, pushing my legs apart. His arousal brushed against my center, and I hissed as my inner muscles clenched with need. How could I still be so hungry, after he'd already given me so much pleasure?

But I was hungry, and I knew I wouldn't be sated until we went all the way. I gripped his hips, urging him forward, and he laughed as he buried himself completely inside me. We moaned in unison at the instant rush of pleasure, and I instinctively clamped my legs around him, drawing his body tight against me. My lips sought his as he began a slow, steady rhythm, and I lifted my hips to meet his, thrust for thrust. As equals.

Our bodies trembled with the effort of holding back, the desire to savor our first time greater than our need for completion. But instinct eventually won out, and Iannis's thrusts came faster, harder, deeper. Our souls were still joined, doubling the pleasure for both of us, and I dug my fingernails into his shoulders to try and find purchase in this crazy, relentless storm of sensation.

"More," I demanded, arching into him. He used his magic on me, intensifying the pleasure of each thrust, turning me absolutely molten with need. When I came again, the rush of euphoria was so intense I was, for a moment, without sight or sound. There were only the waves of fierce, almost violently pleasurable sensation, followed by the sweetest relief I'd ever experienced.

I felt Iannis's body stiffen against mine, sight and sound coming back as he surged deep inside me with a groan. He buried his face in my hair, shuddering as he came, and I wrapped my arms around him, holding him tight as he rode it out, savoring his orgasm as it rippled through my own body. And as I stroked his trembling back, I knew I would never let him go, no matter what life decided to throw at us next.

24

"So you still won't agree to marry me?" Iannis demanded, sounding highly offended.

I rolled over to face him, smiling at the confounded look on his face. We'd spent the night on the beach, unwilling to stop touching each other long enough to move and find a better spot. There was sand in my hair and ingrained into every inch of my skin, and I felt way too fantastic to care. A night of hot sex could do that to a girl, especially if it was with the right guy.

And *boy,* did I have the right guy.

"You don't have to look so insulted about it," I said, cupping his cheek with my left hand, then dropping a light kiss on his nose. "Remember, marriage is forever. A long time for me, and even longer for you."

"And here I thought you were the impulsive one." He sighed, passing his hand through his dark red hair. "I know it is forever, Sunaya. That's the whole point. Of course, if you need more time to think about it, we could stay here a while longer. This is the first time in weeks we have a chance to talk without constant interruptions."

"Yes," I murmured. "I've missed you. A few stolen minutes here and there aren't enough as your apprentice, let alone your lover."

He smiled. "The last few weeks were far from normal, and you know it." He looked around the beach. "After last night, I find myself developing a fondness for this deserted island." He cupped a hand between my legs. "If you are only willing to be with me here, I guess we'll have to stay longer. As long as it takes for you to agree."

"Beast," I gasped as he pressed the heel of his hand against my sweet spot. The burst of pleasure sent a flush to my cheeks, and I arched my hips, seeking more. "It has nothing to do with the island."

To my frustration, the hand retreated. "By Resinah, darling, what do I have to do to make you see reason?"

I sighed, realizing Iannis wasn't going to drop this subject. "I'm not saying that I don't want to marry you," I said, levering myself onto my elbows so I could look him in the eye. "In fact, if it means we can do this every night, I'm all for it. It's just... I've got some concerns."

Iannis frowned, rolling off me and onto his side again. "What sort of concerns?"

"Well, for one, I have no idea what's going on at home. Are we still in the middle of a revolution?"

"No, of course not," Iannis said. "Two days after Thorgana's capture, the Shiftertown residents decided to withdraw their support of the Resistance and attempted to kick them out. Between the clans and the Mages Guild, we managed to overwhelm them, and those who have not been killed have been taken prisoner." He sighed. "I will need to sort that out when we return. Prison Isle is far too small to hold so many."

"That's fantastic though!" A weight lifted from my chest now that I knew the city was safe, or at least on its way to being safe once more. I grinned. "You know, I may have had something to do with the shifters deciding to change sides."

"Somehow, that doesn't surprise me at all." Iannis kissed the end of my nose, eyes twinkling. "You're becoming quite the unstoppable force." His expression grew serious again. "But none of that has anything to do with our future. Tell me why else we can't get married."

I squirmed beneath the weight of his stare. "Everyone will think we're rushing into this to silence all those rumors and gossip. I want to be with you, but I don't want this to look like we got married just to solve a problem. And what about the fact that we're supposed to be master and apprentice? I thought carnal relations with your apprentice were frowned upon among mages." That was what I had always understood, though I was not entirely sure how bad it was. Mage customs and laws were not well understood among the other races.

Iannis smiled ruefully. "It is indeed unusual, but for mages, marriage – or at least the intention to marry – trumps every other consideration. The formal bond between a couple is respected by everyone. There have been some precedents of marriage between a master and apprentice, though not recently, and it is certainly going to cause talk. Still, an illicit affair would be considered much worse, and it would be impossible to hide in our position."

"I see," I said dubiously. "But could you still continue to teach me magic?"

"Yes, of course. I certainly would not want my fiancée or wife subject to the authority of *another* master." From the expression that twisted his face, I could tell the very notion was repulsive to him.

"I suppose I could ask Fenris to teach me when you don't have time, and Janta to tutor me in Loranian," I mused. "But you would still be in charge of my training." Yes, that might work. I sighed.

Even if I got Iannis to promise to devote more time to my training, after the experience of the past few weeks, it was ten to one that something would happen to interfere with our regular times.

"As for rushing into marriage," Iannis continued, "I only wish that were possible. Marriages between mages are a highly formalized matter, with lots of rules, and usually preceded by at least one year's engagement. Ideally, we would wait until your graduation, but that is too long in our case." His voice was firm. "Anyway, less than a full year would raise lots of comment, but I'm willing to go right ahead, if you are."

"No, that's fine," I assured him, relieved. "That is, we can still, umm, be together, while we wait for the ceremony?"

"Just try to keep me away." He kissed me again.

I grinned against his mouth. "In that case, a long engagement is a good idea." After all, marriage was irrevocable while both partners lived. It only made sense to be very certain beforehand. If either of us were to change our mind, I'd rather it be before the wedding when it was still safe to back out.

Not that I wanted to back out.

"Good," Iannis growled, grabbing me by the waist and pulling me on top of him. "Now, let's stop talking and finish what we started earlier."

"I thought you'd never ask," I said, then he pulled my mouth down to his again, effectively shutting me up.

EVENTUALLY, the sun climbed high enough in the sky that we determined it was too hot to stay out any longer. Besides, we were both in desperate need of a bath, so I led Iannis into the forest and to the sweet water of the spring I'd been bathing in for the last week. Somehow, we managed to wash up without making love again, which was a good thing because I really wanted to get off this island.

"Do you have anything you need to take before we leave?" Iannis asked as he dressed. "Such as clothing, perhaps?" He arched an eyebrow.

"What, you don't like what you see?" I gasped, pressing a hand against my chest in mock offense.

"You know well enough that I do," Iannis said dryly. "But that doesn't mean I want to share your charms with the world. You'll need suitable clothing when we arrive at the mainland and meet any other mages."

"Well, I've still got my pants," I told him. "They're in my cave."

"Cave?"

I took him up the hillside, through the cave entrance, and down the tunnel leading to Messindor's underground room. Iannis grumbled a little along the way – fitting through the cave entrance and traversing the tunnel was difficult for a man his size – but the expression of amazement when I finally led him into the room was worth it.

"Astonishing!" He crossed over to the shelf, running his finger along the leather-bound spines. "Some of these magical texts are quite rare." He carefully extracted a book from the shelf, opened it up, and scanned a page. "I don't think a copy of this book has been seen for several hundred years."

"Well, that's not surprising," I said, sitting down on the cot. "Messindor's last journal entry was around three hundred years ago."

"Messindor?" Iannis asked, frowning.

I explained to him about the diary I'd found, showing him the journal entries, the maps, and the pouch of gold. "The one thing I still haven't figured out is this damned chest," I said, jerking my head toward the stubborn chest that defied my attempts to open it. "I have no idea what's in it."

Iannis set the book in his hand aside and crouched down to examine the chest. After a few moments, he shook his head, laughing softly as he ran his fingers over the wood.

"What's so funny?" I demanded.

"Nothing," he said, pressing his fingers into one of the runes. To my surprise, the carved piece of wood popped out, revealing a tiny knob that held it in place. "You can't be expected to know about puzzle chests, as they went out of fashion long before your time."

"Puzzle chests?" I asked, watching him press his fingers against the other runes. The next two did nothing, but the third one popped free as well, and so did the one on the opposite side of the chest.

"Yes," he said, eyes narrowed as he sat back on his haunches. "They're rather like a safe combination. You have to find the hidden knobs, and then you have to twist them into the right order."

He fiddled with the knobs for a few moments, twisting them this way and that. A loud click echoed through the room, and the chest popped open.

"By Magorah!" I exclaimed as I stared at the contents. The chest was filled to the brim with glittering jewels.

"And that," Iannis said, taking my hand in his and pressing a kiss to my knuckles, "is your engagement present."

25

By noon, Iannis and I were on the small, but speedy sailboat he'd arrived in, with my gold and jewels safely stowed away next to Messindor's collection of books. Iannis was fascinated with them, and the diary in particular – he told me that one of the books held a handwritten alternative recipe for recharging *gulayas* more quickly, with ingredients that were legal and easily obtainable. The texts also contained rare spells for magical defense that were thought to be lost.

On the mainland, a small, private dirigible was waiting already, courtesy of the local government. It took us to the Southlands, the country that took up the southern section of the Northia continent, directly below the Federation. There Iannis took me shopping for more suitable clothing – I was dressed in my torn leather pants and one of his button-up shirts – while the pilot restocked food and drink supplies and the coal needed to heat up the air inside the dirigible.

Once again, Iannis and I had vastly different ideas about what clothing was considered suitable. He wanted me to arrive in mage robes, to pave the way of our engagement announcement, which I adamantly refused. Resinah had said to embrace both halves, not become a mage completely.

Eventually, we compromised, and I boarded the dirigible in a red-and-black dress with three-quarter length sleeves and a skirt that fell just below my knees. My bare feet were properly covered by a pair of cute, low-heeled boots, and I crossed them at the ankles as I settled into my cushy leather seat for take-off.

"So," I said, once we were in the air, alone in the small, but well-appointed cabin. "We really need to talk."

"About?"

"Changing the system."

Iannis nodded slowly. "I agree that the current set-up cannot continue as it was. I had already planned to discuss possible reforms with the Council and Director Chen."

I arched a brow at that. "You're all mages. Do you *really* think you guys are going to be able to come up with anything workable on your own, considering how out of touch most of you are with the shifter and human communities?"

Iannis sighed. "It wasn't always that way, you know. We used to know more about the people and their political inclinations than they did themselves."

I blinked. "Is that so?" I couldn't even imagine such a thing.

Iannis smiled slightly. "I know you don't fully agree, but we mages are best suited to ruling." I opened my mouth to argue, but he held up a hand. "Hear me out, Sunaya. The average lifespan of a mage is many times longer than that of the average human, which means we cannot help but amass more knowledge and experience, and take a wider perspective. There is also the fact that through magic, we are able to create wealth without being forced to exploit the workforce. Believe it or not, when mages first came to power, there were various experiments with human self-government. In case you haven't noticed, we do still allow the humans a certain measure of self-government today, as well as the shifter clans. But giving them too much power has never ended well."

"That may or may not be true," I argued, "but you mages govern without giving the shifters or humans any opportunity to voice their opinions or concerns. Why are there no human or shifter representatives on the Council, for instance?" Iannis's brows rose, and I took his lack of immediate response as encouragement. "Having them there would help prevent such barbaric customs as the magic-wipe law, for example. That practice needs to stop, and the Mages Guild needs to set up some sort of training facilities for those who *are* manifesting mage powers."

"The constitution of Canalo does not allow the inclusion of non-mages in the Council," Iannis pointed out. "The current Councilors are already troublesome enough, and the weekly council meetings a great waste of time I can ill afford. If there were humans and shifters on it too – it does not bear contemplating."

"And why should humans and shifters heed that constitution, or the Council, if they had no say when it was established?" I demanded. "The public won't be content to be kept in ignorance forever."

"What you suggest is not something that can happen overnight," Iannis warned. "I have already suspended the magical testing in the public schools until a better solution can be reached, but keep in mind that many human families may still want the option for their children to remain human. Training them as mages means taking them from their families, a thing that very few parents desire. Shifter families might be even less happy at sending their offspring to the mages for training. Of course, mages are hardly ever born into the clans – you are an exception only because your father was a mage."

"Right." I bit my bottom lip as I considered that. It was true that many families might prefer their children never inherit magic powers, but... "Don't you think the child should also have a say? It's their powers, after all, and their life that is being forever altered when those powers are taken away. If you're going to keep the testing, it should be done at the latest possible age, so that the child can be consulted."

"Twelve years old is still very young for such a momentous decision," Iannis mused, gazing thoughtfully out the window. "Most children are likely to embrace their magic, once that option exists. But perhaps further testing and questioning could be done to determine whether each individual child is best suited for life as a mage, or if the child would be better off raised with their human family, as a human."

I pressed two fingers to the side of my forehead – I was starting to get a headache just thinking about the ramifications of all this. "Obviously, this needs way more thought and discussion," I said. "But back to my original question...what did you mean when you said that mages used to know the shifter and human populations better?"

"It used to be common practice for us to mingle with the other races in disguise, much as you do now," Iannis explained. "Doing so allowed us to understand their needs and concerns better, and also to predict and head off any societal disruptions or catastrophes. But around one hundred years ago, the Federation mages decided to eliminate that part of apprentice training. The Chief Mages considered it a waste of time. Besides, sending mages into the population in disguise led to undesirable entanglements and friendships."

"You mean like my mother and father?"

"You could say that," Iannis said carefully. "Certainly, there were more shifter-mage hybrids born back then, and the Mages Guild didn't know what to do with them. Many had their powers suppressed, as you did, and ended up outcasts who lived and died miserably, their lives often ending well before their time. Others were sent out of the country by their parents, either to live in hiding or to settle in other countries that were friendlier to their kind."

I let out a breath. "I guess I was lucky Roanas decided to take me in." He'd caught me stealing food at a market stall, and instead of a thief, he'd seen a grubby, starving kid with nowhere to go. As the Shiftertown Inspector, he could have prosecuted me, but instead, he'd taken me into his home and raised me as his own.

What would my life have become, if not for that fateful day? Would anyone have helped me? Or would I have grown up on the streets, perhaps killed before ever reaching adulthood?

"You were very lucky," Iannis murmured, his eyes on me again. "I wish I could have spared you the pain of your childhood, but your unique background is the reason why you are so good at what you do. I would have probably uncovered the Benefactor and her plan on my own at some point, but by then, it would likely have been too late to squash the rebellion without resorting to genocidal methods."

I shuddered. "Well, I guess you could call that a silver lining."

"Indeed." Iannis's eyes twinkled. "In the meantime, though, you have demonstrated to me that withdrawing from the population was a mistake, and one that will be rectified immediately."

I didn't know how I felt about the idea of mages walking among the shifter and human populations in disguise, keeping tabs on us. There had to be a better way of ensuring the safety of Canalo's citizens, without resorting to espionage.

You've done it yourself, you know, a voice in my head reminded me. *Don't act so hypocritical.*

"You're thinking too much," Iannis said, and the next thing I knew, he'd yanked me into his lap. "Let's postpone the rest of this discussion, as my mind is far more occupied with what lies beneath this dress." He slid a hand up my bare thigh.

"Well, don't let me derail your train of thought," I gasped as his fingers moved higher. He covered my mouth with his to muffle my cries as he found my sweet spot, and I decided that, for now, this flight was better spent doing things other than talking about social issues. They would be waiting for us when we landed, and, for now, I wanted to savor the alone time Iannis and I still had left.

WHEN IANNIS and I disembarked from the dirigible, what seemed like the entire Mages Guild was waiting for us on the front lawn of the Palace. They clapped and cheered in unison when the two of us emerged together, and I wasn't sure if they were cheering because Iannis was back, because he was successful in rescuing me, or both.

"Welcome back, Lord Iannis!" Director Chen beamed as she and Fenris stepped forward to greet us. They bowed. "We are all very relieved you have safely returned, and of course, that Miss Baine is with you." She inclined her head to me as well, though the enthusiasm in the gesture left much to be desired.

"Yes, we are very glad to see you *both*," Fenris added, putting firm emphasis on the word *both*. He stepped forward to embrace me then. As I hugged him back, he whispered in my ear, "And especially you, My Lady."

"Flatterer," I muttered with a grin. I knew from the look in Fenris's eye that he could scent evidence of our recent lovemaking, and that he'd already deduced what that meant. But neither of us said anything more about it, and he retreated to Director Chen's side again.

"Thank you," Iannis said, raising his voice to acknowledge the crowd of mages as well. Turning back to Director Chen, he asked, in a lower voice, "I hope your relief does not stem from any serious problem that has occurred in my absence."

"Oh no, Lord Iannis," Director Chen said confidently. "Everything is under control right now. The rioting has all but ceased in the streets, and the enforcer patrols have ensured that citizens are discouraged from looting. We do have hundreds of captured insurgents awaiting your disposition, and there is the matter of all the civilian criminals as well."

"I will address all of that shortly," Iannis promised Director Chen. "But right now, I have an announcement to make."

"Of course." Director Chen stepped aside so that Iannis could address the crowd, and a little thrill shot through my veins when Iannis twined his fingers through mine.

"I would like to inform you all of my engagement to Miss Sunaya Baine, daughter of the Baine Clan, and also a mage by birth. The wedding date will be announced in due course. We hope you all share in our happiness," Iannis added with a broad smile, which was rare for him in public.

Director Chen went utterly white, and Fenris grabbed her by the elbow to steady her. For his part, he simply grinned at us, and the rest of the crowd broke out into applause. Sincere applause, I realized with some shock. Many of the ones closest to us came forward to shake our hands and congratulate us, and though the Council Members in particular did not seem thrilled about the engagement, most of the good wishes we received were genuine. Maybe mages weren't as rigid and closed to change as I'd thought, if they were willing to accept the idea that I would be their new lady, as Fenris had called me.

"Come," Iannis murmured, drawing me away from the crowd. "I've an engagement present for you."

"An engagement present?" I asked as he led me through the

gardens and up the steps to the Palace entrance. "I thought the jewels in the box were my present."

"Don't be silly," he chided. "I was only joking about that. I may have opened that chest for you, but you found it, so the contents were rightfully yours to begin with."

"Oh." Flustered, I said nothing more as I followed him up the curved double staircase and to his rooms in the West Wing. I really hadn't expected any kind of engagement present from him.

"I don't have a present for you," I blurted out as we stepped into his sitting room.

Iannis turned, then gently cupped my chin with his long fingers and tilted my head back a little. "You can count the books you found as a present, if you like," he said, smiling. "Or use one of those many gems to get me something, if you absolutely feel you must. But as far as I'm concerned, the only thing I want from you is what you have already given."

"A pain in your ass?" I half-joked as he dipped his head toward me.

"No." His mouth curved against mine as he kissed me. "Your love."

His hands found mine, fingers curling around them as he kissed me deeply, and I gasped as power surged through me, forming a circuit between us. The sensation was familiar – he'd done the same thing the last two times he'd accessed the lock my father had placed on my power in order to give me more access. This time, though, the current that ran through me was hotter and brighter than before, and my body trembled from the force of it. By Magorah, but what was Iannis doing to me now?

A sudden tug at the center of my body ripped a cry from my lips, and something cracked wide open. Power spilled through me so suddenly that my knees buckled, and Iannis grabbed me about my waist and pulled me tight against him to keep me from falling.

"That is one of your gifts," he murmured into my hair. "You have more power than you realize, and it will take some getting used to now that you have access to all of it."

"All of it?" I looked up at him in surprise. "You've broken the lock my father put on my magic?"

"Permanently." Iannis grinned at the stunned expression on my face. "It wouldn't do to have my future wife handicapped in any way. Besides, you've gained enough control over your emotions that I can trust you won't blast someone into smithereens whenever you get angry."

"I'll do my best," I said dryly, and he chuckled, pulling away. Lifting my hand, I directed my magic toward a small, potted tree by the window, willing it to sprout a few blossoms. Power surged through me, and I gasped as the branches exploded with dozens of tiny purple blossoms – quite a few more than I'd expected.

"I guess I need to recalibrate," I thought, scratching my head as Iannis laughed. Yesterday, I would have had to push harder to get the same effect.

"Indeed." Grinning, Iannis kissed the top of my head, then pulled a key from my sleeve and placed it in my hand. "Your second gift," he explained when I frowned down at the key in puzzlement. "You'll find a brand-new steambike with your name on it when you next go snooping in the garage."

"Wow." I stared at him, at a complete loss for words. "You don't know how much that means to me," I finally said as I threw my arms around him and kissed him hard.

Sometime later, Iannis lifted his head, breathing heavily. "Much as I would love to continue this, we do have other matters that need attending," he reminded me. "I must call a council meeting and determine what to do with the prisoners."

"Of course." Sighing, I unwrapped myself from around Iannis's body, then stepped back. "You're inviting me to this one, right?" I asked, giving him a beady eye.

"I wouldn't dream of doing otherwise."

26

Several hours later, I left the council room exhausted, but triumphant. I'd lobbied hard for lighter sentences for the shifter and human civilians who had been incited to violence by the rebellion, insisting that it would be more productive to put them to work rebuilding the city via community service projects than having them languish on Prison Isle, or relegating them to back-breaking mine work. The council had grudgingly agreed, especially when Iannis threw the weight of his approval behind me.

As for the Resistance soldiers themselves, that was a tougher battle, particularly as the Resistance was still active in other states of the Federation. I argued that because the Resistance had brainwashed the shifters with propaganda and false promises when the plan all along was to kill them, the shifter soldiers should be given lighter sentences. Between the higher taxes levied against the shifter community, and the Herald's successful attempt to turn the population against shifters, they could hardly be blamed for latching onto the promise of a system where they would be treated fairly.

The council members contended that regardless of the reason, these shifters had willingly participated in heinous crimes against civilians, and needed to be punished accordingly. But a few of them agreed with me to give them a second chance, and Iannis pointed out that, at this time, goodwill toward the community was needed far more than punishment. Eventually, we came to an agreement that the shifter members of the Resistance would be sentenced to a maximum of five years' hard labor in the mines, depending upon how long they'd been with the Resistance, and whether or not they'd directly contributed to acts of terrorism.

As for the humans, the higher ups were facing execution after their trials, and the regular soldiers either many more years of hard labor in the mines than the shifters, or some equally gruesome sentence. I suppose I could have argued for some of the soldiers as well, but honestly, I didn't give a shit. I remembered all too well the congregation that had applauded Father Calmias's sermon – they hadn't been an oppressed people looking for fair treatment. They'd been a group of elitists, ready to commit genocide to get what they wanted.

I found out at the council meeting that though Chartis had gotten away yet again, Yantz was in custody, as were Thorgana Mills and my cousin Rylan. I wanted a face-to-face conversation with the last two, so after the meeting dispersed, I left the Palace and rode my new steambike to the Port to catch a ferry to Prison Isle.

News of my engagement to the Chief Mage had spread across the city like wildfire, so when I arrived at the island, the prison staff practically tripped over their feet to accommodate me. I informed the warden on duty that I wanted to speak to Rylan Baine, and I was promptly led to a private visitor's chamber to wait while they brought him in. I was amused when one of the hulking prison guard mages offered me refreshments – they'd never been this accommodating when I'd come here on enforcer business. My first impulse was to decline the offer, but I figured Rylan might want something to eat or drink. So instead, I asked for whatever they had available.

When two guards led Rylan into to the room, he arched his brows at the sight of the platter of sliced cheeses and meats and the pitcher of milk that was sitting on the steel table. I didn't miss the gleam of hunger in his yellow shifter eyes though – his face was thin, eyes sunken, and the loose fit of his black-and-white striped prisoner's uniform told me he hadn't been eating enough.

Not exactly surprising, I thought to myself. The easiest way to keep a group of shifters under control was by keeping them undernourished. Our superior strength and agility depended on large quantities of food. Anger sparked in my chest at the idea that the shifters here were being starved, but there was nothing I could do about it, and besides, they *were* criminals.

"Why, cousin," Rylan drawled as he sat down in the chair opposite mine, "a tea party, for me? You shouldn't have."

"Don't be an asshole, Rylan." I shoved the platter at him. "Eat. You look like something the cat dragged in."

"No kidding," Rylan agreed. His wrists were bound with steel manacles engraved in runes that prevented him from breaking them, so he couldn't shovel the food into his mouth as fast as he wanted to. Nevertheless, he managed to clear the plate in less than ten minutes, and downed three glasses of milk besides that.

"Thanks," he muttered when he was finished.

"No problem," I said dryly. My stomach gave a hollow pang at the sight of the empty platter – I'd yet to have dinner, but I hadn't wanted to eat any of the food since Rylan clearly needed it more than I did.

"So, did you come here just to feed me?" Rylan asked. "Or did you have something to say?"

"I wanted to bring you some news," I told him. I started in with the Benefactor's plans for the shifter community, telling him what I'd learned at the Ur-God temple and from talking with the humans individually, and also that I'd convinced the Mages Guild to lighten the sentences of shifter soldiers in view of the recent injustices.

Rylan's lips were pressed together when I finished. He looked pained, but resigned. "I know you're not lying, and what you say unfortunately lines up," he admitted with a sigh. "Over the past few months, the human officers were suddenly being given access to ridiculous amounts of money and way more information than we were, and shifters were excluded and ignored more and more in meetings and decisions. Believe it or not, we used to avoid things like blowing up bridges and setting buildings on fire. But not only were we starting to do it, but shifters were also being sent in to carry out the worst and most dangerous missions."

"I suspected as much," I told him, a little sadly now. "I couldn't believe it when you guys tried to blow up the Firegate Bridge. It had never occurred to me that the Resistance would go that far."

"We shouldn't have." Rylan's shoulders slumped, and he scrubbed his hands over his face before looking me in the eye again. "Look, despite everything that's happened between us, I'm glad you're safe. I fought hard against the kill order that was put out on you, but it came down from the top, and there was nothing I could do."

"I know," I told him. I didn't want him to feel guilty about this. Thorgana was at fault here, not him. "And you did warn me about going to the Convention."

"I also told you not to warn the Chief Mage," Rylan growled, anger lighting his eyes now. "But I knew you wouldn't listen, so I took extra steps there to ensure your safety too."

I froze. "What do you mean by that?"

"I was in town when I called you, so after I hung up the phone, I went down to Witches End and had a witch cast a spell to make you forget to tell the Chief Mage whenever you were near him."

"What the fuck?" I shot to my feet so quickly that my chair clattered to the floor. "How the hell did you manage that?"

"I filched some hair from your apartment the last time I was there," Rylan admitted, looking more than a little uncomfortable now. "The witch was able to use it to cast the spell on you."

"You bastard!" I slammed my hands down on the table, sending the empty milk pitcher crashing to the ground. It shattered, scattering shards of pottery across the floor as I shoved my nose in Rylan's face. "You almost got the Chief Mage killed, and you made me think it was *my* fault by making me forget to warn him!"

"Yes, and I also saved *your* life," Rylan shouted back, not backing down one bit. "The Resistance would have killed you for sure if the Chief Mage hadn't gotten on the dirigible that day."

"Yeah, and so what?" I sneered, shoving back from the table. "They put a hit out on me anyway, didn't they? At least if you hadn't messed with my head, I could have warned Iannis, and we could have potentially saved hundreds of lives. Their blood is on *your* hands, Rylan."

Disgusted, I had the guards take him away, then asked them to leave me for a moment so I could regain my composure. I was shaking with rage, so angry at Rylan's betrayal that I wanted the guards to bring him back in here so I could beat the shit out of him. But that wouldn't solve anything, and besides, he would be sent off to the mines soon anyway.

When I was composed again, I asked the guards to bring Thorgana in. Unlike Rylan, she didn't appear undernourished, but her platinum-blonde hair hung limp around her heart-shaped face. Without her makeup, she looked brittle and colorless.

"Miss Baine," she said in a cool voice, crossing her legs as she sat down in the chair. Somehow, she managed to make her prison uniform look elegant, and she sat in the hard chair with the posture of a queen. "I would say it's nice of you to visit, but I'm afraid the very sight of you turns my stomach."

"Is that because I'm a shifter, or because I'm a mage?" I asked casually, refusing to react to the malice glittering in her eyes. "I hear you hate both of them equally, which is kind of strange."

She shrugged. "The mages are cruel and unjust, and the shifters barbaric and dangerous. I console myself with the certainty that their days are numbered, no matter what becomes of me."

"And yet," I said, glancing down at the runed manacles on her wrists, "you're a half-shifter yourself, aren't you? That's why you're so strong, and why you look younger than your age. And I bet it's also helped you gather information at your little parties. You've got shifter senses."

"An unfortunate curse," Thorgana agreed, her mouth twisting into a sneer. "But I learned early in life that if I wanted to succeed, I had to use every advantage I could."

I shook my head. "How can you say that? You were raised in a wealthy family, had every human advantage there is, *and* you have some useful shifter abilities." I eyed her again. "I'm assuming you can't actually shift, though?"

"Even if I could, I would hardly care to turn into a filthy animal," Thorgana said coldly. "My late father was less fastidious – he had a dalliance with a wolf-shifter servant girl that resulted in my birth. Because his own wife was barren, he kept me as his child and got rid of the servant. That part of my heritage was never alluded to in the family, and I was glad enough not to be reminded."

"So you *are* his heir then, and not just an empty-headed fool," I murmured. No wonder she hated that part of herself, if she had been brought up to hate and despise her shifter heritage all her life. "As his only child, he would have taught you the family business."

Thorgana didn't confirm that – she simply turned her gaze away and began examining her nails. "Did you come here to waste my time and yours with nonsense and pointless questions, Miss Baine?"

"No," I said evenly. "I came here to look you in the eye and tell you that I know what you are, and that you may as well give up whatever details you're still hiding before they're uncovered. The Finance Secretary has already impounded all your businesses in Canalo and alerted the rest of the Federation to do the same, and the Minister is demanding your extradition. Don't you think you'd be better off here, than at the capital?"

Thorgana laughed. "What difference does it make, when I'm slated for execution either way?"

She had a point, but I wasn't going to tell her that. "The Chief Mage of Canalo is a reasonable man. He may be willing to cut you a deal, such as seeing that your husband is spared, if you cooperate."

"What a generous offer." Thorgana smiled coyly, looking back up at me again. "I think I'll take my chances in Dara just the same, but I appreciate you coming here to negotiate on the Chief Mage's behalf. Congratulations on your engagement, by the way. It is not likely to last very long, so you'd better enjoy it while you can."

Frustration bubbled in my chest at the blasé attitude she seemed to hold toward her execution – it was almost as if she wasn't worried. As if she had a plan. And by the way her eyes gleamed in satisfaction, I could tell she knew I was frustrated. After all, her shifter senses would be able to tell her, just as surely as I was able to read her emotions.

"I'll be sure to pass on your felicitations," I told her, standing. "And of your preference for returning to Dara." Her eyes narrowed at that. "By the way, what was that glass thing you threw at us in your mansion, when you were arrested?"

"Glass thing?" She pressed the tips of her fingers against her mouth as she tittered. "Oh, you mean the pendant from my necklace. What of it?"

"That wasn't just a damned pendant," I growled, bracing my hands against the table and leaning into her space. "You were trying to kill us somehow. What the hell was that red, smoky stuff?"

"I'm afraid I can't provide you with any information on that," she said sweetly. "But it certainly seemed quite alarming, didn't it? If I were you, I would watch my back, Miss Baine. With the amount of attention you've drawn from the Resistance, you're a dead woman walking." Her smile turned fierce.

Nervous energy rippled down my spine at the conviction in her voice. Of course it would be foolish to assume that all the secret supporters of the Resistance who were in Solantha had been identified. My stomach sank a little as I remembered the talk of 'secret weapons' I had overheard in the Maintown Ur-God temple. What if they were talking about more than just guns?

"I'm not done with you, Thorgana Mills," I said, straightening again. After all the dangers I'd survived, I was not about to let this bitch of a half-human rattle me. "You might be leaving here soon, but you'll never get far enough away that I won't be able to find you."

She only smiled.

With nothing left to say, I called for the guards to remove Thorgana, then headed back to the ferry. I sincerely hoped I never had to deal with that horrible woman again, but somehow, I doubted this would be the last time I saw her.

27

The rest of the day, and the evening, were so completely jammed with meetings and paperwork that I was totally exhausted when my head finally hit the pillow. I woke up in the morning with a tension headache, and decided then and there that I needed a break from all this crap. I needed to just be Sunaya Baine for a moment, and I also needed to see my friends.

"Are you sure this is a good idea?" Iannis asked as the wheels of the carriage rumbled beneath us. He sat across from me, dressed in a pair of dark red robes today, his hair pulled back from his face and tied at the nape of his neck. Part of me wanted to run my fingers through it until it was wild and free again, but I knew that we couldn't go walking around looking like we'd just had sex *all* the time.

Though carriage sex wasn't a bad idea.

"Why wouldn't it be?" I asked. "We're engaged now, and my friends need to get used to the idea. Not to mention, *you* need to get used to being around them, because once we're married, they'll be coming around the Palace. A lot."

"Naturally," Iannis muttered, but he smiled. "I am glad that you want to include me in other areas of your life."

The carriage rolled to a stop outside Witches End, and Iannis helped me out of the carriage. To my relief, the two burly shop-keepers were gone, and the barrier had been removed from the pier entrance. As we walked up the pier, I saw that all the rubble had been cleared away, and the stores were open for business again. It seemed like it was just yesterday that all the windows were boarded up, but then again, I had been gone for over a week.

A bell tinkled as I pushed open the door to Comenius's shop, and I was pleased to see there were several customers perusing his wares. It was a little sad to see him ringing up the sales behind the counter without Noria's assistance, but at least he was safe.

"Sunaya!" he greeted me, and then his eyes widened at the sight of Iannis standing behind me. "My Lord," he said, dropping the small bag in his hand and bowing. The rest of the people in the shop instantly did the same, and I fought against the urge to squirm uncomfortably. How the hell did Iannis *deal* with all this genuflecting?

"Thank you," he said, waving a hand graciously. "Please, don't pause on my account. Sunaya and I are happy to wait until you are free." He moved toward the small sitting area on the other side of the room.

"Are you sure I can't get you anything? Tea, or –"

"Com." I turned back to him, a little exasperated now. "It's me, Sunaya. It's okay."

Comenius seemed to relax a little then, and he turned back to the customers. It didn't take him long to help everyone – the customers seemed anxious to get out of the shop, uncomfortable with being around Iannis. I slipped my hand into his and squeezed it as we sat next to each other on the wicker couch, actually feeling a little sorry for him. By education and nature, he wasn't very approachable, and his position required that he maintain his stern persona. He needed to remain formidable, even if he did have feelings and desires just like the rest of us.

As soon as the shop was empty, Comenius flipped the sign closed, then came to join us in the sitting area. I stood up before he could bow again and wrapped my arms around him in a brief, but fierce hug.

"Congratulations on your engagement," Comenius said, eyes twinkling as he stepped back to regard Iannis and me together.

My eyebrows went up. "Word travels fast around here, doesn't it?"

"It's been the talk of the town," Comenius agreed as we took our seats. "It's a historic moment, the prospect of a legally binding union between shifter and mage. I imagine your match will spark debate across the country."

"No doubt." Not wanting to think about that, I turned toward Iannis. "I'm sure you already know, Iannis, but this is my friend, Comenius Genhard. He's a hedge-witch."

"Pleased to meet you." Iannis leaned forward, holding out a hand, and Comenius shook it after a moment's hesitation. "Hedge-witches are very well respected in my home country, Manuc, particularly for their formidable herb lore."

Comenius beamed at that. "Thank you," he said. "I'm more than happy to provide the Palace with any assistance in that area, although I'm sure you are more experienced than I am."

"Nonsense," Iannis said mildly. "I hardly know everything, and I've recently discovered a variation on a magical recipe that I could use some help with, as it requires herbs."

They immediately launched into a technical discussion about the new *gulaya* recharging spell Iannis had discovered in Messindor's diary, and I let them go at it for a little bit. It was nice to see the two of them getting along so well, especially since Comenius and I used to be lovers.

"I'm assuming that one of the reasons you came here was to find out if I've received any ether pigeons from Elnos," Comenius said once he and Iannis had exhausted that topic of conversation.

"Well, yeah." I leaned forward a little. "It's been almost two weeks since they left, Com. Shouldn't we have heard something by now?"

"As a matter of fact, I received a message yesterday." Troubled lines settled into Comenius's face. "It turns out that Noria was slated to be sent out of state to an area to assist another group with technical work, and they don't know when or if she'll be coming back. Annia and Elnos have not been discovered so far, but they are still trying to wangle their way into following Noria without compromising themselves. They say even before she left, Noria was always sequestered away with the other technological specialists."

"Shit," I muttered, dragging a hand through my hair. Noria was a genius inventor, and in the hands of the Resistance, she could do some serious damage. The idea that they had so many specialists working for them also sounded ominous – just what the hell were they planning? "We have to get her back."

"First, we must find out exactly where she is, Sunaya," Iannis reminded me. "I can contact the Chief Mage of that area, once we do. The entire Federation is on the alert for any activity by the Resistance – any of my colleagues will be more than happy to mobilize forces and shut down this operation."

"No," I snapped. "I'm not going to throw Noria to the wolves like that. I need to get her out of there before we call in the authorities, or she'll end up getting killed. Not to mention Annia and Elnos, who are there undercover. Elnos is smart, but he's young, and I don't know if he'll be able to defend himself and Annia well enough if he gets caught in the crossfire."

Iannis sighed. "I'm guessing this means you want to take a hand in the rescue yourself, if it becomes necessary?"

"Yes." I paused. "I was hoping you'd come with me."

"I can come too," Comenius offered. "You might have need of me."

Iannis was silent for a moment. "There is much still left to do here in Solantha, and I've promised the Minister to hold myself in readiness for that task force I'm supposed to lead," he finally said. "But you cannot leave your friends in danger, nor can we ignore a potential threat from the Resistance. I will think on this and see what I can come up with."

We said our goodbyes to Comenius, then got back into the carriage and headed to the Palace. Anxiety crawled up my spine, tightening my neck muscles as I wondered just what the hell Noria had gotten herself into.

"It'll be all right." Iannis took my hand into his bigger one and squeezed it reassuringly. "We'll figure out how to take care of everything. Together, we can solve just about any problem, Sunaya."

"Okay." I squeezed his hand back. As I stared out the window, watching the city pass by, I determined that I *would* make it all right. With Iannis firmly on my side now, I had access to all kinds of resources even if he ended up too busy to stand by my side.

And now that I had full access to my magic and control over my shifter instincts, nothing was going to stand in my way.

The End

SUNAYA BAINE'S adventure continues in **Betrayed by Magic**, Book 5 of the Baine Chronicles. Make sure to join her mailing list so you can be notified of future release dates, and to receive special updates, freebies and giveaways!

Join at www.jasminewalt.com/newsletter-signup

Did you enjoy this book? Please consider leaving a review. Reviews help us authors sell books so we can afford to write more of them. Writing a review is the best way to ensure that the author writes the next one as it lets them know readers are enjoying their work and want more. Thank you very much for taking the time to read, and we hope you enjoyed the book!

GLOSSARY

Baine, Sunaya: a half-panther shifter, half-mage who hates mages and has a passion for justice. Because magic is forbidden to all but the mage families, Sunaya was forced to keep her abilities a secret until she accidentally used them to defend herself in front of witnesses. Rather than condemn her to death, the Chief Mage, Iannis ar'Sannin, chose to take her on as his apprentice, and now she struggles to balance her shifter and mage heritage.

Baine, Melantha: Sunaya's cousin, and daughter to the Jaguar Clan's Chieftain.

Baine, Mafiela: Chieftain of the Jaguar Clan and Sunaya's aunt.

Baine, Mika: a young jaguar shifter, daughter of Melantha Baine

Baine, Rylan: one of Chieftain Baine's least favored children, and Sunaya's cousin. He is an active member of the Resistance, with the rank of Captain.

Benefactor, the: the name the Resistance call their anonymous, principal source of financial support. According to Sunaya's investigations, this mysterious criminal has many different irons in the fire.

Bosal ar'Nuris: mage, Secretary of Education and Culture of Canalo, member of the Canalo Delegation to the Convention

Canalo: one of the fifty states making up the Northia Federation, located on the West Coast of the Northia Continent.

Canalo Council, usually just the **Council:** a governmental body composed of eight senior mages, supposed to advise the Chief Mage and substitute for him in case of sudden death

Chen, Lalia: the current Director of the Canalo Mages Guild in Solantha. She serves as deputy to Iannis ar'Sannin, the Chief Mage.

Chartis, Argon: former Director of the Canalo Mages Guild, dismissed by the Chief Mage for insubordination and attempts to undermine the Chief Mage's authority.

Chieftain: a title used to distinguish the head of a shifter clan.

Canter: an elderly mage often manning the reception at Solantha Palace.

The Cat's Meow: a diner in Shiftertown, owned by the Tiger Clan.

Coazi: a group of related tribes controlling large parts of Mexia and adjoining states

Comenius Genhard: a hedgewitch from Pernia, owner of the shop Over the Hedge at Witches' End. Close friend of Sunaya Baine, employer of Noria Melcott, and lover of the witch Elania.

Creator: the ultimate deity, worshipped by all three races under different names.

Dira: female mage, the receptionist at the Mages Guild.

Dara: capital of the Northia Federation, located on the east coast of the Northia Continent.

Elania: girlfriend of Comenius; a witch specializing in potions, with a shop in Witches' End

Enforcer: a bounty hunter employed by the government to seek out and capture wanted criminals. They operate under strict rules and are paid bounties for each head. While the majority of them are human, there is a strong minority of shifters, and even the occasional mage.

Enforcers' Guild: the administrative organization in charge of the Enforcers. Also, the building from which the various Enforcer crews work under their respective foremen.

Faonus: one of the three founding mages of the Federation

Fenris: a clanless wolf shifter as well as good friend and confidant of Chief Mage Iannis ar'Sannin. No known last name.

Firegate Bridge: Solantha's best-known structure, a large red bridge spanning the length of Solantha Bay. It is accessible via Firegate Road.

Captain Galling: the human captain of the Enforcer's Guild in Solantha City, appointed by the former Chief Mage and Council.

Coman ar'Daghir: Member of the delegation of Rhodea to the Convention, Legal Secretary of that state

Garai: the largest and most populated country on the Eastern Continent. Garaians are known for slanted eyes and ivory skin as well as their complicated, rune-like alphabet.

Garidano, Cirin: Finance Secretary of the State of Canalo.

Great Accord: a treaty struck by the ruling mages centuries ago which brought an end to a devastating war known as the Conflict. It is still the basis upon which mages rule their countries and territories. All new laws passed must be in accordance with the provisions of the Great Accord.

Gulaya: a star-shaped charm, usually made of metal, that is anchored to a specific location and can take its wearer back there at need. Rare, and difficult to recharge.

Hennis: a jaguar shifter, butler in the home of Mafiela Baine, the Chieftain of the Jaguar Clan.

Herald, The: the main newspaper in Solantha City, geared towards the human majority population.

Iannis ar'Sannin: Chief Mage of Canalo. He resides in the capital city of Solantha, from which he runs Canalo as well as the Mages Guild with the help of his deputy. Originally a native of Manuc, a country located across the Eastern Sea.

Jeremidah: one of the three founding mages of the Northia Federation ("The Founding Trio") together with Faonus and Micara

Kalois: a rare foreign plant which masks the smell of silver so well that shifters can be drugged or poisoned despite their sensitive noses.

Kan Zao: a mental and physical martial art tradition from Garai.

Lakin, Boon: a jaguar shifter from Parabas, recently appointed as Solantha's new Shiftertown Inspector following Roanas's death. Sunaya and he are friends and occasional allies. It was a case he investigated and discussed with Sunaya, that led to the eventual exposure of the Shifter Royale.

Loranian: the difficult, secret language of magic that all mages are required to master.

Mages Guild: the governmental organization that rules the mages in Canalo, and supervises the other races. The headquarters are in Solantha Palace. They are subordinate to the Chief Mage.

Magi-tech: devices that are powered by both magic and technology.

Main Crew: the largest group of Enforcers in the Guild. They are generally favored over the other crews and get the most lucrative dockets.

Manuc: an island country off the west coast of the Central Continent.

Magorah: the god of the shifters, associated with the moon.

Melcott, Annia: a human Enforcer. She is a close friend of Sunaya's, and Noria's older sister.

Melcott, Noria: Annia Melcott's younger sister. A gifted inventor, she regularly tinkers with mechanical devices in between her college classes and her part-time job at Comenius's shop

Micara: one of the mages that made up the Founding Trio of the Federation, together with Faonus and Jeremidah

Mills, Thorgana: human socialite, who inherited ownership of The Herald in Solantha and several other newspapers, as well as other companies across the Federation. She only resides in Solantha part-time. Sunaya used to do occasional bodyguard gigs for her in the past.

Minister, the: See entry for **Zavian Graning**

Nebara: one of the fifty states that make up the Northia Federation.

Northia Federation: a federation consisting of fifty states that cover the middle of the Western Continent. Canalo is part of this federation.

Over the Hedge: a shop at Witches' End selling magical charms and herbal remedies, belonging to Comenius Genhard.

Pandanum: a base metal used, inter alia, for less valuable coins

Pernia: a country on the Central Continent, from which Sunaya's friend Comenius Genhard hails.

Polar ar'Tollis: Fenris's former name, from when he was the Chief Mage in Nebara.

Prison Isle: an island in the middle of Solantha Bay that serves as a prison for Canalo's criminals.

Privacy Guard: a company leasing uniformed guards to governments and other institutions all over the Federation.

Ragga, Elnos: Noria Melcott's boyfriend. He is a student at Solantha academy and one of the few mages who believes in equality amongst the races. He and Noria can often be found working together, developing new magi-tech devices.

Recca: the world of humans, mages and shifters

Residah: the mages' book of scripture that holds Resinah's teachings

Resinah: the first mage, whose teachings are of paramount spiritual importance for the mages. Her statue can be found in the mage temples, which are off-limits to non-mages and magically hidden from outsiders.

Resistance: a movement of revolutionaries and malcontents planning to overthrow the mages and take control of the Northia Federation. Over the past months they have become bolder and more aggressive, using terrorist attacks with civilian casualties. They are financially backed by the still-to-be identified Benefactor.

Rowanville: the only neighborhood of Solantha where all three races mix.

Sandin Federal Bank: a bank with branches in all fifty states of the Federation; its Canalo manager was Danrian Warin. It was shut down after Sunaya brought a scheme of "interest-free loans," financed with illegally mined gold, to the Chief Mage's notice.

Serapha charms: paired magical devices that allow two people, usually a couple, to find each other via twinned stones imbued with a small part of their essence. Normally, only the wearer can take a serapha charm off.

Shaman/Shamaness a spiritual leader of the Coazi tribe, highly adept at nature magic, healing, divination and mind magic

Shifter: a human who can change into animal form and back by magic; they originally resulted from illegal experiments by mages on ordinary humans.

Shifter Courier: Solantha newspaper specifically geared towards the shifter population.

Shifter Royale: an illegal underground betting concourse where kidnapped and drugged shifters were forced to fight against each other, sometimes to the death. Discovered and exposed by Sunaya, with help from Boon Lakin and Annia Melcott, after her cousin Mika had been kidnapped by the organizers.

Shiftertown: the part of Solantha where the official shifter clans live.

Shiftertown Inspector: a shifter appointed by the Shiftertown Council to police shifter-related crime. He has deputies who assist him. The position is currently held by Boon Lakin, a jaguar shifter, appointed after the murder of his predecessor Roanas Tillmore.

Solantha: the capital of Canalo State, a port city on the West Coast, home of Sunaya Baine.

Solantha Palace: The seat of power in Canalo, where both the Chief Mage and the Mages Guild reside. It is located near the coast of Solantha Bay.

Taili the Wolf: in shifter legend, the very first shifter (a female).

Tanzarite: a rare semi-precious stone.

Tillmore, Roanas: The former Shiftertown Inspector and father figure/mentor to Sunaya. He was poisoned while digging into the silver murders, prompting Sunaya to take over the investigation.

Tua: a legendary and highly dangerous race of very long-lived beings with powerful magic, who sometimes cross from their own world into Recca, most frequently in Manuc

Turain: a small town north of Solantha, where the Shifter Royale took place

Ur-God: the name the humans call the Creator by.

Witches' End: a pier in Solantha City, part of the Port, where immigrant magic users sell their wares and services.

Yantz, Petros: the former Chief Editor of the Herald. He fled the city after Sunaya discovered he was behind the silver murders, and is still at large.

Zavian Graning: mage, Minister of the Northian Federation. Elected by the Convention for an indefinite term, he is charged with coordination of governmental business and particularly Foreign Affairs, between the Convention sessions that he prepares and presides.

ACKNOWLEDGMENTS

First off, I'd like to thank my beta readers. They're an absolutely stellar group of people who give me excellent feedback on short notice, and this book would not be the same without them.

Thanks again to Mary Burnett, my writing partner and editor. Publishing four books in less than a year is a big deal, and we've accomplished much more than I think either of us expected.

I'd also like to thank Jason Cipriano and Michael-Scott Earle. You two are the best indie author buddies a girl could ask for. And your books aren't half-bad either. ;)

And of course, a BIG thank you to Judah Dobin, my illustrator and snuggle buddy. Somehow, you manage to be talented at both. Love you lots. <3

ABOUT THE AUTHOR

New York Times and USA Today Bestselling Author Jasmine Walt is a devourer of books, chocolate, and all things martial arts. Somehow, those three things melded together in her head and transformed into a desire to write, usually fantastical stuff with a healthy dose of action and romance. Her characters are a little (okay, a lot) on the snarky side, and they swear, but they mean well. Even the villains sometimes.

When Jasmine isn't chained to her keyboard, you can find her working on her dao sword form, spending time with her family, or binge-watching superhero shows on Netflix.

Want to connect with Jasmine? You can find her on Twitter at @jasmine_writes, on Facebook, or at www.jasminewalt.com.

ALSO BY JASMINE WALT

The Baine Chronicles Series:

Burned by Magic

Bound by Magic

Hunted by Magic

Marked by Magic

Betrayed by Magic

Deceived by Magic

Scorched by Magic

Tested by Magic (Novella)

Forsaken by Magic (Novella)

The Nia Rivers Adventures

Dragon Bones

Demeter's Tablet

Templar Scrolls

Serpent Mound

Eden's Garden

The Gatekeeper Chronicles

Marked by Sin

Hunted by Sin

Claimed by Sin

The Dragon's Gift Trilogy

Printed in Great Britain
by Amazon

62151023R00149